Fated Hearts

NEW YORK TIMES & USA TODAY BESTSELLING AUTHOR
KELLY ELLIOTT

Fated Hearts
Book 8 Southern Bride Copyright © 2021 by Kelly Elliott

Cover photo by: Shannon Cain/Photography by Shannon Cain
Cover Design by RBA Designs
Interior Design & Formatting by: Elaine York, www.allusionpublishing.com
Developmental Editor: Kelli Collins
Content Editor: Rachel Carter, Yellow Bird Editing
Proofing Editor: Andrea Varnyken, Yellow Bird Editing
Proofing Editor: Elaine York, www.allusionpublishing.com

No part of this book may be reproduced or transmitted in any form or by any means, electronic or mechanical, including photocopying, recording, or by any information storage and retrieval system without the written permission of the author, except for the use of brief quotations in a book review.

This book is a work of fiction. Names, characters, places, and incidents either are products of the author's imagination or are used fictitiously. Any resemblance to actual persons, living or dead, events, or locales is entirely coincidental.

For more information on Kelly and her books, please visit her website www.kellyelliottauthor.com.

Fated Hearts

Chapter 1

Roger

"I'M SORRY, MR. Carter, but all flights out have been canceled due to the snowstorm."

I sighed but then quickly flashed the older woman behind the American Airlines counter a smile and a wink. I traveled enough to know that if the issue was weather-related, they didn't have to put you up in a hotel, and I knew things would be booked fast because of the storm. "It's not your fault. Can't control the weather, even if you do have lovely blue eyes."

She blushed and leaned in closer. "We don't normally do this when it's weather-related, but I can offer you a hotel room over at the Grand Marshall since it looks like you may be stuck here for at least two nights."

"Two nights?" I asked with a frown.

"It's a pretty intense storm that's moving in."

I took a quick glance around the airport. Hotels were going to be booking up fast, and the Grand Marshall was a luxury one with a nightclub on the top floor. I'd be stupid to turn it down. I looked back at the lovely lady. "I think I should take that room before they're all g–one."

With a grin, she replied, "I'll get you all taken care of. They always hold a few rooms for us just in case."

An hour later, I stepped into my room at the Grand Marshall right outside O'Hare Airport. I walked straight to the bedroom, dropped my one bag by the window, shut the curtains, and then face-planted on the bed.

"Christ on a cracker, I'm fucking tired."

I had been on the business trip from hell, and I swore it was the longest trip I'd ever taken. Considering it was only supposed to be two days, for me to think that showed how messed up the entire thing had been. Delayed flights getting to Chicago. Too much pizza and beer, and meeting after meeting. I hated negotiations, I hated pompous-ass businessmen, and I hated flying. I hated business trips, in general, and I hated being stuck in the frigid north where the temperature outside was cold enough to freeze my goddamn balls off. Not to mention I was hungry. The whole way here in the Uber, I had debated whether I should eat or just go to sleep. Considering I had made it to the hotel alive despite the daredevil driver, I decided to go for sleep.

My phone buzzed and I rolled over to pull it out of the back pocket of my jeans.

"What?"

"Hello to you too. What has you so grumpy?"

The voice on the other end of the phone was my brother Truitt's. It was his fault I was stuck in Chicago in the first place. It should have been him here, but he had asked me to do him a favor. Never again.

"First off, asshole, it's nearly midnight. I'm stuck in Chicago for what looks like another two days if this storm is as bad as they say it will be, and I haven't gotten laid in at least six months. No...longer. Oh, and I'm hungry as shit."

"Dude, that sucks big time for you. How did the meetings go?"

"Is that all you care about, the stupid meetings? Do you even care if I'm sleeping in a chair in O'Hare right now?"

Truitt laughed. "Please. I know you, and I'm almost positive you've sweet-talked yourself into a hotel room—and not only a hotel room, but most likely one that's right there at the airport so you can get on a plane at a moment's notice when they start flying out."

I sat up and stared straight ahead in the dark. "My God. How is it you know me so well? They put me up at the Grand Marshall."

Truitt whistled. "How young was the ticket agent?"

"I'd say she was around Mom's age."

Truitt laughed. "It's scary how well I know you. Now, the meetings?"

With a sigh, I fell onto my back again. I could hardly keep my eyes open. "Truitt, I'm so fucking tired I can barely think straight. I'm so tired I'm not even going to eat. I've been sitting in a small, cramped boardroom with stuffy producers, directors, and suits from the network since seven this morning. It's now almost midnight, and I haven't eaten, I haven't taken a shower, and all I want to do is sleep."

"Fine, we can talk tomorrow, but can you at least tell me—"

I hit End on my cell phone, turned it off, and tossed it onto the side table. I got up and stripped out of my clothes before sliding into the bed. I didn't even care that I hadn't taken a shower. I didn't even care enough to take the top cover off. I was that exhausted. I knew the moment my head hit the pillow, I was going to be out.

The sound of a hotel door opening and closing had me pulling the pillow over my head. Fucking thin walls. How could they call it a luxury hotel when I could hear every damn thing the person in the next room was doing? The couple next door had been having sex for the last hour and had only just stopped. One of them must have left, which would explain the sound of the door opening and closing. Now, it was finally peaceful, and I could get some sleep. I moved my pillow back under my head and closed my eyes.

I heard the soft click of the bathroom door shutting, and then water started to run.

I opened my eyes and sighed before I pulled the pillow over my head again. As much as I hated that I could hear everything happening in the next room, the sound of the muffled water caused me to drift off to sleep once again.

Next came a woman's soft voice. "Where's the damn light?"

No, we don't need the light on in my dream, baby. Just come to bed.

Even with the pillow over my head, I saw a bright light fill the room—and then the sound of a woman screaming had me jumping out of the bed and damn near falling on my face as I tripped over my luggage.

"Oh my God! Oh my God! You're naked! Why are you naked!?"

I rubbed at my eyes to make sure I was awake and not dreaming. After blinking several times and letting my eyes adjust to the bright light, I saw a woman standing on the other side of the bed.

"Why are you in here?" she shouted. "And you're naked!"

I blinked again, still half-asleep. "Yes, you've already mentioned that. Why are you in *my* room? I was fucking sleeping—that's why I'm naked!"

Her lip curled back in a snarl as she jerked her head back and looked at the bed, then me. "Who sleeps naked in a hotel bed? That's just...gross!"

I scrubbed my hand over my face, pausing for a moment to take in what I was seeing. *Holy mother of God.* The stranger was dressed in nothing but a white tank top and lace panties. Her blonde hair was pulled back in—oh, Jesus—two pigtails.

That was fucking hot.

I did a quick sweep of her insanely gorgeous body before I finally looked at her face. She looked like a goddess. No, a princess. Both?

"Oh, shit," I whispered. "You're beautiful."

Her mouth opened as if she was going to say something, but then she quickly snapped it shut.

I was staring at the most beautiful woman I had ever seen in my life. She had the bluest of blue eyes, and they stared back at me in utter disbelief.

"Your hair... It's...it's in pigtails."

She frowned and placed her hands on her hips. "Really? *That's* what you're going to focus on right now?"

"I'm sorry. A beautiful woman nearly naked *and* wearing pigtails is in *my* hotel room. What else am I going to notice?"

The corner of her mouth twitched before she sighed and dropped her hands. "I believe you're in *my* hotel room."

Laughing, I looked around and motioned with my hands. "I do believe I was here first, princess."

She growled. Holy shit, she actually growled. "Don't call me that. I am not your princess. I happen to have a name."

I stood there and waited for her to give me said name. With one brow raised, I watched as she finally took in my body. She made absolutely no attempt to hide the fact that she was appraising me. And, of course, I noticed the extra few moments she spent on my cock. I smirked and asked, "Are you finished checking me out?"

Her gaze jerked back up to mine. "What?"

"What's your name?"

"Oh...um...it's Annalise. Annalise Michaels."

"Roger Carter."

Annalise looked all around the room, completely avoiding any eye contact—or any other part of my body. "Could you please put some clothes on, Roger?"

"Can you?"

She turned back to me. "I'm not the naked one."

I huffed. "Please, I can see your nipples through that thin white tank."

She quickly covered her chest with her arms and let out another growl, followed by, "Could you at least try to act like a gentleman?"

I reached down and opened my suitcase, searching for a pair of sweats. After finding them, I slipped them on as Annalise pulled a sweatshirt over her head to cover herself. She then started to put on yoga pants. It was hilarious watching her struggle to pull them up. She hopped, twisted, then finally fell on the bed and pulled them on. All the while, I stood there and watched in amusement.

Once she was dressed, she focused her attention back on me. "Okay, so what are we going to do about this?"

I shrugged and headed into the other room to see if there was any water. Two bottles sat on the counter, and I grabbed one to open it.

"Wait! Don't drink that!"

I glanced at the water and then at Annalise. "Why not?"

"They'll charge me, like, five dollars for it."

I twisted it open, and she frowned. "No," I said, "they'll charge *me* the money because this is *my* room."

"Well, this is the room they gave me a key to. So, it's mine."

"I was here first."

She narrowed her eyes and looked to be thinking really hard for something to say. "Well…well… Listen here…mister. Um…you're wrong!"

"I'm wrong that I was here first?" I asked with a humorless laugh.

"Yes. No, I mean, yes, you were here first, but…but…oh, my gosh." She brought her fingers to her temples and rubbed while mumbling something to herself.

Tilting my head, I let out a laugh. "Let me guess, you're the type of person who'll be lying in bed hours later, and you'll think of the perfect comeback and then get mad because you couldn't think of it when you needed it."

Her eyes widened. "How did you know that?"

I rolled my eyes. "Lucky guess, princess."

"Ugh, stop calling me that. Roger, I'm exhausted. Can we please just go down to the front desk and find out what happened?"

"I'm not changing rooms. I was here first."

She pointed at me and said, "Well, I took a shower first! Ha!"

I stared at her. "And that trumps me actually walking into the room, crawling into the bed, and sleeping, well before you showed up?"

Annalise shot me a smirk, knowing damn well I was in the right, and she was not.

It dawned on me then that it hadn't been a dream. "That's what the water sound was."

She frowned. "Excuse me?"

I waved my hand dismissively. "Nothing. Come on, let's go fix this."

Walking back into the bedroom, I grabbed the key I'd put on the side table and then started for the door.

"Um, aren't you going to grab your things?" she asked.

"No, because this is my room. You grab *your* things. I was here first. Dibs."

She laughed. "Oh, my God, did you seriously just call dibs on a hotel room? What are you, ten?"

I glanced back at her and winked. "You're just pissed you didn't think of it first."

Annalise drew her brows down, inhaled a deep breath through her nose, and exhaled. "Damn it, you're right. I don't want to pack up all my bathroom stuff, though. It's late. I'm so tired."

It was my turn to laugh. "Now who's acting like a ten-year-old? Whine much?"

She followed me out of the room and into the hallway. "You didn't put on shoes."

I shrugged. "It's two in the morning. I don't care."

Folding her arms over her chest, she glared at me.

"You really think you're going to get this room?" I asked her.

"I certainly do."

I pressed the button on the elevator and then turned to face her. "Want to bet on that?"

Her perfectly arched brow rose, and I was able to get a better look at how truly beautiful she was in the bright light of the hallway. "Are we talking 'money' bet?" she asked.

"Do you want to talk money bet?"

She nodded. "Hundred bucks you're the one leaving."

I reached for her hand. "Hundred you're the one leaving."

After a firm handshake, we both turned and waited for the elevator. The doors opened, and we both stepped inside and faced the front.

"Not gonna lie, I'm totally turned on that you bet money just now," I said.

She made a fake gag sound. "Ugh, gross."

From the corner of my eye, I saw her take a quick peek down at my junk. It took everything I had not to laugh.

Chapter 2

Annalise

DAMN HIM! WHY did he say he was turned on, and why did I look down at his dick? His rather impressive dick too. When he'd jumped out of that bed sans clothes, I'd nearly choked on my own tongue. I don't think I've ever seen a man with such an incredible body. Or such an impressive dick.

No, no, no! Do not picture him naked, Anna. Do not.

"Wow, okay, is it getting hot in this elevator?" I asked, fanning myself with my hand.

"Nope. Feels good to me."

Oh, no. Now everything he said I was going to associate with something sexual.

"It's hot," I said. "Their heater must be set to high."

"If you say so, princess."

With a look that I hoped told him he was two seconds a–ay from being junk-punched, I huffed. "Annalise. That's my name. Not princess, baby, sweetheart, darlin', pumpkin, puffy, lover, sweet-pea—"

Roger held up his hand to stop me. "Wait. Did you just say 'puffy'?"

I felt my cheeks instantly heat. "No."

"Yes, you did. Did some idiot actually call you puffy? Oh, my God, tell me why. I have to know."

Folding my arms over my chest, I looked away from him. "I'm not talking to you any longer."

He laughed, and I hated the way it made my body feel all warm and tingly. Just like I hated how damn handsome he was. And his body—don't even get me started on how insanely hot his body was.

I stole a glance at him and nearly groaned. He had dimples. Why, Lord above, did you have to make him hot, big in the Netherlands, *and* give him dimples?

The elevator dinged as the doors opened, and we both walked out at the same time, bumping into each other. Roger took a step back and motioned for me to go first.

"By all means, you go first, puffy."

"Oh, my God! I want to punch you so hard right now, you don't even know."

He chuckled and walked past me to the front desk. The young woman who had been there earlier came walking out and gave me a sweet smile. But when she saw Roger, her smile grew into a full-on grin.

"What can I help you with, sir?"

He smiled back, and I was pretty sure my knees wobbled slightly. Apparently, so did the clerk's because she held onto the counter. That was when I knew I was screwed. She had nearly melted on the spot. And then I noticed his blue eyes. If it was at all possible, they were even bluer than mine. Add that smile that should be rated R, and I knew I was going to be the one finding another room.

"Heidi? Is that your name?" Roger asked.

She nodded and sighed. "How did you know?"

"It's on your nametag," I stated dryly. She ignored me while Roger cleared his throat in an attempt to hide his laugh.

"Heidi, there seems to be a problem," he said. "I checked into my hotel room a few hours ago. The American Airlines agent arranged for me to stay here for the next two nights—and imagine my surprise when a complete stranger walked into *my* room."

Roger pointed to me when he said "stranger." Heidi looked at me and raised her brows as I attempted to give her my best smile.

"She came into your room?" she asked with an accusatory stare.

Wait. What in the hell? She's the one who gave me the key to his room!

I took a step forward. "Yes, because when I checked in, *you* told me my room was sixteen thirty-three. So, I went to that room. My key worked, I walked in, and lo and behold, he was in there sleeping in my bed. Naked!"

Heidi snapped her head back to Roger and gave him a slow once-over, most likely imagining him naked.

Damn it. I messed up...again.

Roger smirked, and it took everything I had not to slap that smug smile off his face. Gah, why did he have to be so handsome and witty? If I didn't already think he was a jerk, I was positive I'd have gotten caught up in his charms too.

Wait. What?

Heidi cleared her throat as I shook the weird thoughts away. She stared down at her computer. "Let's see if we can fix this."

Roger and I looked at each other. He lifted his hand and rubbed his fingers together. "Get ready to pay up, princess."

I shot him a dirty look, and when I knew Heidi wasn't looking, I gave him the finger.

"Feisty. I like it."

With a roll of my eyes, I replied, "You would."

She typed for a good minute before just staring at the computer screen for what seemed like forever. Then she frowned. Lifted her brows. Chewed on her lip. Glanced up at us, then back down at her screen.

"I'm starting to lose that warm and fuzzy feeling that says you're going to fix this for us, Heidi," Roger stated.

Swallowing hard, she looked at me and then Roger. "The hotel keeps a few rooms on hand if they need them for flight crew or passengers. Somehow...I don't know how the system did it, but when it booked you into the room, Mr. Carter, it never marked it. So, it booked Ms. Michaels into the same room as well."

This was an easy fix. I leaned forward and in my sweetest voice asked, "Okay, well, can you just give one of us another room?"

"Her," Roger said with a wink in Heidi's direction.

This time, his charm had no effect. "I wish I could," Heidi said, "but there are no more rooms available."

"None?" Roger and I asked in unison.

Heidi slowly shook her head. "None. Not a single room. I'm so sorry."

Roger sighed as he threaded his fingers through his brown hair. Heidi let out a weird little groan, and I forced myself to look away.

"Well, looks like we're bunking together, Annalise," he said.

I jerked my head up and stared at him. "What?"

Heidi had the same reaction. "Wait, you're staying in the same room?"

We both ignored her. "Together? You want to stay in the hotel room together?" I asked with a disbelieving laugh.

He leaned closer, narrowed his eyes, and asked, "Do you want to sleep in the airport? Or out here in the lobby?"

"Oh, we can't allow that," Heidi said. "No sleeping in the lobby."

I frantically shook my head. "No, I don't want to go back to the airport. I almost died driving here. I'm pretty sure the Uber driver had never seen snow before."

With that brilliant, dimpled smile of his, Roger replied, "Then come on, roomie. I'm exhausted."

He turned and started back toward the elevator. I glanced over at Heidi, who had been watching him leave. She turned to look at me.

"I'm so jealous of you right now," she whispered.

With an overly exaggerated sigh, I followed after Roger.

Once we were back in the room, Roger went straight into the bedroom. He pulled his T-shirt over his head but luckily kept his sweats on. He crawled into the bed, then looked at me with a questioning expression. "What?"

"Um...where am I supposed to sleep? The sofa in the living room isn't big enough for either of us."

With a wide smile, he slapped the large, king-size bed. "Crawl in, princess. Don't worry, I'm so fucking tired I won't even know you're there."

My mouth fell open. "You want me to sleep with you?"

He had closed his eyes, but he opened one of them again. "As intriguing as sex with you might be, no. I don't want to sleep with you. I want to *go* to sleep. You can sleep next to me."

"I am not getting in that bed."

Roger pulled the pillow out from under his head and buried his face in it. His voice was muffled as he said, "Then sleep on the sofa or the floor. I'm tired, and I'm going to sleep."

As I stood there and debated what I was going to do, I heard a soft snore come from Roger.

How had he fallen asleep that fast? Geesh, he really must have been exhausted.

After looking at the bed, then the floor, then the bed again, I decided it would be safe to sleep in the bed. My gut was telling me I could trust Roger; besides, if he had any ill intentions, would he have dragged himself down to the front desk to get me out of the room?

I chewed on my lip a few moments and then decided it would be okay. Roger was all the way on the other side. I could put a pillow in between us. I was such a heavy sleeper, I was positive I wouldn't even move in the middle of the night.

I slipped the sweatshirt off but kept my yoga pants on.

With a deep breath in, I whispered, "It's okay, Anna. It's fine. He'll stay on his side. I'll stay on mine."

Gently slipping into the bed, I turned and faced Roger. His massive chest rose and fell slowly with each breath. I could feel my eyelids growing heavier and heavier as the weight of today finally came crashing down. I tried to force myself to stay awake a bit longer, but my eyes drifted shut until I finally gave up the fight and let sleep take over.

Warm. I was so comfy warm. A hotel bed had never felt so freaking comfortable before, and I made a mental note to stay at more luxury hotels from then on whenever I traveled. You'd think I would anyway since I had been working for one the last few years.

The feel of something warm lightly blew on the back of my neck, and I wanted to sigh like a contented cat. Was the heater blowing on me?

A sense of complete warmth surrounded me—but when I went to move and stretch out my legs, I instantly froze. I slowly opened my eyes and concentrated on what was up against me.

Roger. My back was against him. No, not just against him, tucked next to him with his arm draped over my side.

Oh. My. God. We're spooning.

How in the hell did that happen? Where was my buffer pillow? And was he…?

I slowly pressed my ass backward and felt the hard length of his ridge against me. I paused again as I held my breath. *Oh, he is big.*

Shit, it's getting hot in here.

Slow, steady breathing came from behind me, and I relaxed some. Roger was still asleep.

Think, Anna, think. How are you going to slip out from his hold? And do you even want to slip out of it, or would it be better to simply pretend to be asleep and let him continue to hold you? It had been so long since a man held me close. So long since I had felt such warmth. And his dick…my God…how wonderful would it be…?

No! No! No! Stop this thinking at once, Annalise Margaret Michaels! No sexy time with the grumpy, hot stranger. You don't even know him.

I paused in my mental chastising. Okay, but how bad would it be to simply lie here and let him hold me? No harm, no foul.

I froze when Roger moaned and pushed his hips against mine, causing his dick to press into my ass. I bit back a moan of my own and remained as still as I could.

Breathe. Breathe, you fool!

One slow and steady breath in. Then out. Repeat.

Roger moved again, then paused. He was awake. His body went rigid when he realized we were spooning.

"Shit," he whispered as I stayed focused on breathing in and out. I decided to pretend I was still asleep to keep either of us from having to face this awkward moment.

Roger slowly lifted his arm off me, then carefully rolled onto his back. Was it my imagination, or was he suddenly breathing heavier?

I felt the bed slowly move as he got out. It sounded like he grabbed his bag before he tiptoed into the bathroom and softly shut the door. The moment I heard the click, I let out a very quiet sigh and buried my face in the pillow.

His dick had been right up against me. His arm around me. His hard, firm chest pressed against my back. I groaned into the pillow as I felt an ache grow between my legs.

Damn him! Damn this Roger Carter for being one of the hottest guys I've ever seen. Damn him for spooning me and getting me all hot and bothered.

The shower turned on, and I rolled onto my back and stared up at the ceiling. "I need to find another hotel," I whispered. I sat up and noticed I was in the middle of the bed. My so-called safety pillow was nowhere to be found. One of us had most likely tossed it out of the bed last night.

"Who spooned who?" I mused as I reached over to the side table and grabbed my phone. Goodness, it was nine in the morning. I had one missed text from my mother.

Mom: Darling, you never sent a text when you got to the hotel. Did you find a room? Please tell me you found a room and you're safe.

Ha! How did one inform their mother that they did indeed find a room, but with a hot-as-hell naked guy who was now in the shower only a few feet away? For all I knew, he was a serial killer.

Me: Hey, Mom! Sorry I didn't text, but by the time I got to the hotel and sorted out a problem with the room, it was well past two in the morning. Looks like I'll be stuck in Chicago for a few days. All flights out of O'Hare are canceled. It's a pretty wicked storm.

If I knew my mother, she would either be carrying her phone with her like it was glued to her hand, or she'd left it somewhere and it would take her the whole day to find it. Since she had been waiting on a text from me, I was going with her having it on her. Sure enough, her reply came through almost instantly.

Mom: *So glad you're in a hotel! What was the problem with the room?*

Me: *I'll call later and explain. Give Daddy a big hug and kiss for me. Love you!*

Mom: *Will do! Love you back, sweetheart!*

I opened my email and quickly skimmed my inbox. I had informed my new boss I was stuck up north because of the weather and wouldn't be making it there for at least a day, most likely two. This wasn't how I wanted to start the next chapter of my life, but what was a girl to do? Couldn't control the weather.

Sure enough, there was a message from her.

Subject: *RE: Stuck in the snow*

Dear Annalise,

Please don't worry about it. It sounds like all of the north is getting packed with storms. Don't stress and we will see you when we see you!

The sound of the shower turning off had me placing my phone on the side table and scrambling back under the sheets. The last thing I wanted to do was face Roger. Not after his junk was nearly all up in my trunk.

I closed my eyes at the sound of the door slowly opening. I could hear Roger moving quietly through the room. He walked back over to his side of the bed and put his bag down. A few seconds later, the door to the room opened and then clicked shut.

I threw the sheet down and exhaled. "Two days. I cannot be stuck in this hotel room with that man for two days."

Deciding to get up and get dressed so I could hit the gym after a quick stop by the front desk, I threw on some different yoga pants and a Dry-Fit shirt. I walked into the bathroom and noticed that Roger had put his toiletries to one side, and neatly moved mine to the other. You could tell a lot about a man by what he used for his bathroom routine.

He had an electric toothbrush. Used Colgate peppermint toothpaste—gross, Crest-lover here—and floss. Oh, nice. We had a man who took care of his teeth. Come to think of it, when he had smiled, it had looked like an awfully nice one.

I shook my head and kept snooping. Speed Stick deodorant and a black bag that I was guessing held his shaving items. Had he shaved? No, he wouldn't have had time to shave. Lord, how I loved a man with a five o'clock shadow.

What made me smile, though, was the way all his items were neatly pressed to the other side of the bathroom sink. I had unpacked mine last night and had left everything all over the sink. He could have been a jerk and pushed mine to the side in a pile, but he hadn't. Why did that make my stomach flutter?

"Oh, for the love, Anna. It's been too long since you've been with a guy."

After I brushed my teeth and exchanged my pigtails for a ponytail, I headed to the front desk. It was my lucky morning because Heidi was gone. A younger man stood behind the counter, and when he saw me, he grinned.

"Good morning. How may I help you?"

"Yes, I'm in room sixteen thirty-three, and it was double-booked. I was wondering if..."

He shook his head, and I stopped talking. Clearly, he already knew the situation. "Ms. Michaels, I'm so sorry. Mr. Carter was here only minutes ago. I'm sorry to say we still have no available hotel rooms, and with the way this storm is continuing, I doubt we will. I've called to a few of our sister hotels to see if I might be able to find a room, and I haven't had any luck yet."

I sighed. "Well, it was worth a shot. Do you think you could keep checking?"

"I've already made a note of it and put it in our daily pass-down so that the next person on shift will be on the lookout as well."

Smiling, I said, "Thank you so much—" I glanced at his nametag—"Hunter. Thank you."

"It's my pleasure, Ms. Michaels."

With that a bust, I headed back to the elevator and to the gym, which was on the third floor. The entire time I walked down the hall, I tried to think of a solution to the sleeping problem. Maybe they had a rollaway bed I could ask for.

Shit! Why hadn't I thought of that last night?

Pushing open the door to the gym, I saw a man about my age running on one of the two treadmills. There were two elliptical machines and two stationary bikes as well. I walked over to the other treadmill and stepped on. I hit the buttons and started a nice, fast walk to warm up before my run.

When I glanced up and looked into the mirrored wall, I tripped over my own freaking feet.

"Roger," I whispered, taking in the sight of him lifting weights. He had on headphones, and his eyes were shut while he concentrated on doing bicep curls. My tongue instantly went to my lips to moisten them.

The man was dressed in shorts and a T-shirt that said, *"Born and Raised Cowboy."* I knew I'd heard a hint of southern in that accent.

It looked like the damn shirt was painted on him, it fit so snugly.

"Right? He's hot, isn't he?"

My head snapped to the right to find a girl on one of the elliptical machines. She was also watching Roger work out in the mirror. Her dark hair was up in a ponytail, and she looked close to my age, maybe a few years younger. For sure in her late twenties.

"When he started working out, my best friend was running on the treadmill and missed a step. She went flying off the damn thing, and he touched her!"

I screwed up my face in confusion. "He...touched her?"

She laughed. "Not like that. He ran over and helped her up. Asked if she was okay and all of that. I swear the little bitch did it on purpose. Although, she did have to go back up to the room because her elbow was cut open and bleeding."

Gasping, I asked, "Is she okay?"

Elliptical Girl shrugged. "No clue. I told her she was on her own. No way I was leaving this front-row seat. You should see when he does one-legged squats. He has an ass that you could bounce a quarter off of."

I shook my head as I kept walking. "Wait, your friend got hurt, and you stayed here just to watch Roger?"

Her eyes snapped from the mirror to me. "Oh, my God. Like, is he your man? I'm so sorry! He's just so...handsome isn't even the word. He's so pretty, hot, built, fine...I could go on."

I laughed.

"You're so lucky. He's a gentleman. He helped Lynn and asked if she needed him to go get help. You look good together. With you looking like Cinderella and all, and him...Prince Charming."

I rolled my eyes. Good Lord, this man had a powerful effect on women, that was for sure. "He's not my boyfriend."

She nodded. "Husband then. Lucky bitch," she whispered.

Before I had a chance to correct her, I heard my name.

"Annalise, princess. What are you doing here?"

I turned and looked in the mirror to see Roger walking up. Elliptical Girl had to slow down, probably for her own safety.

"Roger," I replied with a smug smile. "I'm about to run a few miles."

The guy on the treadmill next to me had just slowed down and gotten off. Roger glanced at the now empty machine, then back to me.

"A run, huh? How about a little friendly competition?"

I lifted a brow. I loved a good challenge. Widening my smile into a full-on grin, I asked, "What did you have in mind?"

Chapter 3

Roger

SHE WASN'T JUST beautiful. She was fucking thrilling as hell. The way she lit up when I issued a challenge... It was nice to meet a woman who wasn't afraid to spar back with me. Something told me Annalise Michaels liked to win at everything.

Giving her a quick once-over, I had to concentrate on not going hard just from the sight of her. "First person to stop running loses."

"Oh, this is going to be good," the girl on the elliptical said.

Not even bothering to look at her, I said, "Put your bets in, folks."

Annalise laughed but quickly stopped when the guy who had vacated the treadmill called out, "I've got ten on the girl giving up first."

"I'll take that bet!" Elliptical Girl said, coming to a stop and walking over to the guy.

"Wait, what?" Annalise asked as she stared at the two strangers standing off to the side.

"I'll up to twenty," Runner Guy said.

Elliptical Girl turned and walked toward Annalise, gave her a good look-over, and then turned back to Runner Guy. "She looks like she's in good shape."

Annalise grinned. "Thank you."

"I'm upping it to fifty."

I laughed when Annalise's mouth dropped open. "So, this is what happens when people are stuck at hotels during a winter storm, huh?" I joked.

"Done. Fifty it is. How's this going to work?" Runner Dude asked in a serious voice.

Annalise and I looked at each other, and she shrugged. "Rules?"

"It's simple: Get on the treadmill and run," I explained.

"No set speed or incline?"

"Let's keep it simple, princess. It's all about endurance, and trust me when I say I'm like the Energizer Bunny. In all aspects."

She rolled her eyes as Elliptical Girl said, "Oh, my."

Annalise shot me a dirty look. "Fine. Be prepared to get your ass beat."

"Ha!" I mused, taking my place on the treadmill next to her. "You have no idea what you've just gotten yourself into."

With a smug expression, she started to jog. "Maybe now would be the right time to inform you I went to state three years in a row in high school for cross-country. Oh, and I ran cross-country on scholarship in college."

I was positive my jaw hit the treadmill. How I didn't fall and launch off the damn thing like Elliptical Girl's friend earlier, I will never know.

I let out a disbelieving laugh. "You little liar. You're trying to get into my head."

She winked at me. She actually fucking winked at me. My dick instantly went hard.

Then she said, "Guess you'll have to wait and see."

The door to the hotel gym opened and Runner Dude, whose name was Dylan, walked in. "How's it going, Mary?"

Mary, also known as Elliptical Girl, smiled as she looked at me. "He's wearing down, I can tell."

"I...am...not...," I gasped.

Dylan shook his head. "Dude, she's hardly busting a sweat. She's kicking your ass. Not only has she gone farther, she's running faster than you. Move, man!"

"You get up here if you think it's so easy, Dylan! I'm trying! She's a fucking machine!" I retorted.

Mary fist-pumped from her place on the floor where she was watching some stupid YouTube video. "Yeah, she is! Keep going, Annalise!"

Annalise smiled and pulled out her earbud. "What was that?"

Mary gave her a thumbs-up. "Keep going, girl. You're kicking his ass!"

Pulling her eyes from Mary's reflection in the mirror, Annalise turned to me, maintaining her pace on the treadmill. "Oh dear, Roger. You look a little red in the face. You okay?"

"How...are you...talking so...normal?" I gasped for air between each breath.

With a shrug, she replied, "State champ, three years running."

"Don't give up, Roger!" Dylan chanted from the other side of me.

A pain shot through my right leg. "Muscle. Cramp!"

"No!" Dylan cried out at the same time Mary yelled, "Yes! Yes! Yes! He's going down!"

If I didn't stop soon, my fate was going to be the same as the girl who had fallen on the treadmill earlier. And I would be damned if I let Annalise see that happen.

I hit stop while Dylan cried like a baby next to me.

"You can pay me at dinner tonight, Dylan." Mary walked up to Annalise, who was still running, and high-fived her. "Thanks, Annalise. See you at dinner."

When I stepped off the treadmill, my legs felt like jelly. Dylan had to grab hold of me so I didn't fall to the ground.

"How long...were we running? Like, what...five? Six hours?" I asked.

Dylan glanced at the clock on the wall and then back at me with a look of utter pity. "Almost two hours."

"That's it!" I cried out as my hamstring went into a full-throttle cramp, and Dylan dropped me like a hot plate.

"Roger!" Annalise shouted and got off the treadmill to come to my side.

"Oh, my...God! Everything hurts! Can't breathe...heart...attack!"

Kneeling beside me, she rolled her eyes while she stretched my leg and said, "You need to get up."

"Can't. Move."

"You need to get some water into you. Have you not been drinking any?"

I opened my eyes and looked at her. She *had* been sweating after all, thank God. A weird sensation in my chest made my breath hitch as her eyes stared into mine. I was hit by the urge to kiss her, and I had to look away. How could a woman who just ran for two hours straight look so fucking beautiful?

"I ran out," I said, drawing in a deep breath while Annalise continued to stretch my leg.

"Is the cramp gone?"

"It is, but I feel like the second I go to stand, it'll come back again."

Mary rushed back into the gym. "Here! I bought some water and Gatorade. That should help."

Annalise took both drinks. "Thank you, Mary."

I nearly drank the whole damn bottle of Gatorade after Annalise handed it to me. Her eyes went wide, and I knew she was trying to hold back a smile.

"Take deep breaths in your nose for three seconds, then let them out for four," she instructed.

I did as she said, feeling better as the seconds passed by.

"The cramp is gone." I looked up at Dylan. "Sorry you lost, dude."

He glanced at Mary and smiled. "I'm not. I got myself a pretty girl for our double date tonight."

Frowning, I looked at Annalise. "You're going on a date tonight?"

She laughed. "No, Mary and Dylan invited us to eat with them tonight. You said yes."

"You can't ask me questions when I'm in an exercise-induced state of confusion!" I argued.

Her smile instantly fell, and she shrugged casually. "It's okay, you don't have to go. Mary's friend Lynn will be there, as well, so it wasn't a date on our part if that was what you were worried about."

"It is on ours," Mary giggled as she and Dylan headed for the door. "It's been fun. See you later, Annalise!"

Annalise gave them a smile, and I was struck again by how pretty she was.

"See ya around, Roger!" Dylan tossed over his shoulder as if we had been the best of friends forever.

When Annalise turned back to me, her smile once again faded away. "Do you need help getting up?"

"No," I snapped, instantly feeling like a dick when I saw the hurt look in her eyes. "I didn't mean to snap at you like that. I'm just tired."

"It was a good run. You should run marathons if you don't already."

I stood and shot her a weary expression. "Annalise, does it appear to you that I'm a runner? The longest I've ever run was three miles once, and I thought I was going to die."

Her smile was back, and I liked knowing I had put it there.

"Well, it was fun," she said. "I like a little bit of competition."

A thrill of excitement rushed through me. "Is that right?"

She reached for a towel and wrapped it around her neck. "Did you want to take a shower first?"

Being in that hotel room while knowing she was naked was not a good idea. "I'm going to do some more weights, maybe some stretching. You go on up and take your time."

"Okay." She nodded. "And just so you know, the front desk has my name down in case any rooms open up. I'm going to swing by and see if they have any rollaway beds."

"Yeah, they, um, they told me they would give one of us a call should something come open, and I asked about the rollaways. They don't have any."

We both turned and looked out the window at the far end of the gym. The snow was coming down fast and hard.

Annalise sighed and said, "I have a feeling we won't be flying out tomorrow if this keeps up."

"Well, let's hope it stops soon."

When she turned and met my gaze, something passed between us. I couldn't put my finger on what exactly it was.

"Let's hope," she whispered before she grabbed her phone off the treadmill and headed toward the exit. "I'll see you in a few."

"Yeah, see ya."

The moment Annalise left the gym, I reached for my own phone that was in the cup holder of the treadmill. I pulled up Truitt's name and pressed Call.

"Hey, how's it going?" Truitt asked.

"Things could be better. The hotel double-booked my room."

"What do you mean?"

With a frustrated groan, I ran my fingers through my hair. "I mean at two in the morning, I woke up to a half-naked girl in my room. The hotel booked her in my room by mistake."

"Holy shit!" Truitt said, laughing. "Tell me she was pretty, at least."

I glanced back at the door Annalise had just walked through. "Yeah, she's pretty alright. And a pain in the ass."

"Okay, why do I feel like there's more to this story?"

"Because there is. They don't have any open rooms—no hotels around the airport do because of all the stranded travelers. So, we're sharing the room."

The line was silent for a moment. "You're sharing a hotel room with a stranger?"

"Yep. A gorgeous, hot-as-hell, stubborn-woman-who-likes-competitions stranger."

"Do I even want to know what you've already challenged her to?"

"It was just some running. The little minx didn't tell me she'd won state in cross-country in high school and went to college on a track scholarship until after we'd made the bet."

Truitt laughed. "I like this girl. Where's she from?"

"No clue."

"What does she do for a living?"

"I'm not sure."

With a grunt, he asked, "Do you at least know her last name?"

"Yes, I know her last name. That's about all I know of her, and all I care to know."

"Well, it looks like Chicago is getting pounded with snow, and it's forecasted to last well into tomorrow, so you might want to get to know her a little better if y'all are gonna be bunking. I can't wait to tell Ryan."

I rolled my eyes and went over to the workout bench. Ryan was one of our best friends and happened to be the brother of Truitt's wife, Saryn.

"Get a good kick out of it now while I'm not there."

"Are you sleeping on the sofa?"

"Hell, no! It's like a love seat. We slept in the same bed. It's a king."

"Wait. You're sleeping with a pretty—"

"Gorgeous. And hot. Did I mention she has a fucking amazing body?"

Truitt chuckled. "You mentioned something along those lines. Anyway, you're sharing a bed with her?"

"It's not what you're thinking. She made a pillow barrier between us. *Although*," I said with a grin, "I did wake up this morning spooning her. Not sure how in the hell that happened."

Truitt busted out laughing. "Holy hell. You're gonna have blue balls by the time you get back home."

I laughed. "Probably. Anyway, this couple invited us out to eat with them tonight. I think I might have hurt Annalise's feelings by turning them down."

"Why did you turn them down?"

Scoffing, I replied, "I don't want her to think it's a date."

"For fuck's sake, Roger. You're stuck in a hotel room with her. You're never going to see her again. Why would she think it was a date?"

I shrugged, even though he couldn't see me. "I don't know. The other couple is clearly fixin' to hook up. They met in the gym while Annalise and I were trying to see who could outrun the other."

"That's kind of cool."

"What? That the other couple met like that?"

"Yeah, it's cool."

"If you say so."

I heard him sigh. "Just go to dinner. What harm is it gonna do? If you're stuck in Chicago, you might as well deal with it and have a good time."

"I guess. Anyway, I'll let you go."

"Roger...you know it's okay to be attracted to someone in more than a physical way. It's been how many years since—?"

"Don't. Don't say her name, Truitt."

The silence over the phone was deafening.

"That has nothing to do with this," I continued.

"Right. Well, hopefully, a miracle will happen, and the storm will move out, and you'll be on your way back to Texas tomorrow."

"Yeah. Hopefully. Kiss the kids for me."

"I will. Talk to you later."

Hitting End, I stood and took in a few deep breaths. I would take the long way back up to our room and hope that it gave Annalise enough time to shower and change.

"God help me," I whispered as I headed out of the gym.

Chapter 4

Annalise

IT HAD BEEN an hour since I'd left the gym. Surely Roger couldn't still be working out? I glanced at the clock and sighed.

I didn't want to admit it at the time, but when Roger declined dinner, it made my heart drop with disappointment, and that had both surprised me and made me a bit angry. Not that he'd declined the dinner but the fact that his refusal hurt.

Grabbing my purse and the hotel key, I decided to head down to the sports bar in the lobby to see about an early lunch.

When I walked in, I noticed all the TVs had different sports games playing. High tables were spread throughout the room, with a large bar running along the back, and more TVs mounted above all the glasses and liquor.

I decided to sit at the bar since it was just me. I drew closer but paused when I saw Roger. He was already sitting there, and next to him was a young woman. She smiled and placed her hand on his arm as she laughed. I pulled my gaze from the point of contact and cleared my throat, walking toward the opposite end of the bar. Roger hadn't seen me, of course; he was too busy flirting with the young blonde to even notice me walk by.

When I sat down, the good-looking, younger bartender walked up and grinned. "What can I get you?"

"I was wondering if I could order some lunch?"

"Of course. Let me grab you a menu. Can I start you off with a glass of wine?"

Shaking my head, I replied, "Give me your favorite local craft beer."

He winked and said, "You got it."

I took a glance at where Roger was seated. The young woman let out another laugh at something he said, and I found myself rolling my eyes as I turned away.

"Here's the menu and your beer."

With a smile, I took the menu from the bartender. "Thank you so much. So, is this pretty normal? This snowstorm?"

He glanced over the bar toward the large windows and doors at the front of the hotel. "I mean, we get storms, but this one is shutting down the entire city. I'm stuck here. Can't even get home."

"That's awful," I commiserated.

He laughed. "I'm going to guess you're stuck here as well?"

I nodded. "Yes. And forced to bunk with a stranger because they double-booked the room."

His eyes went wide. "Wow. That's no good. They can't find you a room anywhere?"

Again, I shook my head. "Nope. But it's okay, he's pretty nice."

"It's a guy? You're staying in a hotel room with a guy you've never met?"

I shrugged. "It beats sleeping in the airport."

He nodded. "I guess so. There are a few of us bunking in a suite. Not the best situation, but it could be worse. We could lose power."

"Don't say that!" I warned, and he laughed.

"I'll let you look at the menu. Be right back."

I liked the bartender's smile, and I watched him as he walked toward the other end of the bar. The sound of a woman's laughter pulled me from my thoughts, and I glanced over to find Roger looking at me. The young woman on his left was attempting to get his attention again, but his focus was purely on me. I smiled and held up my beer before I quickly focused on the menu.

Something about the way he looked at me started a shiver up my back, making my body shudder.

After deciding on what I wanted, I put the menu down and looked up at the baseball game on the TV.

"Know what you want?" the bartender asked as he appeared in front of me.

"Yes. The grilled chicken salad and a baked potato, loaded, please."

He nodded and started to walk away but then stopped and faced me. "Listen, there's a nightclub on the top floor of the hotel. A few of us are going later. You're more than welcome to come with me, or all of us—I mean, if you'd like to."

I smiled and took him in. He couldn't have been more than twenty-three if that. Cute as hell with what looked like an amazing body. "I'm pretty sure I'm at least ten years older than you," I stated as I picked up my beer and took a sip.

With a shrug, he replied, "That doesn't make you any less beautiful."

I could feel the heat of someone's eyes on me and turned to see Roger staring once again.

I dug my teeth into my lip and turned back to the bartender. What would a little harmless dancing do for one evening? I might as well have a bit of fun while I was stuck in Chicago.

"I'll meet you there. What time?"

A wide smile appeared on his face. "Eleven, at the front of the club?"

"Eleven it is," I said with a soft laugh.

He reached over the bar and extended his hand. "The name is Roby, by the way."

I shook his hand and replied, "Annalise. It's nice to meet you."

"Same." With a wink, he said, "Let me go get your order in."

I watched Roby walk over and enter my order.

"A little young for you, isn't he?"

Jumping at the sound of Roger's voice near my ear, I turned and shot him a dirty look. "You scared me."

"Sorry, didn't mean to interrupt your gawking."

I rolled my eyes. "I wasn't gawking."

"So, where are you meeting your new little friend?"

Taking a drink of my beer, I glanced over toward Roby. "There's a nightclub on the top floor of the hotel. I'm meeting him there later this evening."

Chancing a look at Roger, I almost laughed when I saw him scowling at poor Roby. "Is he even twenty-one?" he asked.

"Stop it," I said with a chuckle. "Who's the pretty little blonde you were chatting up?"

"That's Lynn, Mary's friend. She fell off the treadmill earlier. I saw her sitting at the bar and asked if she was okay. She invited me to dinner tonight."

I stiffened. "Did you accept?"

"Yes, I did."

That made me jerk my head to the side. "You mean the dinner you were invited to earlier that you turned down?"

He reached over for my beer, then took a long drink. He set it down with his brows raised. "That's good."

My eyes bounced from my nearly half-downed beer to Roger. Ugh. I wanted to punch him in the face.

"To answer your question, I already ran into Dylan and told him I would join y'all for dinner tonight," he said.

"You said you didn't want to go."

He looked at me and grinned. "I changed my mind."

"Because of Lynn?" I asked, hating that I voiced my thought out loud.

Roger simply grinned at me.

"Another beer, Annalise?" Roby asked.

"On a first-name basis, I see." Roger extended his hand to Roby. "Roger. I hear you and my roomie are meeting up later at the club."

Roby's gaze turned to me. "This is the guy?"

Roger stared at me as I answered, "Yes, this is the guy."

He gave Roger a look. "Is it cool that I asked her out?"

My mouth dropped open. "Wait a minute, Roger and I are not together. At all. I mean, please."

"Hey, I take offense to that," Roger said. "Would it be so wrong if we were together?"

"We're not, so it doesn't matter," I countered.

"But what if we were...? Would that be so bad?"

Roby glanced back and forth between us as if watching a tennis match before he finally walked away.

I turned to face Roger. "Why are we even having this conversation?"

"Because you acted like being with me would be a bad thing. No, a disgusting thing."

Laughing, I shook my head as I said, "Nonsense."

Roby walked up with my replacement beer, and I smiled at him. I noticed he set one down for Roger, as well, before he headed off to help other patrons.

Roger leaned toward me on his barstool. "Then why did you have to throw a 'please' on the end as if the idea was insane?"

I swiveled on the barstool and stared up into his eyes. They were still the most beautiful shade of blue I had ever seen in my life. It was like looking at the sky on a perfectly clear day.

For a moment, I lost all train of thought. "You have the most stunning blue eyes."

"I could say the same thing about you, Anna."

Hearing him use my nickname made my heart thump against my chest.

"Thank you," I whispered before clearing my throat. "I hardly know you, Roger, so how could I know what being with you is like?"

A slow, unbelievably sexy grin moved across his face. "We could go up to the room and I can show you right now."

I raised a brow. "Are you asking me to sleep with you?"

He let out a soft laugh. "We did that last night, Anna. I'm asking if you want me to fuck you and show you just how good we could be together."

An instant rush of wetness gathered between my legs, along with a throbbing I hadn't felt in a very long time. Before Roger could read my face, I turned away from him and reached for my beer.

"Aren't you the romantic," I stated dryly. I took a drink, praying he wouldn't notice the effect his words had on me.

He laughed, reached for his own beer, and took a drink. When he put it back down, I could feel his eyes on me, but he didn't say anything else. Was he waiting for me to say something?

"Has anyone ever told you that you look like—"

I cut him off and asked, "Cinderella?" Sighing, I went on. "Yes. All the time. I actually played the part in a high school play. I've always wanted to go to Disney's Magic Kingdom."

"You've never been?" Roger asked.

"Nope," I replied with a shake of my head. "Someday. This is probably silly, and I know I'll regret telling you this, but I've always dreamed of having my honeymoon there."

Roger smiled. "Why would I think it's silly?"

With a half-shrug, I said, "I don't know. I'm too old to believe in fairy tales anymore, but..." My voice trailed off before Roger bumped my arm. "I've always wanted to meet her...Cinderella."

I felt my cheeks heat up, and I turned to look at him. He stared at me with the strangest expression. Probably thinking of how he could get rid of the crazy woman staying in his room.

He shook his head. "I'm going to head on back to the room and clean up." He stood, leaned down, and pressed his mouth against my ear. "Enjoy your lunch, Annalise."

Even if I wanted to say something in return, I couldn't physically do it. My entire body was on fire from those four damn words. It was the smell of him. That outdoorsy, musky smell that I knew was simply a mix of his cologne and sweat. God, why did it turn me on so much? Or was it the way his hot breath tickled down my neck and seemed to spread throughout my entire body?

All I could do was nod and then watch as he walked out of the bar while I tried not to imagine what being with Roger Carter would feel like. No, as I tried to not imagine what being *fucked* by Roger Carter would feel like.

Chapter 5

Roger

THE DOOR TO the bathroom opened, and Annalise stepped out in a dress that nearly had me swallowing my own tongue.

"Wow. You look...beautiful."

She glanced down at the form-fitting black dress and smiled. It was long-sleeved, but one sleeve was lace from wrist to shoulder. When she turned, I had to fight to hold in a moan. The back of the dress was low-cut enough to tease me with the soft skin of her back. When she finished her spin, I let my eyes roam her entire body. It was a sexy-as-fuck dress, but not too sexy. It fell just above her knee, and showed enough cleavage to make my dick harden in my pants.

"You look pretty nice yourself," she said. "Do you always have suits with you when you travel?"

"When you're a lawyer and in meetings for days on end, you do."

She lifted her brows. "A lawyer, huh?"

It was then I realized that the only thing we truly knew about each other was our names. "Yes, I was in Chicago on business, mostly for my brother. He's in negotiations to do a show on a cable network, and he couldn't make it, so I stepped in."

"Wow, that's kind of cool. What does he do for a living?"

"Builds playhouses."

I could see the confusion on her face, so I took out my phone and pulled up the latest playhouse Truitt was building. It was castle-themed.

"Holy shit! That isn't a playhouse, it's a mini castle! That's for someone's kid?"

Laughing, I said, "Yeah. You'd be surprised at what he's made. He's done playhouses for a few actors, and a couple of singers, as well."

"That's amazing."

I pushed my phone back into my pocket and watched as Annalise made her way over to her suitcase and pulled out a small clutch.

"What do you do for a living, since we're sharing?" I asked.

"I'm in hotel management. I was most recently employed at the Lotte New York Palace in New York City."

"Shit, that place is nice."

She smiled. "You've stayed there before?"

With a nod, I replied, "I have. A college friend of mine got married there. It's beautiful. How long did you work there?"

"Six years."

"Why did you leave?" I asked, watching her grab a pair of black high heels. She bent slightly to slip them on, and I stared at her perfect ass, my pants suddenly feeling a bit too tight.

"I was tired of living in New York. A smaller hotel was looking for a general manager, and I needed a change. I interviewed for it twice, and they offered me the position. I was supposed to start tomorrow."

"Shit, that sucks."

Annalise shrugged. "They know I'm stuck in Chicago, so it's not that big of a deal."

I got up from the couch when I saw that she was ready. We both started to head for the door.

"Will it be a big change for you?" I asked.

"A *huge* change! But one that I'm looking forward to. I'm only thirty-one, but I feel like I need to slow down. I want wide-open spaces and room to breathe. New York City was fun when I was younger, but not so much now."

As we walked to the elevator, I contemplated how much personal information we should share with one another. I wanted to ask her where the new hotel was but decided not to. She hadn't asked me any more information about my personal life, so I wouldn't pry into hers.

Annalise hit the button for the floor and said, "Mary said we're supposed to meet them at the Andiamo."

I placed my hand on her lower back and tried to ignore the way it sent a jolt of heat through my entire body. I also ignored the way my heartbeat seemed to speed up as well. Ever since I'd made that stupid suggestion about fucking her, I hadn't been able to get it out of my head.

Every time I closed my goddamn eyes, I saw Annalise naked under me. Naked on top of me. Naked in the shower. Naked in every possible way I could think of.

"Roger? Roger?"

Snapping out of my thoughts, I looked around.

"Are you coming?" Annalise asked with a slight chuckle, standing half-in and half-out of the elevator.

I shook my head. "Shit, I must have been lost in thought. I don't even remember the elevator ride."

With a smile and a wink, she said, "I hope they were good thoughts."

My gaze fell to her mouth, which only moments ago I had pictured wrapped around my cock. "Very good," I said, clearing my throat.

"Shall we?" she asked.

I nodded and motioned for Annalise to start walking. Man, she looked so beautiful in that dress. It was a damn good thing I was never going to see this woman again because if I had to look at her every day, I was pretty sure my hand would cramp from jerking off to her image.

"Annalise! Roger! Over here!" a female voice called out.

"There they are," I said as I pointed to the table where Mary, Dylan, and Lynn were sitting with some other guy I hadn't met.

"I'm glad you joined us for dinner, Roger," Mary stated. She stood to hug Annalise, then turned and smiled at the guy sitting next to Lynn.

"Annalise, Roger, this is Monty, Dylan's business partner and friend. He's stuck here as well."

I reached out and shook his hand. "Nice to meet you, Monty."

Monty smiled at me and then focused on Annalise. He made no secret of the fact that he was checking her out, letting his eyes take in every inch of her body in a slow perusal. "Dylan said you were beautiful, but he didn't say you were stunningly beautiful."

For fuck's sake, had he really just used that line on her? When I took a quick glance over at Annalise, she didn't seem the least bit impressed. Instead, she looked at Lynn and extended her hand.

"I don't believe we've met yet, Lynn."

Lynn gave her a smile that was fake as hell and quickly shook Annalise's hand, letting her gaze bounce from me to Annalise. "No, we haven't had the pleasure."

I pulled out a chair for Annalise, then sat next to her while Monty continued to stare. I glanced at Lynn and caught her staring at *me*.

Good grief, dinner was going to be long.

Twenty minutes into the meal, and I was fighting the urge to reach across the table and knock the shit out of Monty. He was obnoxious, and his endless flirting with Annalise was not only getting on my nerves, but everyone else's as well. Never mind the fact that Lynn kept trying to pierce me with her fuck-me-now eyes.

"Annalise, what are you doing after dinner?" Monty asked.

Looking up from her meal, she replied, "I'm actually meeting someone up at the club on the top floor of the hotel."

I tried to ignore the way that made my blood boil. Why should I care if Annalise was hooking up with some bartender? She was a grown woman, and one I hardly even knew. And if I didn't care, why did the idea of Roby or Bobby, or whatever the hell his name was, touching Annalise make me want to hit someone?

Jackass Monty raised a brow and looked over at me. I smiled and went back to eating.

Suddenly, Lynn clapped her hands, which had us all looking at her as she bounced in her seat like a five-year-old. "We should all go to the club tonight. I mean, if we're stuck in this godforsaken hotel, we might as well take advantage of it, right?"

Monty leaned back in his chair and grinned like the Cheshire cat. "That's a great idea, Lynn. Who's up for a trip to the club?"

Mary and Dylan exchanged a glance before they both agreed as well.

Lynn pinned hopeful eyes on me and asked, "What about you, Roger? Will you go too? I would love to dance with you."

I could feel Annalise looking at me. "Sure, a little dancing never harmed anyone."

When I turned to her, she smiled and then looked across the table at Lynn. She frowned, and I followed her gaze, only to find Lynn eye-fucking me again.

"Does that mean you'll save me a dance or two?" Lynn asked me.

Ignoring her, I focused on Dylan. "What do you and Monty do for business?"

Dylan let out a chuckle, clearly catching on that I wasn't the least bit interested in Lynn. "We own a consulting firm."

"Really?" I asked. "What sort of consulting firm?"

"A large, very profitable one," Monty added.

"What do you do, Roger?" Mary asked.

I gave a one-shoulder shrug. "My father owns a ranch. I help with the cows."

Annalise laughed but then quickly covered it with a cough.

"What about you, sweetheart?" Monty asked, staring at Annalise.

"The name is Annalise," she said with a frown. "Not sweetheart, babe, baby, darlin', *or princess*."

I couldn't help but smile as I reached for my beer and took a sip.

"And I'm in hotel management," she added.

"Here in Chicago?" Monty asked.

Annalise reached for her wine, but before she took a drink, she answered with one word. "No."

"So, you sound like you're from the south, Roger. And your daddy owns a ranch. How exciting. I've always wanted to…two-step with a cowboy." Lynn slowly ran her tongue across her lips.

"This is not your lucky night then, Lynn," I said. "Sorry, but I don't know how to two-step."

The girl actually pouted. Monty turned to her and said, "I know how to two-step. I'm from Dallas."

Christ above, please don't let this douche be on my flight back to Texas.

Lynn clapped her hands again and then wrapped her arm around Monty's. "Then you get the first dance."

"What if it isn't a country song, Lynn?" Mary asked.

Monty's and Lynn's eyes were locked, almost as if seeing each other for the first time. "Who cares?" Lynn purred as she tilted her head and winked at Monty.

Annalise leaned over and whispered in my ear, "I feel like we've just been saved in some weird way."

I smiled and turned my head, nearly brushing my lips against hers. Annalise drew back in surprise, but the smile stayed on her face.

"Let's hope," I said.

Chapter 6

Annalise

THE MOMENT ROGER placed his hand on my lower back when we stood from the table, I felt my body tremble again. It was subtle enough that I knew he wouldn't notice—like he hadn't noticed when he'd gently guided me onto the elevator and then over to the table. Every damn time he touched me, my heart felt as if it was about to leap right out of my chest.

We pulled ahead of the rest of our group, and Roger leaned down to speak quietly to me.

"I'm pretty sure Lynn was trying to play footsy under the table with me."

I laughed. "She was. She kept hitting my leg, and I finally kicked her foot away. That was about the time she started to pay attention to Monty."

He chuckled, and I loved how the sound rumbled in his chest. "Thank you, then. I thought at one point she was going to jump across the table and attack me."

"Me too! And what about that clown, Monty? Oh, my gawd, could he be any more stuck on himself?" I asked as I tossed a quick look over my shoulder. Monty and Lynn were pulling up the rear, deep in conversation.

"Well, at least you won't have to worry about him when you meet up with your date later."

I stumbled, and Roger reached for my arm to steady me. "Sorry, not used to walking in these heels," I said. "And by the way, it's not a date."

We stopped at the elevator, and Roger pushed the arrow pointing up. The rest of the group slowly made their way toward us. "Your bartender friend probably thinks it is. You told him you'd meet up with him, Anna. That's a date."

Why did I love the way he said my name? It was that southern accent of his and the way he didn't use a long "A."

"Well, it's not. I told him I would meet him and his friends. I didn't say I planned to spend the entire night with him."

Roger laughed again. "Good, because there's no bringing anyone back to our room."

I huffed and replied, "Like I would ever do that."

He simply shrugged.

A thought hit me right in the middle of my chest. What if *Roger* met someone and wanted to bring them back to our hotel room? A strange sensation rushed through me.

Holy hell. Is that...jealousy?

"What's the matter?" Roger asked.

I shook my head. "Nothing, just silly thoughts running through my mind."

He raised a brow. "Care to share?"

"No, I do not."

He winked and my stomach flipped. *Damn this man and the way he makes me feel.*

Roger and I rode up in the elevator in silence as the rest of our group chatted on and on about the club we were going to and how amazing it would be. I exchanged a look with Roger as we were getting off the elevator and nearly tripped. He was smiling at me. With those dimples. Ugh.

Quickly looking away, I focused on the entrance to the club in front of me. Roby would be standing on the other side of the door, and I suddenly realized how stupid it was of me to agree to meet him here. I had done it purely out of spite because Roger had been talking to Lynn in the bar earlier. *Why, hello there, jealousy. I see you're back again already.*

"You're a little early if you're supposed to meet him at eleven," Mary said as she walked up next to me.

I glanced at her and said, "I'm not that worried about it—it was just an excuse to get out, to be honest."

Mary nodded and looked back over her shoulder at Dylan. "I'm really glad you came into that workout room this morning. If you hadn't, I would have never even spoken to Dylan."

I followed her gaze. "You like him?"

Her eyes met mine, and she smiled brightly. "I really do. We've spent all day together. Talking, walking around the hotel, and getting to know each other. I'm sorta hoping Lynn hooks up with Monty so Dylan and I can be alone tonight."

My brows shot up in surprise. "Oh, wow! You really...*really* like him."

Mary blushed. "Yeah, I think the feeling is mutual."

I glanced over to where Dylan stood, talking to Roger.

"But where does he live? Where do *you* live?" I asked.

"He lives in Philadelphia, and I live in Houston."

"So, it would be long-distance."

She nodded. "But I can work anywhere for my job, which is a plus."

"What is it you do?"

"I design websites, so I work one-hundred percent from home. Not that I'm saying I would up and move. I haven't even known him for twenty-four hours," she said with a chuckle. "At first, I thought it might be a fun adventure to have a bit of a love affair, and for all I know, it could still turn out to be just that. For once, I'm not going to listen to my head. I'm going to live in a fairy tale land for a while."

I nodded and stole a look at Roger. Chewing on my lip, I let myself wonder what it would be like to have a love affair, as Mary called it, with Roger. No strings attached, just sex. Hot, amazing sex, because if the man could make my body burn with desire simply from smiling at me and touching my back, what in the hell would he do to me in bed?

Mary leaned in closer to me. "Just do it, Annalise. I see the way the two of you look at each other. Have you never had a one-night stand?"

"I have, and I regretted it the moment I did the walk of shame the next morning. This time, I'd still be stuck with him and not even able to leave if I wanted to."

We both laughed as Mary intertwined her arm in mine and walked us toward the nightclub's entrance. "Well, if you want my vote, I say go for it. You only live once, right? Besides, after this snowstorm is over, you'll never see Roger again."

I forced a smile. Why did the thought of not ever seeing Roger again make me feel…sad?

Good Lord, maybe I did need to get laid.

After we all showed our IDs and paid to get in, we stepped through a door that led into the nightclub. It was dark in the club, but not dark enough that you couldn't glance around and see everyone. I was impressed that you couldn't hear the music outside in the hallway except for a slight beat of the bass. A bar ran along the back and sides of the club, with a large dance floor in the middle. Not very many tables and booths were scattered about, leaving more room for the dance floor. There weren't a lot of people in the club since it was most likely only the guests of the hotel and maybe some hotel employees. Yet the few tables they had were mostly all taken. There were people of all ages here.

Lynn let out a squeal, and then she and Monty took off toward the dance floor and never looked back.

The bass of the music moved through my already-tense body, and I felt a strange sensation as I drew in a slow breath. I felt eyes on me, and I swore I could feel the heat of them boring into me. Was it Roby, maybe?

No. He wouldn't make me feel like that.

Turning, those blue eyes met mine, and I knew the heat I was feeling was from Roger. Then he looked past me and frowned.

Following his gaze, I saw Roby in a small crowd. I couldn't help but laugh at the sight before me.

"Looks like he didn't want to wait," Roger quipped.

Roby was locked in a kiss with a woman who appeared to be closer to his own age. A sense of relief washed over me, and I turned back to look at Roger. "I actually feel relieved."

He laughed and shook his head. "Drink?"

Nodding, I let him take my hand and lead us over to the bar. Mary came rushing up to us.

"Dylan found a table. Do you mind getting us drinks?"

Roger shook his head. "Don't mind at all."

"Same as what we had at dinner, please. We're over in the corner right there!" Mary pointed. I stood on the balls of my heels but couldn't see anything. Roger, on the other hand, nodded.

Looking down at me, he asked, "What do you want, princess?"

Normally, a guy calling me princess would drive me up the wall, but when Roger said it, it actually made me feel like one. When most guys said it, they were trying to get under my skin, knowing that people always told me I looked like Cinderella. And then, of course, when a former boss of mine began saying it, all it did was creep me out. Maybe I was already in that fairy tale land Mary had talked about. I had always been a sucker for the whole happily ever after. I tried to hide my smile behind a deep sigh. "Whatever beer you're drinking, please." Turning to Mary, I said, "I'll help Roger bring back the drinks."

Mary glanced around quickly and then shouted, "Nothing for Lynn and Monty—I have no idea where they went."

Nodding, I placed my hand on Roger's arm and nearly gasped. Lord Almighty, the man was built like a brick house. He dropped his head to hear me better.

"Nothing for Lynn and Monty."

He gave me a thumbs-up before stepping closer to the bar and yelling out our order. I reached into my purse to pull out my credit card, but he brushed my hand to the side. "I've got the first round."

"Thank you," I replied with a smile.

Soon we had our arms full of drinks, and I tried not to spill mine as we made our way through the people and over to the table. Bodies pressed against me, and I quickly remembered why I stopped going to clubs. I hated crowds. Big or small ones. Finally, I saw our table. Mary and Dylan had their heads together, deep in conversation.

After handing them their drinks, Roger motioned for me to slide into the booth, and then he slid in next to me. The feel of his body so close to mine caused a rush of emotions. Lust, excitement, nervousness, curiosity... You name it, I felt it. There was no denying the reason I felt so hot, and it had nothing to do with the heat of the club.

The music vibrated through my entire body, and the longer I sat there, the more I realized how much I wanted to dance. I slid my gaze over to Roger, who was looking out over the dance floor. He must have sensed me staring because his eyes moved to me.

He bent closer and placed his mouth against my ear, and the warmth of his breath made me shiver. "Want to make a bet?"

"What kind of bet?" I asked with a suspicious look.

He laughed. "I'm going to guess that your bartender boy toy is keeping a close eye on the time and will indeed be waiting for you to meet him."

I glanced out over the crowd to where I had last seen Roby. I couldn't see him since the nightclub was darker and there was a good group of people in the place, but from the way he'd been lip-locked with that girl, I highly doubted he'd be looking for me still.

Turning back to Roger, I asked, "How much?"

His eyes sparkled with excitement. I loved that he got just as much of a thrill out of betting as I did.

"A hundred dollars says he'll be there at eleven."

My eyes drifted down to the wide smile on his mouth. I couldn't help but wonder if his lips would be as soft as they looked.

"Fine. A hundred on him not being there," I stated.

Roger slowly shook his head. "Princess, have you looked in the mirror lately? Why do you think he won't be there?"

I gave a half-shrug. "I think he likes to flirt and will most likely assume I'm a no-show, especially considering I'm older."

Roger reached for his beer and took a long, slow drink before he placed it back down. He looked at his watch and then back out over the crowd.

"I guess we'll find out in five minutes," he shouted as he kept scanning the dance floor.

"Five minutes!? How long were we up at the bar?" I called over the music.

Mary gestured to me. "Are you going to go and see if he shows up?"

I nodded and jammed my thumb toward Roger. "Made a bet with Roger, so I need to go see. He says he'll show. I say he won't."

Dylan laughed and shouted back, "He'll show!"

Mary nodded. "Hell, yeah, he will. Have you looked in the mirror lately?"

I felt my cheeks heat at Mary's compliment, or maybe it was from Roger leaning into me as he said, "I told you."

Glancing back at him, I sucked in a breath at how close we were. All I had to do was lean into him a *little bit more*, and our lips would meet. Roger's eyes fell to my mouth, and I instinctively swept my tongue out over my lips. His gaze jerked back up, and for a moment I swore he was going to kiss me. Instead, he grinned wickedly and leaned back, once again scanning the dance floor.

It was only when he took his eyes off me that I realized I had been holding my breath. I exhaled slowly and leaned against the back of the booth.

"Jesus Christ, the sexual tension between the two of you is off the charts!" Mary said into my ear. "Just fuck him already and put both of you out of your misery."

Laughing, I pushed her away. "You're crazy!"

She tilted her head and regarded me before she said, "Maybe, but I know *I'm* getting laid tonight."

Her voice was a bit loud since there was a slower song playing now, and Roger and Dylan both looked at us.

Dylan grinned from ear to ear and then focused on me. "Mary and I'll stay here while you two go see if your date arrived. That way we don't lose the booth."

Roger slid out and reached for my hand. The moment our fingers touched, I felt that jolt. Roger's eyes met mine, and there was no doubt about it—I saw the desire in them, and I was positive mine mirrored it back.

Or he was simply excited to see who was going to win the next bet. That thought wasn't as thrilling, though, so I pushed it away.

Roger laced our fingers together as he guided us toward the entrance, pushing through the crowd of people. I glanced over to where I had seen Roby, but he was gone.

"Wait," I called out, pulling Roger to a stop.

"What's wrong?" he asked.

"Dance with me!" I shouted.

His brows snapped down in confusion. "What?"

I pulled him toward the dance floor. "Dance with me."

With a slight shake of his head, he glanced toward the entrance and then back to me. "What about Roby?"

"It doesn't matter to me if he's there or not. I don't want to see him."

Roger looked confused. "Why not?"

I swallowed hard and decided to follow Mary's advice. "I'd rather spend the night with you."

He pulled his head back in surprise, and I felt my stomach drop in horror. It didn't even occur to me that maybe Roger *wanted* me to meet up with Roby so he could...

"I mean, unless you'd rather be free to um...um..."

He tugged at my hand and pulled me up against him. "No, I'd rather dance with you—and only you."

A heated pool of desire built in my lower stomach, and I couldn't help the smile that grew on my face.

The song ended; "Coño" by Jason Derulo started. My goodness, the heavens were on my side tonight. Roger must have thought so, as well, because his sexy grin with those full dimples appeared, and he backed me toward the dance floor. My heartbeat matched the rhythm of the song as Roger pulled my body against his and proceeded to move in ways I would have never imagined. He moved his hips like we were in the middle of one of those hot salsa dances.

Good God, can this man dance.

It wasn't long before I relaxed and matched his movements with my own. When his hands traveled up my sides, then my arms, then back down in a slow, sensual way, I followed his lead. For someone so big and built, he moved fluidly.

I turned and pressed my ass against him and nearly lost my ability to think when I felt how hard he was. Roger placed his hands on my hips and moved us in ways that should honestly be illegal to do in public.

If we kept this up, I'd be dragging him back down to our room.

Roger turned to me and drew my body up against his as the song changed again. "My Oh My" started. He gave me a crooked smile that said his thoughts were as wicked as mine, and my knees nearly buckled out from under me. That smile said so many things, and I found myself returning one of my own. Or at least, I sure hoped mine came across as sexy.

He placed his hand behind my neck, threaded his fingers into my hair, and then pulled, causing my head to fall back. I gasped at the shock of the slight pain and pleasure mixed together that came over me.

My chest lifted and fell, and it had nothing to do with dancing.

God, kiss me already!

Apparently, the man could read minds as well. Roger pulled me closer and lowered his mouth to mine.

His tongue swept over my lips, prompting me to open to him. The moment I did, and his tongue met mine, I moaned in glorious delight. A growling sound from deep in Roger's throat made me stretch up to deepen the kiss, while his other hand pressed against my lower back, drawing my body to his. He obviously needed us closer in the same way I did. If I could have, I would have crawled into his body and explored it all night long.

Roger tore his mouth away, and we both opened our eyes and locked gazes. He was breathing just as hard as I was.

His eyes searched my face as if making sure he was reading all the signs right.

Hell to the yes, he is. What was it Mary had said? You only live once?

Drawing in a breath, I wrapped my arms around his neck and drew those soft, luscious lips back to mine in another mind-blowing, heated kiss. In my entire thirty-one years, no one had kissed me as senseless as Roger Carter was doing.

That should have been my first warning sign.

Chapter 7

Roger

WHEN ANNALISE PULLED me back down to kiss her, I had to fight the urge to push her into a dark corner and explore more of her body. Yes, I wanted to sink deep inside of her, but what I wanted to do *most* of all was strip her dress off and kiss every fucking inch of her soft skin. She was perfect in every way, and God, did I want to learn more. Never mind the fact that she smelled like a springtime garden. Roses and something else had been hitting me all night, nearly driving me mad.

"Roger," she murmured against my mouth as I pulled us off the dance floor and over to a nearby wall. I pressed her body to the hard surface and captured her lips once more. Her hands moved up my chest, and we both moaned at the added contact between our bodies.

Dragging her mouth from mine, Annalise gasped for air while I placed kisses down her neck.

"We need...to leave," she shouted over the roar of the nightclub.

I slowly drew back and looked down into her eyes. "If we go back to the hotel room right now, Annalise, I'm going to strip that dress off of you and fuck you until you're so damn exhausted your body can't even move."

Her mouth fell open slightly before she closed it, swallowed hard, and then whispered what I thought was a yes.

"Is that a yes, you do want me to take you back to the room?"

Her head bobbed up and down. "Yes. I desperately want and need for you to take me back to the room. Now!"

Clasping her hand in mine, I pulled her through the nightclub and to the exit.

Once outside, my pounding heart competed with the bass of the music drifting through the entrance.

"Wait," Annalise said, yanking me to a stop. Shit, if she told me that we needed to slow down, I was going to have to go take a very cold shower.

"Shouldn't we let the others know we're leaving?"

I stared at her like she'd lost her damn mind. "I think it's okay, Annalise. I highly doubt they'll miss us."

A smile appeared on her face, followed by a slight blush on her cheeks. My God, she was the most beautiful woman I had ever laid eyes on. I couldn't wait to see where else on her body she blushed.

She giggled. "Right. Let's go."

I pressed my hand to her lower back and guided her away from the club and around the corner to the elevators. It was getting harder and harder to ignore the way my body reacted anytime I came in contact with Annalise. Honestly, it should have scared the living hell out of me. But now was not the time to worry about it, so I pushed it aside.

I motioned for another couple to step into the elevator ahead of us. They did and stood off to the side. When Annalise and I stepped in, it was as if the other couple suddenly had blinders on. They embraced and started kissing.

Annalise's mouth dropped open and her eyes went wide as she pulled her gaze from the couple to me. All I could do was wink and fight the urge to show that stupid bastard the correct way to kiss a woman senseless. No, what I wanted to do to the woman standing beside me needed to be done in private.

The elevator descended and finally stopped on our floor. The ding of the door opening caused the other couple to stop sucking face to see what floor it was. As we walked out of the elevator, I glanced back to see the guy lifting the girl and pushing her against the wall.

Annalise gasped. "Oh, my gosh, are they going to…?"

"Fuck in the elevator?" I asked.

"Yes. Are they?"

Laughing, I tugged her a bit faster. "Pretty damn bold if they are."

"Here, I've got my key."

I heard the sound of the door unlocking, and it made me pause for the slightest moment. I put my hand on the handle, turned it, but barely cracked the door open. Looking down at Annalise, I asked, "Are you sure? We don't have to do this."

She smiled up at me as she placed her hand on the side of my face. "I want to do this. I think I've wanted you since the moment you jumped out of the bed naked."

Smiling, I dipped my head and kissed her quickly before fully opening the door. We probably needed to go over some things before we did anything. Like the fact that we would most likely never see one another again after the next day or two.

I stepped back from her and tried to think straight. Her kisses had left me shaken.

Clearing my throat, I motioned for her to walk in and said, "We both need to agree there are no strings attached. We don't ask personal questions."

Annalise nodded. "I agree, it has to be no strings. No personal information."

When the door clicked shut, she faced me. All she had to do was smile, and I was lost to her. She dropped her purse, and we both took a step toward one another, within touching distance. Her hands were everywhere on me. Pulling my shirt out of my pants, fumbling with the buttons on my shirt, all while I attempted to unzip the dress she had on.

"The fuck, is this thing Roger-proof?" I asked, tugging on the zipper.

Giggling, she reached behind her back and slid it down with ease. "You need to use gentle hands."

My cock instantly got harder in my pants if that was at all possible.

I pulled my shirt open, and buttons flew everywhere. Annalise let out a squeal, but then sobered when I reached for her dress and pushed it off her shoulders and down her stunningly perfect body. It pooled at her feet, leaving her dressed in only a black bra and black lace panties.

"Please tell me those are a thong," I whispered.

With a wicked smile, she stepped out of the dress, took a few steps back, and slowly turned her body in a full circle.

Annalise, dressed in black heels, a bra, and a lace thong, was my new favorite thing in the entire world.

"Fuck me," I whispered as I started to undo my belt and then my pants, all the while keeping my eyes on her. She ran her finger along the line of her panties. "You are beautiful, princess."

I waited for her to reprimand me for using the nickname, but all she did was hook her thumbs into her panties and slowly push them down.

The room swayed, and I suddenly felt lightheaded when I watched her kick the thong to the side. Then she reached up behind her and unclasped her bra, letting it slide down her arms and to the floor. She was perfection in every way. Her body was slender, yet she had curves in all the right places. Obviously, she worked out, but she wasn't stick-thin, and I loved that.

"I need you to know something, Roger."

All I could do was nod as I took in the naked goddess who stood before me. If I touched my dick right now or stroked it, I would come within seconds.

Kicking off one heel, she kept talking. "I've never done anything like this before. I don't want you to think..."

Her voice trailed off, and she dropped her gaze from mine. I wanted to tell her the same thing—that I hadn't had any meaningless one-night stands. But it was far from the truth. I wasn't a manwhore, but I had been with plenty of women in my day. Something about Annalise, though, was so different. The last thing I wanted to do was dwell on the fact that she made me feel things I hadn't ever felt before.

"Tell me what you want, Anna."

Her eyes lifted to mine again. "If all we have is the next twenty-four hours, give or take, to spend together, I want to spend it learning every inch of your…"

Her voice trailed off once more, and she watched as I slipped my pants and my boxer briefs down in one movement. My dick sprang out and bounced against my stomach muscles. Annalise licked her lips, staring at my cock as I kicked off my shoes and finished undressing.

"You were saying," I softly prompted, walking over to her.

"I, um… I want to…to…um…" With a quick shake of her head, she lifted her eyes to meet mine. Nothing else needed to be said as I took the final step, cupped her face with my hands, and kissed her.

She wrapped her arms around me, and we both moaned when our bodies pressed fully against each other's.

"Oh, God, Roger."

My name coming off those pink lips was enough to almost make me lose my damn load right then and there.

I reached down and swept her up into my arms and carried her into the bedroom. I was just starting to lay her on the bed when she said, "Wait! Take the top cover off! I don't want my body touching it."

Chuckling, I set her down, ripped the comforter off, and then grabbed her and tossed her onto the bed while she laughed.

She crawled up the mattress and lay down completely. Her blonde hair splayed across the pillows, creating the most erotic image I'd ever seen. Never in my life had I ever wanted to be inside a woman as much as I did with Annalise.

I moved over her and kissed her gently on the lips before brushing my mouth along her jawline and down her neck.

"Birth control?" I asked.

She panted and then stilled.

I drew back and looked at her. "I have condoms. I wasn't sure if you were on the pill or not."

Nothing like *the talk* to kill the mood.

"I'm on the pill, and I want to feel you... All of you. I'm clean, by the way. I mean, no sexual diseases."

I swallowed hard. "I've never had sex without a condom before."

"If you—" she started before I pressed my mouth to hers to end that conversation. If she wanted me to go bare, I was going to fucking go bare.

"I want to feel you, too, Anna. I'm also clean and was tested a few months back and haven't been with anyone since then."

She smiled, and I felt a strange pull in my chest.

"I'm going to learn every single thing about this beautiful body and what brings you pleasure."

Her chest rose and fell as she dug her teeth into her lower lip.

"First place is here," I whispered, rubbing my thumb over one peaked nipple. I placed my mouth over the other, gently sucking.

Annalise gasped, laced her fingers through my hair, and tugged. I had to fight the urge to move and bury myself inside of her.

Slow down. Take your damn time and savor each moment.

I wanted to memorize every single thing about Annalise and this night. If this was the only time I'd ever be with her, I needed to remember it.

Her body arched as she pushed her breast farther into my mouth. I gently bit down on the nipple while I twisted the other.

"Roger!" she softly cried out, her fingers digging deeper into my hair.

Christ, she was so sensitive.

I moved my mouth to the other nipple to give it equal attention before I placed soft kisses down her stomach. Her breath started to come faster, and when I glanced up and saw her watching me, I had to reach down and pull on my cock to ease the ache.

"Spread your legs for me, Annalise. Let me see you."

Her mouth opened slightly before she ran her tongue over her lips and did as I asked.

I groaned when I got a look at her. Everything about Annalise Michaels was perfection. Spreading her lower lips open, I slowly pushed my finger inside her.

"Fucking hell, you're so tight."

"It's...it's been a while since I've been with anyone."

My eyes darted up to hers. "How long?"

She seemed dazed and distracted as I slowly rubbed her clit with my thumb, moving my finger in and out of her. She was so wet and ready.

"A year or so."

I slowly shook my head. "That's a damn shame, Anna. A pussy this beautiful should be worshiped daily."

Her head dropped back down on the pillow and she moaned. "A dirty talker. Good God, help me."

I chuckled and moved closer, dying to get a taste of her. When my tongue swept over her core, Annalise nearly shot straight up out of the bed.

"Oh, my God! Yes, please, Roger. Oh, please!"

"You don't ever have to beg me, princess," I whispered, pressing my mouth to her and nearly expiring on the spot. Her taste was so different. Why was everything about Annalise so fucking different? Why did it feel like she'd reached into my soul and claimed it all for herself? I suddenly wanted to make her come over and over so I could hear my name falling from her mouth.

I sucked on her clit and then flicked it with my tongue as I slipped another finger inside of her.

Her back arched, her hands went back to my hair, and she pulled me in closer, guiding me to where it felt the best.

"So...close...," she gasped.

Covering her clit with my mouth, I sucked in, and Annalise fell apart.

She slammed her hands over her mouth as her entire body shook with the force of her orgasm. Instead of relenting, I sucked more, curling my fingers and hitting that spot inside of her that made her body shake even more.

This time she covered her face with the pillow while she screamed my name into it. I couldn't help the fucking smile that spread over my face when she used her hand to push me away.

Removing my mouth, I slowly kept pumping my fingers inside her. Annalise started to pull away from me, but I took hold of her, moved her body, and positioned myself at her core.

She threw the pillow to the side and stared up at me as I pushed inside of her.

"*Fuuuuuck*," I groaned. She was so goddamn tight, but with how wet she was, I slid right in.

"Roger, I'm going to…! Oh, my God!"

The feel of her pussy pulsating around my cock nearly had me coming right along with her. I paused, not moving a muscle as she dug her feet into my body to pull me into her while she moved her hips.

I dropped my head and buried it in her neck.

"Anna…if you don't want me to come, stop moving for a second."

Her breaths came in short gasps. "I came…again. Oh, my God. I've never come with a guy inside of me before."

I lifted my head and met her gaze. "Score one for me and my amazing dick."

She laughed and looked away, her cheeks turning pink.

"Don't look away. I want to see you when I start to make love to you."

I froze, every inch of my body going rigid as I realized what I just said.

I never *made love*. I fucked. That was it. I wasn't the type of guy who gave himself to a woman like that. At least, not anymore.

Annalise felt the change in me. "What's wrong?" she asked.

Swallowing hard, I smiled and then pressed my lips to hers. I slowly pulled almost all the way out before pushing back inside.

We both moaned at the feeling of our bodies connecting.

"You feel so good, princess," I whispered against her lips.

Annalise wrapped her arms around my body and held on to me as our bodies moved together in a beautiful rhythm. I wasn't sure what was happening to me, and I wasn't about to stop and analyze it. All I wanted to do was be in this moment with her.

"Roger," she whispered, her fingertips moving lightly across my back. "Faster. Please."

My dick demanded that I do what she asked. But the feel of her was too delicious. I knew the moment I moved faster, went harder, I would come, and it would be over.

"Why the rush, princess?" I asked, covering her body with kisses between each word.

She wrapped her legs around me and drew me as close as she could. "Don't stop."

I dropped my forehead to hers as we moved together. "I won't. God, I don't *ever* want to stop."

More words slipped out before I could stop them.

What in the living fuck is happening to me? What is this woman doing to me?

After a few minutes of slowly making love to her, I lost the battle. I sped up. Drew out and slammed back into her, causing Annalise to gasp and then quickly follow it up with a moan.

"Yes! Roger, yes! Please!" she begged. "I…I feel like…oh, God!"

I reached between our bodies and pressed on her clit. It didn't take her body long to respond, just as I knew it wouldn't.

"Holy shit!" she cried out.

"Should I pull out?" I asked as I realized I was on the verge of spilling into her. How the hell I had the fortitude to even think clearly was beyond me at that point.

Her head thrashed from side to side; I wasn't sure if she was trying to tell me no, don't pull out, or no, don't come in her. I'd never come inside a woman unless I had a condom on, but something in me wanted to come inside of Annalise. Fuck, I wanted to mark her as mine. Claim her. Spill every drop of myself inside her.

"Annalise!" I cried.

"Don't pull out!" she managed to say as she dug her heels into my ass and pulled me in deeper. I groaned when her pussy tightened around me, and she came again.

When my own orgasm hit, I swore I nearly lost consciousness. I had never experienced such an intense release before in my life. The pleasure that ripped through my body had me crying out her name, and I buried my face in her neck and thrust in hard and fast until I was spent.

When our bodies finally started to return to some sort of normal state, I realized I was nearly crushing Annalise with my body weight. I lifted off her some, only to have her pull me back.

"Wait. I don't want you to move yet," she said.

I looked into those sky-blue eyes of hers and smiled. "Did that feel good, princess?"

Her grin nearly had my dick coming right back up. "That was the most amazing sex of my entire life."

I tilted my head and replied, "Why, thank you."

Annalise blushed and let out the cutest fucking giggling I'd ever heard. My damn cock twitched inside of her as the sound traveled through me.

"You're a dirty talker, Mr. Carter."

"Am I?"

I instantly stared down at her when she dug her teeth into her lower lip. "You are, and I liked it."

"Well, if you let me rest for a bit, I'll be sure to show you more."

Her eyes sparkled with excitement. "Is that a promise?"

"You were the one who said you wanted to use the time we had left to your advantage."

A lazy smile moved over her beautiful face. "So I did."

"Let me clean you up."

I pulled out of her, rolled off the bed, and headed into the bathroom. After cleaning myself off, I wet a washcloth with warm water and made my way back to where Annalise was lying on the bed.

She reached for the cloth, and I shook my head. "Let me do it."

"What? I can do it—"

I brought my fingers to her lips to get her to stop talking. "I want to do it. Open your legs for me, Annalise."

Her throat worked to swallow as she did what I asked. She slightly hissed through her kiss-swollen lips, and I glanced up. "Sore?"

"A little. I haven't been with anyone in a year. Not since I broke up with someone I was dating off and on."

A surge of jealousy hit me at the thought of another man between those legs. I continued to gently wipe my cum off her while I tried to get my head straight. All these emotions were not something I ever experienced with a woman. Especially one I had only known for twenty-four hours.

"Roger?"

"Yeah?" I asked as I looked up.

When our gazes locked, a strange pressure built in my chest. I nearly fell back onto my ass when I realized what was happening. Why this felt so different, so good.

I was falling for her. I liked her. Wanted her for more than just a quick romp in bed.

I shook my head and quickly stood. Annalise must have seen the change in me because she reached for the sheet and covered herself up. Fuck, the last thing I wanted to do was make her feel uncomfortable.

Forcing a smile, I leaned down and kissed her softly. It was hard to ignore the instant rush of tingles that jumped from her body to mine, but I knew I had to. I wasn't going to let *that* happen again. There was only one other time in my life when I'd felt like this, and that was with Kerri. The one and only girl I had given my heart to... and then watched in horror when she was taken from me.

"Do you want to take a shower with me?" I asked, hoping to erase the confused expression on her face.

"Shower with you?"

I laughed. "You've showered with a guy before, right?"

With a shake of her head, she blushed. "I can't say I have."

I was stunned to feel myself growing hard again so quickly.

"Well," I said as I took her hand and pulled her off the bed, "I think we're going to have to change that."

She laughed. "Roger, that shower is not big enough for both of us."

Winking, I leaned in, lowered my voice, and said, "It will be once I'm inside you."

Chapter 8

Annalise

OH, MY GOODNESS. How in the world had I just experienced three mind-blowing orgasms and yet my body was already tightening with need for Roger once again? I was still reeling over the fact that he'd cleaned me off, and I'd spent the whole time fighting the urge to get turned on again. It was the sweetest thing anyone had ever done for me after sex. Granted, I hadn't had that many lovers, but I wasn't an innocent either, and no man had ever stopped to pay attention to my needs after sex.

There was also the whole having-sex-with-no-condom thing. That was new too. I was on the pill and not worried about pregnancy, but I hadn't even known this man for twenty-four hours and I was letting him come inside of me. I was suddenly hit by the memory of him on top of me only moments ago, and I felt my core tighten.

Who am I right now? And who in the hell knew I would love a dirty-talking man!

"I've heard sex in the shower is uncomfortable," I said.

Roger gave me a perplexed look. "Is that yet another challenge, princess?"

I had all but given up on getting Roger to stop calling me that. Even though I would never admit it, I actually was starting to like it. Another thing that was not my norm.

"Oh, believe me, you seem like the type of guy who could manage to have sex anywhere he wanted."

Roger faked a wounded expression. "Ouch, are you calling me a manwhore?"

I let my eyes travel down to his erect dick. "I mean, you've certainly had practice with that thing."

He covered himself with his hands as his mouth dropped open. "Why, I never! I happen to just be that good."

My mouth twitched with a hidden smile. "It was rather nice."

"Nice?" he asked in a low, rumbly voice.

With a half-shrug, I turned and headed toward the bathroom. "Yes. Nice."

"Excuse me, but I believe you came three times. Three."

I reached in and turned on the shower before glancing back at Roger. "If you really want to impress me, three isn't the magical number, Mr. Carter."

His eyes grew dark, and I swore his nostrils flared. "What *is* the magical number, Anna?"

I dug my teeth into my lower lip. "I won't know until I hit it."

Growling, Roger pushed me into the shower, pressed me against the cold tile, and captured my mouth with a kiss so mind-blowing, I nearly forgot how to stand. Then he dropped down and lifted one of my legs, hitching it over his shoulder.

He licked his lips as he prepared to devour me.

"I need another taste of you."

All I could do was reach for the metal bar in the shower and hold on for dear life while he took me to heaven again.

"Roger," I panted as my orgasm quickly built up.

He didn't stop. He sucked, licked, and gently bit as I moaned.

Then it happened. I exploded into another orgasm that shook my entire body. I felt my legs give out, and before I even knew what was happening, Roger had picked me up and entered me, holding me against the shower wall.

He withdrew, slowly pushed back inside, and then smiled. "Was that the magical number, princess?"

I couldn't think. I couldn't speak. All I could focus on was the delicious way his body moved inside of me. I had never in my life had more than one orgasm at a time with a man, maybe two...and the second one was fleeting, at best. But now...now it felt as if I was on the verge of yet another.

"Kiss me," I demanded.

His dimples appeared when he gave me a sexy grin. "Your wish, princess."

The moment his tongue touched mine, I tasted my own pleasure. A bolt of lust and desire raced through me. Roger angled me and went deeper inside, hitting a spot that nearly had my eyes rolling to the back of my skull.

"There is...no way!" I said, feeling that familiar buildup again.

"I need you to come, baby. I'm so close."

I opened my eyes and locked onto his. Gracious, his eyes were beautiful. Like the summer sky after an afternoon rain shower. So blue and bright, they nearly brought me to tears. I could feel the pressure in the back of my eyes growing.

"Anna. Now!"

His command—or maybe it was the way he said it with such raw need and passion—sent my orgasm tumbling over the edge. It wasn't as strong as the last one, but Lord, it still packed a pleasure-filled punch.

I dug my fingers into his shoulders and dropped my head back against the shower, letting out moan after moan as I felt the tears I had struggled with moments ago be set free. They mixed with the shower water, and for that, I was thankful.

"Yes, that's it. I'm coming, Anna! God, it feels so good."

By the time Roger stopped moving, I was spent. Exhausted.

I forced my body to move and lifted my head up to look at him. "*That*...was the magical number."

I felt the bed move and opened my eyes. A small stream of light filtered in through the curtains, just enough to see Roger's gloriously naked body as he stood and stretched. Heat instantly pooled in my lower stomach.

He leaned down and grabbed a pair of shorts, which he slipped on before starting toward the bathroom.

When I heard the door click shut, I rolled over and softly groaned.

"Oh, my gosh," I whispered, every muscle in my body aching. After our shower, I had nearly passed out from exhaustion. Roger had dried me off and then carried me to the bed. I was out the moment my head hit the pillow.

Around five in the morning, he had woken me up with soft kisses around my breast and up my neck. When I opened my eyes and saw him smiling at me, the instant desire I felt shocked me. I wanted him like I had never wanted any other man. Regardless of the fact that he'd already made me come five times earlier that night.

Five. Holy hell.

I had never come so many times, and honestly thought it was impossible. Okay, not *impossible*, but unlikely it would ever happen to me. The guys I'd been with in the past were certainly not capable of making me feel the way I felt with Roger.

I smiled as I thought back to how bold I'd been when I'd whispered that it was my turn and pushed him onto his back and crawled over him. It was then we heard the couple in the next room moaning from the other side of the wall. They followed it up with cries to go faster.

I had looked down at Roger, only to see one of his brows lifted. "I think you could beat her," he said.

And the gauntlet had been dropped. It hadn't been hard, really. Being on top of Roger, feeling his body rub against my clit as he lifted his hips to meet me thrust for thrust, caused me to lose my mind. Of course, it helped when he encouraged me to be a bit louder as I told him exactly what I wanted.

I had never been so open with a man during sex before. I wasn't sure if that should bother me or not. Why was it so different with Roger? Was it because I knew it would all end soon...this fairy tale world we were living in? Or maybe he simply brought out another side of me. A side I rather liked.

"Tell me how good it feels, princess," he had said with a wicked smile.

"Feels so good!"

Then he said the magic words that made my entire body explode. "Fuck me harder, Anna."

I had come so hard and so intensely, I wasn't sure if I was calling out to Roger or God or to the whole hotel. When I finally collapsed on his chest, we heard soft moans of pleasure from the other room, followed by silence.

Roger had rolled me over and made the sweetest love to me after that. He'd kissed me gently and moved in a way that would ruin me for all men after him. The connection I felt with him was nothing I had ever experienced before, and I knew a part of me needed to pull back because once it was over, I could see my heart breaking. Roger was so tender in everything he did, and I couldn't help but wonder if he was this type of lover with everyone.

After he'd cleaned us both off, I'd drifted to sleep in his arms with that same thought rolling around in my head.

Now, staring up at the ceiling, I thought about what it was going to be like when we both walked away. It was clear there was a connection. I knew what held me back—a long-distance romance was not something I wanted. What held Roger back? The same thing?

The shower turned on, and a wicked thought occurred to me. After all the pleasure Roger had given me throughout the night, it was time to return some.

As I stood up to go join him, the room phone rang. I reached out and answered it.

"Hello?"

"Yes, Ms. Michaels, this is Rory at the front desk. We actually have a room that has come available for you. It looks like the airport will be closed at least until tomorrow with this new round of snow coming in, and you'll need to spend one more night with us at least."

My heart pounded in my chest as I stared at the closed bathroom door. Chewing on my lip, I thought back to the amazing night I had spent with Roger. Did I really want our time together to end?

"Thank you so much for letting me know, Rory. I'll pass on the room, though."

"Um, but it says in the notes you needed another room because—"

"Yes," I said, cutting her off. "It appears the situation has worked itself out, and I don't need a room. Mr. Carter and I are fine sharing."

A moment of silence occurred before my words seemed to sink in. "Ohhhh, okay. Great! I'm glad things are…um…working out for you both then. I'll go ahead and remove this note. As far as the bill for the room?"

"We'll figure that out when we check out. Thank you."

Before the nice front desk girl could respond, I quickly hung up. I brought my hand up to my mouth as I sat there in stunned silence.

"What did you just do?" I whispered to myself. My eyes darted over to the bathroom door while my heart pounded rapidly in my chest. A giggle burst free, and I shook my head. Who in the world was I anymore?

I stood and took a step closer to the bathroom door.

Okay, this is what you want, Annalise Michaels. Go take it.

Slowly, I made my way over to the bathroom door. My hand shook as I reached out and opened it. The clear glass shower was slightly fogged up, but I still had a perfect view of Roger's incredibly fit body.

Wow. To think I'd slept with that man. He had been inside of me. And now—now I was about to drop to my knees and take what I wanted.

Him.

As if sensing me there, Roger turned and looked at me. A slow, sexy smile spread across his face. "See something you want, princess?"

I pretended to be annoyed with the nickname and shot him a warning look. He winked, and I felt my stomach dip.

My eyes drifted down, and I watched him grow harder. A soft moan slipped free from my lips, and Roger opened the door to the shower.

I lifted my gaze from his midsection to see those baby blues filled with desire. The slow throb between my legs intensified.

"Yes, I do believe I do, Mr. Carter."

He spread his arms wide and teased, "I'm all yours."

It was my turn to smile. I stepped into the shower, shut the glass door, and licked my lips as I dropped to my knees and took him in my hand. He hissed and dropped his head back. I wanted him so much, I could practically feel the aching pain pulsing through my veins, but I was scared to death I wouldn't do this right. What if he hated it, or I sucked too hard? I knew I should use my hand simply from watching a porn or two in my life. Not to mention the times I'd heard my friends talk about giving guys blowjobs. I had never had the desire to give a man one before, and the few guys I'd dated had never asked. Well, one had when he was drunk, and I'd quickly refused.

I inhaled slowly, then let it out as I stared at his hard dick, jumping in my hand with each small movement I made. I decided I needed to be honest with Roger, if for no other reason than for him to be able to tell me what felt good.

Glancing up, I noticed he had moved the showerhead so it wouldn't spray in my face. "I've...I've never done this before," I said.

His brows shot up in surprise. "You've never given a guy a blowjob before?"

I shook my head. "Nope, never. So, I might be bad at this."

A small growl came from low in his throat as he brushed the back of his knuckles against my cheek. "Anna, I can tell you right now, the moment you wrap those pretty pink lips around my dick, I'm going to be fighting not to come. Don't worry, you'll do it right. Trust me."

"I don't think I'll be able to do the whole swallow-and-act-like-a-bad-bitch thing. Will you let me know before you come?"

He nodded and swallowed hard. "Of course, I will."

I drew in a deep breath, looked down at his impressive appendage, and exhaled. I wrapped my mouth around him and instantly moaned at the salty taste that was Roger. He was big and hard, yet so soft. He tasted better than I thought, or maybe that was the soap? No, no, there was a bit of a clean taste to him, but this was for sure him. The small amount of precum had given me a good taste, and I highly doubted the soap was salty.

Oh, God. Concentrate, Annalise!

I peeked up and saw the most glorious sight I would probably ever see. Roger, with one hand braced on the tile of the shower, his eyes closed, and a look of pure ecstasy on his face. I hadn't really even done anything except put him in my mouth and slowly move. His free hand slipped into my wet hair, and he pulled on it gently before he started to help guide me into the rhythm he liked.

"Fucking hell, Annalise. God...it feels so good."

My chest warmed and I decided to experiment with both my hand and my mouth. Rachel, my best friend from high school, had given us all a demonstration one night with a cucumber. What was it she'd said would throw a man right over the edge?

I sucked with my mouth and pumped with my hand as I tried to recall the memory of that day. Her words came back in a rush.

"Play with his balls—guys like that. But be gentle. And if you really want to blow his mind, as well as his load, either gently press your finger against his ass, or slip inside just a little bit. He'll most likely end up marrying you if you pull that move."

I pulled my mouth up along his shaft and let it pop out of my mouth as I gave my aching jaw a quick break. Lord, friends should warn friends about what a jaw workout blowjobs were.

Moving my hand up and down, I looked up to see Roger staring down at me. God, it should be illegal for a man to be so freaking handsome and look at a woman that way. My clit throbbed, and I fought the need to touch it and offer some relief.

I took him into my mouth once again but kept my gaze on his.

"Anna," he panted. "I'm getting close."

I smiled, moving my hand from his shaft to his balls. They were pulled up tight against his body, and he let out a groan as he closed his eyes.

"Fuuuuck. Yeah, touch them like that."

Knowing our time was limited, and this might very well be the last time I would get to do this, I reached between his legs and gently slipped my finger between his ass cheeks. Roger's eyes flew open, and his entire body seemed to react. Moving my mouth faster and sucking a bit more, I pressed my finger against him and felt it slip inside.

"Fuck, yes!" Roger called out. "I'm going to come, Anna! God!"

His voice sounded strained as he tugged at my hair to pull me off him. It was in that moment I decided I wanted every part of what he had to offer. I took him in deeper and pressed my finger into him a little more, causing him to let out a moan of pleasure that echoed in the shower.

"Anna, I'm coming!"

Warm liquid hit the back of my throat, and I quickly swallowed as fast as I could. He tasted like salt and earth and everything I dreamed he would. He dug his hands into my hair, and I loved that I had made him feel so good. I sucked and licked until he had nothing left, and my jaw felt like it might lock into place.

Roger pulled away from me and stumbled back against the shower. I stood and leaned my face into the stream of water, rinsing out my mouth.

"Jesus H. Christ. For someone who's never done that before, you sure knew the right things to do. And what the fuck was the whole ass thing?"

I shrugged. "A friend mentioned once that guys like that, but if you don't, I—"

Before I could finish, he pulled me to him and kissed me. The kiss was deep and different from the others. Exactly how it was different, I wasn't sure. It simply *felt* different. I wrapped my arms around him and melted into his body. I could honestly stay wrapped up in Roger's arms forever and be completely content.

Oh, dear. That kind of thought was going to get me in trouble.

When he finally pulled back, he leaned his forehead to mine. "It felt amazing. I don't think I've ever come so damn hard before in my entire life. I thought I was gonna pass out for a second."

I chuckled and looked up at him. He kissed the tip of my nose.

"Thank you. That felt amazing."

I gave myself an internal fist pump. "Well, it was the least I could do after you pleasured me so much I nearly fell into a coma."

He laughed and then turned me around and reached for the soap. When he started to clean my body, I had to bite my lower lip to keep from saying something stupid like, "Let's move in together and make each other feel good every day!" Or "Tell me where you live, and I'll fly there once a week. We can make this work!"

No. No, none of that would work. One, I didn't want a long-distance relationship, and two, something told me Roger Carter wasn't the type of guy who would be interested in *any* sort of relationship.

"Your skin is so soft," he said, placing the soap back down and massaging my shoulders. I leaned against him and moaned when his hands moved around to caress my breasts.

I dropped my head back against his chest as I said, "That feels so good."

He placed his mouth to my neck and kissed me softly. "You're so beautiful, Anna."

I closed my eyes and tried to keep my heart from beating straight out of my chest. I couldn't deny how I was feeling, and a part of me was scared to death because I knew without a doubt, I was falling for Roger—and falling hard. I needed to remember it would all be over in a day or two. That the wonderful bliss and pleasure I felt was going to end. It had to end. We were two strangers who had been tossed together.

But the attraction we had for one another was undeniable. The first time I saw him, standing there naked, I somehow knew I was meant to meet him. We were meant to spend these few days stuck in this hotel together. Crazy as it sounded, I felt it in my very soul.

Turning to face him, I forced myself to offer a carefree smile. The last thing I needed was for Roger to think I wanted something more than the few days we'd agreed to. "Thank you for saying that."

"It's the truth."

I felt my face heat up, and it wasn't from the warm water in the shower. "Let's go get some food. I'm starving."

His eyes lit up. "So am I! Hopefully, the hotel doesn't run out of supplies with this snowpocalypse."

I laughed and stepped out of the shower while Roger turned it off. Grabbing a towel, I said, "To be honest, I've been scared we might lose power."

"Don't jinx us," he stated as he stepped out and stood there, water rolling down his perfectly chiseled body. I opened my mouth to say something and found I couldn't even form words. No man should look this beautiful.

"You must work out a lot...you're...so built," I stammered.

The moment the words came out, I wanted to hide my face. I was clearly staring at him, but my goodness, a girl couldn't ignore a body as fine as his.

Roger laughed again. "I do work out. I love my Peloton, and I do weights. Run occasionally but not far, obviously."

I let my gaze roam freely over him. I wanted to soak up as much as I could. "Well, it pays off."

He winked. "I'm glad to know."

Grabbing a towel, he quickly started to dry off alongside me.

The fact that this was going to end soon hung in the air like a heavy weight. I wasn't sure if he noticed it as well. If he did, he played it off well. An unbelievable rush of sadness came over me as I wrapped the towel around me and walked out of the bathroom. I needed to get my emotions under control, and I needed to do it fast.

Chapter 9

Roger

SOMETHING HAD SHIFTED.

I felt it surround me the moment her eyes skimmed up my body and met mine. Her expression changed from lust to something that looked like sadness. She forced a smile, wrapped a towel around her body, and walked out of the bathroom.

I took the few seconds of alone time to gather my thoughts. Annalise had blown my damn mind with that blowjob. The way she'd looked up at me, trusting me enough to try something for the first time…a part of me found it hard to believe that *was* her first freaking time. She put her finger in my ass, for fuck's sake.

With an internal groan, I pushed the thought away before I got hard again. That had been one of the most amazing sexual moments of my entire life. I'd never felt this before with anyone, not even—

Before I could conjure her name in my mind, I wrapped the towel around me and walked out of the bathroom.

Clearing my throat, I said, "I got a text from the airline. No flights out today either."

"I'm not surprised. It's still snowing." She pulled the drapes back from the window and looked out.

"Anna, you're in a towel. Maybe you shouldn't stand in front of the window like that."

With a quick peek over her shoulder, she gave me a saucy grin. "Are we not into voyeurism?"

I clenched my fists at the idea of anyone else seeing her naked. With a quick shake of my head, I reached down and grabbed jeans and a sweater from my bag. "No, are you?" I asked, slightly dreading her answer but suspecting she'd say no.

She laughed. "Hardly."

I watched her walk to the dresser and open it. She had unpacked her clothes and put them away, which was clearly a woman thing since my clothes were still in my carry-on.

"I know we said we wouldn't ask personal questions, but you know that I have a brother, so it's only fair you give me something," I said.

Her eyes met mine. "Are you asking me if I have siblings?"

I nodded and slipped on my jeans. Annalise pulled her lower lip between her teeth as she watched me. "Are you not going to put on any underwear?"

Glancing down, I shook my head. "No."

"You're going commando?"

I laughed slightly. "I often do. Plus, I'm running out of them."

She shook her head and went back to searching for clothes. How she'd been able to pack so much in her carry-on was beyond me.

"So, do you? Have any siblings?" I pressed.

"Yes. I have a sister and an older brother. My brother is married with two kids I have yet to meet since he lives in Ireland."

"Ireland? What's he doing there?"

"He works for Intel. He met his wife, my sister-in-law, Kate, over there. They got married and had twins last year."

I pulled a sweater over my head and sat down on the bed to put on my socks and sneakers. "Wow. Twins, huh? Identical or fraternal?"

"Fraternal."

"Is that on your side of the family or Kate's?"

Annalise shrugged. "I think on my dad's side."

"What do you mean, you think?"

She turned and faced me. "My biological parents died in a car accident when I was six months old. My older sister Meg was two, and Jax was four. We were adopted by a family who was only looking for a baby, but then they saw the three of us and took us all in. My parents are amazing. They raised us like we were their own. They told us what they knew about our folks whenever we asked, but we try not to ask too many questions now. I would never want them to think we didn't love them."

I frowned. "I'm sure they wouldn't be upset if you wanted to find out about your roots."

With a warm smile, she nodded. "No, of course not. It's just, I never knew them, and Jax and Meg don't really remember them. So, we don't ask a lot of questions. Twins aren't in Kate's family, so we assume they're on our side."

All I could do was nod. "I get that."

She tilted her head. "What about you, Roger? Just the one brother?"

I paused for a moment, trying to decide how much I wanted to share with her. Did she need to know my father had a bastard son? That my mother and father hadn't loved each other when they'd first gotten married? That my mother had spent more time away from us than she had with us? Of course, now their marriage was strong and solid, but that was a lot to throw at a person. I decided less was best.

"No, I actually have two brothers. Never knew about one until recently."

Her brows rose. "Really?"

"Yeah," I said. With a sigh, I stood up. "It's a boring story."

She nodded, taking the hint that the conversation was over. "I'm ready if you are."

I motioned for her to go first, then followed her out of our hotel room and to the elevator. When the doors opened, Mary and Dylan were standing in front of us.

"Fancy meeting you guys here. Going down for breakfast?" Mary asked with a grin.

"We are," Annalise replied. "How was the club last night?"

"We didn't stay long. Pretty sure Monty and Lynn stayed until it closed down," Dylan answered.

Mary looked between the two of us. "Did you two enjoy your evening?"

"Yes, we did," I answered as Annalise's cheeks turned red. "Very enjoyable evening."

Dylan gave me a knowing smile while Mary and Annalise locked eyes. Something seemed to pass between them.

The doors opened to the hotel lobby, and the four of us made our way toward the restaurant that served breakfast. Mary spun around and faced us before we could walk inside. "Oh, if you want them to service your room, you need to tell them. They're short-staffed and don't have a full cleaning crew. The girl at the front desk told me this morning."

"We don't need the room cleaned, but we could use more towels. I'll go ask," Annalise said.

I gently took her arm to stop her. "No, I'll do it. You go on in, and if you get seated, can you order me a coffee, no cream or sugar?"

She flashed me that brilliant smile of hers. "Of course."

I watched as the three of them headed off in the opposite direction of the front desk. I made my way over and stood behind another couple. Once it was my turn, I stepped up and gave the young guy behind the desk our room number and asked for more towels and an extra pillow. My pillow was so damn flat, it didn't even feel like I was sleeping on one. As I turned to walk away, a thought hit me, and I stopped.

"I believe we have a note attached to our room to give us a call if you have any other available rooms. We no longer need it, so I wanted to go ahead and remove it."

It was a ballsy move on my part, but I was pretty sure Annalise wouldn't want to change rooms either at this point.

He smiled as he typed something in, read for a few seconds, and then looked up at me. "That note has already been removed."

Frowning, I asked, "What do you mean?"

He looked back at the computer and said, "It looks like we had an available room come up this morning, and they called and spoke with...um...Ms. Michaels? She stated there was no longer a need for another room."

I felt my brows shoot up, and I couldn't help the smile that spread over my face.

"Is that correct, sir?" he asked with a concerned expression.

"Yes," I quickly replied. "Yes, that's fine. Be sure to use my card to charge the room and not the other one that's in Ms. Michaels's name."

He nodded. "Yes, sir. It also looks like the last of the snow is moving through. We've just received word that they'll most likely be re-opening the airport tomorrow afternoon unless they can get the runways cleared off faster. If so, then flights will start going out tomorrow morning."

A strange pang hit me in the middle of my chest, but I forced a smile. "That's great news. Thank you."

"Yes, sir. Enjoy your morning."

"You, as well," I said before I turned and headed away from the front desk.

So, Annalise didn't want this to end either. I knew I had a smug smile on my face. Shit, as much as I didn't want to admit it, I was going to miss her. But fate worked in weird ways, and we clearly were meant to have this time together. If all we had left was today, I intended to enjoy it as much as I could. And even though I wanted to drag her back to the room and fuck her until neither one of us could move, I had other plans in mind, starting with breakfast.

When I walked up to the table, I immediately noticed the glow on Annalise's face. Had she always had that, or was it because of the amazing last few hours we'd spent together? I was going with the latter.

"Everything set?" Annalise asked. "We getting more towels?"

"Yes. Also, the front desk clerk told me the airport is opening again tomorrow. Some morning flights going out possibly, but it'll most likely be in the afternoon."

Annalise jerked her head back up to look at me. "Tomorrow morning?"

I didn't miss the disappointment in her voice. "Maybe, if they get the runways clear."

Mary glanced at Dylan. "I just got an email from United Airlines with my new booking information. Looks like I'm flying out tomorrow at two."

"Wow, that's great news," Annalise said as she stared at me. Her voice sounded happy, but those blue eyes of hers said something entirely different. "You'll finally be rid of your unwanted roommate."

"I wouldn't use the word 'unwanted,'" I said with a wink.

She blinked a few times, and something moved across her face that I couldn't read. Truth be told, I hadn't ever gone out of my way to read a woman's expressions before. Not that I didn't care about their feelings—of course, I did. I made sure, though, that I never took a woman to bed whom I knew I wouldn't be able to walk away from afterward, and who wouldn't be able to walk away from me.

Until I met the woman staring at me, that is. With Annalise, everything felt so damn different. A part of me knew it would be hard to walk away from her tomorrow, but I would do it. There was no way I could ever allow myself to open up my heart again. I'd hang on to every single moment in my memories, and I knew I would never forget her. If I were a better man, I'd beg her to come to Texas with me. To let me wake her up every morning with a kiss on the lips before I made love to her.

I shook the crazy thoughts away.

No. I don't make love. I fuck. That's all I know how to do.

"Are you okay, Roger?" Annalise asked, her hand moving to mine.

I drew it away as if I'd been burned, and instantly regretted it when I saw the hurt look on her face. "I'm sorry, I didn't mean to do that. I was caught up in a moment, and you startled me."

She nodded and gave me a soft smile that didn't reach her eyes. I knew it was forced because I'd spent the last few hours seeing a *real* smile on that beautiful face of hers. It made her blue eyes shine like the first rays of the morning sun. Her real smile made her cheeks blush slightly and the corners of her eyes crinkle in the cutest way. She looked away from me now, pretending to read over the menu.

It made my heart feel something I knew I couldn't allow it to feel, let alone let myself even think about.

Before I could say anything else, the waitress walked up and started to take everyone's orders. My appetite had left me the moment I realized I'd hurt Annalise's feelings, but I ordered a breakfast sandwich anyway, and hoped I'd be able to eat it by the time it came out. Annalise ordered avocado toast with a bowl of fruit and a tea.

"So, what are you two doing today?" Annalise asked Mary and Dylan.

"Probably going back to the room to have a movie marathon. What about you guys?"

Annalise shrugged. "I don't know."

"There's a snowman-making contest going on later. I saw the sign for it at the front desk. If you've got warm-enough clothes, we could enter," I said to her before taking a sip of my coffee.

The brightness in her eyes came back. "Really? You'd do that?"

With a laugh, I asked, "Why do you sound so disbelieving?"

She shrugged. "I don't know. I guess I can't really picture you making a snowman."

"I'm wounded, princess. Truly wounded."

Annalise rolled her eyes, but I saw the corners of her mouth twitch with a hidden smile.

A part of me wanted to tell her everything about me. Give her my phone number, tell her to call me whenever she wanted. Hell, I'd even fly out to see her every now and then.

No.

No, that wasn't going to happen.

That wasn't what we had agreed on. No strings attached.

The pang from earlier came back, but this time it felt stronger and more familiar. I had vowed a long time ago that I would never allow myself to feel it again.

Not since *her*.

Not since Kerri.

I closed my eyes and saw her face staring up at me, covered in blood.

"Don't you dare leave me, Kerri! Do you hear me? Don't you dare leave me!"

The corner of her mouth lifted slightly into a smile as she whispered, "I love you, Roger."

"Are you not hungry?"

Mary's voice pulled me from the memory, and I stared down at the breakfast sandwich the waitress had brought. "Sorry, I was lost in thought."

"Seem to be doing that a lot this morning," Dylan stated with a laugh.

I nodded and chanced a look over at Annalise. She was cutting her toast in half and seemed to be somewhere else herself.

After we ate breakfast and talked for a bit more, we all stood to leave.

"We should head on back to the room and grab our coats," I said. "The contest starts in thirty minutes."

Annalise nodded, then focused on Mary and Dylan. "We'll see you both before we all leave, right?"

"Of course!" Mary said. "How about we do dinner tonight?" She looked at Dylan. "Is that okay?"

Dylan nodded. "Dinner sounds good to me."

Everyone swung their heads to look at me. "Dinner sounds great," I said.

Annalise clapped. "Great! Then how about we plan on meeting in the lobby, say, around six?"

"That works," Mary and Dylan said at the same time.

Dylan slid his arm around Mary's waist and guided her out of the restaurant. I placed my hand on Annalise's back as we followed our new friends toward the elevators. A part of me wanted to ask her about the room she turned down this morning, but I didn't want to ruin any part of today. She clearly felt the same way I did. Neither one of us wanted this to end, yet the end was only hours away.

The elevator stopped on Mary and Dylan's floor. They said their goodbyes as they headed down the hall.

"They're totally not watching movies," Annalise stated, and I laughed.

"I'm sure the TV will be on."

She peeked up at me and grinned. "As much as sex with you right now sounds heavenly, you mentioned a snowman contest, and I have my heart set on winning."

My head fell back as I laughed again. "I think I may have met the one person on this Earth who's just as competitive as I am."

She shrugged. "I like to win. I won't lie."

The elevator opened, and we quickly went back to our room. After bundling up as best we could, we soon found our way outside and to the area where the snowman-making contest was about to begin.

"I think we got a good spot here," Annalise said, her game face clearly on. "Lots of loose snow. Look at that family over there, thinking they're so smart. Let's see how smart they are when they realize they don't have enough snow to build a snowbaby."

The hotel had used spray paint to mark circles around their large outdoor area. Everyone got to pick a spot, and the rule was you could only use the snow in your circle to make your snowman.

"I'm going to guess they're doing it just for fun," I said.

She huffed. "Fun. There is no *fun* in this. It's a competition!"

I raised my brows. "I was sorta thinking we might have some fun."

Annalise stared at me. "Don't you want to win?"

"Um," I said as I looked over at the family again. "I think it might be nice to let the kids win. Don't you?"

Her eyes narrowed some before she focused back on the family. They had three kids, and I honestly couldn't imagine being stuck in a hotel room with three young children—those parents deserved a win.

Annalise sighed. "They do look excited. I guess they should win."

I nodded. "Should we give them our circle?"

She spun back to face me. "Hold on now. Let's not get carried away."

It took everything I had to stop myself from pulling her to me and kissing her senseless. Whoever ended up marrying this woman was going to be a lucky bastard. Life with Annalise would never be boring.

An hour later, Annalise and I stood back and looked at our snowman.

I glanced over at the family of five and smiled. Their snowman kicked our snowman's ass. I had heard through the snowman-making grapevine that the dad was a building engineer. They were a shoo-in to win. They had made two snowmen. Both with perfectly round and symmetrical balls. Plus, one of them was turned upside down and wearing a pair of snow boots. They had clearly had more winter clothing to work with since both snowmen had on hats, scarfs, and mittens attached to the ends of their stick arms. I spun around and looked at ours and tried not to laugh.

It was cute, with his baseball hat provided by the guy next to us, and Annalise's scarf and mittens on. I couldn't help but wonder how much longer she would sacrifice them before she ripped them back off and put them on. The hotel had provided carrots and a few other food items to decorate the faces with. When I looked over at Annalise, she wore a proud smile.

"What should we name him?" Annalise asked, just as his carrot nose fell off and landed on the ground.

"Truitt."

She looked back at me. "Truitt?"

"That's my brother's name, and he's the most accident-prone person I've ever met. So far, our snowman has lost his right arm, both blueberry eyes, and now his nose. He needs to be called Truitt."

She giggled, and I loved how the sound of it warmed my body. Not two seconds later, she snagged the gloves back from Truitt the Snowman.

"My hands are freezing!" she said. "These gloves are more for style than warmth, I can tell you that right now."

I took off my gloves and reached for her hands before she slipped them back on. I blew on them before rubbing her fingers between mine. "Better?"

She stared up at me with an expression that said so many different things. But one thing stood out more than the others: She wanted me.

"Should we forgo the judging and head back up to the room?" I asked.

"I think that sounds like a wonderful idea."

As we turned to head back toward the hotel, my phone rang. I pulled it out and answered.

"Hello? Yes, this is him. Oh, great."

I motioned for Annalise to keep walking while I listened to the American Airlines representative.

"Mr. Carter, we've got you rebooked on flight 4906 leaving Chicago at twelve-thirty, nonstop into San Antonio. You'll arrive at three thirty-seven. You should have also received an email with the new flight information, and just to let you know, you've been booked in first class again."

My heart felt like it had just taken a nosedive. "Great, that's great news. Thank you."

"Of course. If anything changes, you'll get both a text and an email."

"Sounds good. Thank you so much."

When I hung up, I noticed Annalise looking at her phone and frowning.

"Is everything okay?" I asked.

She looked up, and I saw the disappointment in her eyes. "I got an email from the airline. They've rebooked my flight."

"When are you leaving?"

"Ten in the morning. I guess they're banking on the runways being cleared."

I gave a nod. "I leave at twelve-thirty."

We both stared at each other for the longest time before she broke the silence. "I don't think I'm ready for my fairy tale to end."

I tilted my head and winked. "Your fairy tale, huh?"

She shook her head as if clearing a thought away. "I don't want to have dinner with Mary and Dylan. Do you mind if we order room service?"

I pulled her body against mine. "Sounds good to me. Once I get you in that room naked, I'm not letting you leave until you need to catch your plane."

A brilliant smile lit up her face. "I like the sound of that plan."

Chapter 10

Annalise

TO SAY MY emotions were on a pendulum would have been an understatement. I was so excited to get to my new life, but the sadness I felt at knowing these were the last hours I would spend with Roger was unlike anything I'd ever experienced. How in the world could a man I'd only known for a few days make me feel this way?

All those times my friends said things like, "It was love at first sight. The first time he touched me, I knew." Now it all made sense. I was a damn cliché.

"I think we're going to need some food if we plan on locking ourselves away in the room," Roger stated as he glanced toward the store in the hotel lobby.

I kept my smile on my face, but inside I was far from happy. It was crazy. I knew when I'd agreed to sleep with Roger it was only temporary, but I felt like I was on the verge of a major breakup with a guy I'd been with for years. It was insane. *I* was insane.

"Hey, are you okay?" Roger asked, placing his hands on my shoulders and drawing me closer.

All I could do was nod.

He gave me a look that said he knew exactly how I was feeling. "Liar."

"It's stupid and doesn't matter."

He frowned at that statement. "Nothing you could be thinking or feeling is stupid, Anna."

God, how I loved it when he called me Anna. I loved it when any words came out of his mouth. "It just feels…" I let my voice trail off, knowing I was about to get choked up with emotion.

He sighed. "I know. I feel the same way."

That caused me to pull my head back slightly. "You do? I mean, how do you know I'm feeling the same way you're feeling?"

Roger laughed. "Are you dreading getting on a plane tomorrow and saying goodbye to me?"

"Yes," I whispered.

"Then we're feeling the same way."

I bit down on my lower lip as I tried to determine how much I wanted to share with Roger about how I was *truly* feeling. The last thing I wanted to do was ruin the few hours we had left by telling him all my emotions. The ones that usually scared guys away, especially when you'd only known them for a few days. I couldn't say: *I think I want something more than a few days of sex. I could see myself waking up next to you every morning.* Or how about: *I want to have your babies.* Or maybe I could completely scare him off: *I think I'm falling in love with you.*

That last one made my heart feel as if it was dropping down into the pit of my stomach. Oh. My. Goodness. Was I truly falling in love with a man I'd known a total of two days?

Instead of telling him all of that, I opted to keep things lighthearted. "Who gets to pick out the snacks?"

He gave me a confused look.

"I mean, look at your body," I said. "You don't really seem like the snack food type of guy, so I think I should be in charge of picking out what we're going to eat for the next ten or so hours."

Roger gave my body a slow perusal. "You don't look like a snack lover either."

I felt my nose crinkle up as I replied, "I'm at least ten to fifteen pounds over where I want to be, and this girl knows how to make a damn good ice cream sundae with caramel, hot fudge, and my secret ingredient. Trust me, I know my snacks."

His eyes turned dark. "The fuck you're ten pounds over anything. Your body is perfect. In fact, if we had more time together, I'd encourage you to eat whatever the hell you wanted so I could feel even more of you while I fucked you."

My face got hot, and I quickly looked around to make sure no one else had heard him. I had dated guys in the past who liked to toss out the word "fuck" every now and then, but Roger didn't mind using it at all. You'd think it would make what we'd been doing feel cheap or wrong. But I knew he didn't mean it like that. Yes, we fucked, and good Lord, did I enjoy it. But I had also seen a tender side of Roger that I didn't think many of his past lovers had gotten a glimpse of.

Of course, that could simply be wishful thinking on my part.

"Stop being bad," I said. "We'll both go get some snacks."

When I turned to walk toward the small gift shop, Roger slapped my ass, causing me to burst out laughing. Everyone in the lobby turned and looked at us. If this was a prequel to how our day and evening would go, sign me up.

I dropped onto the bed and gasped for air.

"Holy shit, Anna. Where in the hell did that come from?" Roger asked, panting beside me.

I turned to look at him. He lay on his back, staring up at the ceiling as he attempted to catch his breath. I had just ridden my cowboy hard and fast.

Was he a cowboy? It was the first time I'd even allowed myself to think about where Roger was from. It was clearly somewhere down south; I knew that much from his southern accent, which, if I was being honest, was a complete turn-on.

"That. Was. Amazing," I panted out.

"That was the best fucking sex of my life. Christ, I think I saw stars."

Laughing, I rolled over and rested my head on my hand. Roger had come at the same time I did, and I loved that I was able to make him orgasm while I was on top. I was pretty sure when I grabbed my nipples and started playing with them, it did us both in. With Roger, this whole other wanton side of me came out during sex, and I loved exploring it. A pang of sadness hit me, knowing I would most likely never have this kind of sex again. I couldn't imagine another man making me feel the way Roger did. I'd had more orgasms with him in the last day than I think I'd had in my entire life.

Roger sat up before making his way into the bathroom. I heard the water turn on, and I knew he was cleaning himself up and would soon be walking out with a warm washcloth for me. It was the sweetest gesture.

"Lie back. Let me clean you up," he said as he emerged.

My heart started racing in my chest, and I did what he asked, knowing that even though I'd had the most mind-blowing orgasm only minutes ago, the feel of him touching me would ignite that flame again.

I closed my eyes when the warm washcloth touched my sensitive flesh. A small moan slipped free, and I felt Roger watching me.

Sure enough, when I opened my eyes, he was staring right at me.

"Sorry," I whispered, closing my legs as a sudden rush of embarrassment hit me.

He winked, and butterflies went off in my stomach.

"Do you want to take a shower?" he asked.

"No," I said with a shake of my head. "I want to just lie here next to you before we both have to get up and leave."

He smiled and tossed the washcloth onto the floor before crawling into the bed. "Fair enough."

I rolled over, allowing him to wrap his arms around me and pull me to him. I had the strangest feeling that Roger wasn't the type of guy who cuddled often, if at all. I wasn't sure why I felt that way—maybe it was something about the way he held on to me so tightly, as if he was afraid to let me go. Maybe it was my imagination, or just me secretly hoping he would beg for my phone number and promise we would meet up at least once a month. Truth be told, I knew the moment I agreed to this, it would be hard to say goodbye. I couldn't help but wonder if Roger was having the same thoughts and feelings.

"I don't do relationships," he said, breaking the silence in the room.

I swallowed hard. "What do you mean?"

"I don't date. I don't have the desire to settle down, and I don't fall in love, ever."

I closed my eyes and prayed my body hadn't sagged in reaction to his words like my heart had. It was crazy, really. I'd only known Roger a few days, so this declaration shouldn't mean anything to me.

Then why did it feel like someone had punched through my chest, grabbed my heart, and pulled it right out? And why had he felt the need to say it at all?

If he was going to be honest, then so was I. Forcing my voice to remain steady and calm, I replied, "It's a good thing we're going our separate ways in a few hours then because I'm pretty sure I could easily fall in love with you."

Roger buried his face in my hair and breathed in as he pulled me closer. He didn't have to say anything; I felt it between us. He had spoken those words out loud to try and push away what he was feeling.

God, I wanted to know exactly what he was thinking. What impact, if any, my words had on him. If we weren't going in two different directions, down two different paths, would he change his mind? Or was this something he did often? He was extremely good-looking, and I wasn't so naïve that I didn't know the man most likely had a very healthy sex life.

"I don't do this, Anna. These last few days have been..." His voice trailed off, and I found myself holding my breath. "They've been amazing and fun, but I..."

"You don't have to say anything else, Roger. We both agreed when we started that it would be no strings attached. I'm not expecting anything from you when we both walk out that door."

He placed a soft kiss on my shoulder, and I could feel his body instantly relax.

"Thank you for giving me some of the most amazing days ever. I'll never forget you, princess. Never."

A tear slipped free as I swallowed the lump in my throat. "I'll never forget you either."

Roger and I stood at the entrance of the airport, staring at one another. Neither of us had spoken a word during the Uber ride there. Roger was way too early for his flight, but he wanted to see me off. I wasn't sure at first if he would come to the airport with me, especially since he'd uttered only a handful of words to me since we woke up. I knew it was his way of putting distance between us, and I couldn't really fault him for that.

"I guess this is it," he said with that smile of his. It made my heart pound in my chest. The dimples didn't always come out, but they were there now.

With a humorless laugh, I replied, "Guess so."

Roger placed his hand on the side of my face, and I leaned into it. "Have a safe flight, Annalise, wherever you're going."

I could feel that lump in my throat again, and when I spoke, my voice sounded strained. "You too."

I reached up onto my toes and kissed him quickly on the lips. I went to step away, but Roger dropped his bag and pulled my body to his. His hand went to the back of my neck before his mouth crashed onto mine.

If I had thought the man could kiss before, this one was mind-blowing. It felt like he was trying to pour every thought and emotion he couldn't verbally say into that one kiss. To say I was being kissed senseless would have been an understatement.

When I wasn't sure I could take any more, he drew back and leaned his forehead against mine. His chest rose and fell with each breath.

"Fuck. We didn't have enough time together."

I took in a shaky breath and sniffled. "This is harder than I thought it would be."

Roger didn't respond to that. He kissed me on the forehead, took a step back, and said, "Goodbye, Annalise Michaels."

My nose stung, and the back of my eyes burned with the threat of tears. I'd never dreamed I could have such feelings for a man I knew almost nothing about.

When I opened my mouth, no words would come out. I cleared my throat and took a step back so that his body was no longer in contact with mine. I needed to be able to think, and having Roger near me like that certainly muffled my thoughts.

"Good...goodbye, Roger." I forced a smile as I held my chin up and fought with everything I had not to break down in tears like some crazy woman.

He gave me one more smile before I turned and started into the airport, leaving him behind to watch as I walked away. My feet felt like lead, and the urge to turn and run back to him was overwhelming.

Each breath came quick and fast, and I pressed my hand over my stomach to settle a sudden rush of nausea.

By the time I made it through security, I couldn't take it anymore, and I looked back. My heart dropped when I didn't see him anywhere.

"Why did you look back, idiot?" I whispered.

I made it to my gate, kicking myself for not asking Roger for his phone number. What harm would having a phone number be?

"No, it's better this way," I said to myself as I flopped into one of the chairs.

My phone suddenly rang, and I jumped. I had never fumbled for my cell so fast. I jerked it out of my purse, hoping beyond hope that maybe while I was in the shower, Roger had gotten my phone number off my phone.

I groaned when I saw it was my sister.

"Hey, what's up?" I asked, trying to sound casual.

"What's up? *What is up?* You've been trapped in Chicago for days, and every time I try to call, you send me to voicemail. When

I text, you say you're busy. What in the hell, Anna? I was ready to call the police, thinking something happened to you. Then Mom told me you texted her to say you had to share a hotel room with some strange man! For all I knew, he murdered you and was simply texting back on your phone!"

When she stopped to take a breath, I cut in. "Oh, my gosh, are you finished yet? I told Mom what was going on, and I *was* busy."

"Doing what?"

"Well, for your information..." I quickly glanced around, then lowered my voice. "I was having the most amazing sex of my life."

The line went silent for a few moments before my sister spoke. "Whaaaat? Sex? With who?" She gasped. "Oh, my gawd! The forced hotel roomie?"

I giggled like a damn schoolgirl. "Yes. Oh, Meg. I am totally ruined for all future men. Roger was... he was...I don't even know the words to describe him."

"Anna Bobana...do you like this guy? How is this going to work? Where does he live? Are you doing long-distance? I'm not sure you're cut out for that type of relationship, but I mean, if the sex is that good, it might be worth it. I hear phone sex can be hot."

Laughing, I shook my head and leaned back in the chair. "I don't know where he lives."

"Wait, come again?"

"That was part of the agreement we made before we...um...had sex. No strings attached, no personal questions. Just a few magical days locked away in a hotel with the best orgasms of my life."

"You got his number, though, right?"

That all-too-familiar pain in my chest came back.

"Nope. No phone numbers. All I know is his name, that he has a brother, and that he's a lawyer."

"You know, you could Google him."

I sighed. "I already thought about that, but...I don't know, it would seem like an invasion of his privacy. I mean, we both agreed it was just for this short time."

My sister and I both exhaled loudly.

"I'm pretty sure he's from down south somewhere," I added. "He had a southern accent."

"Texas?" she asked, a bit of anticipation in her voice.

"I have no clue, and now I'm sitting at my gate regretting the fact that I didn't even ask him for his number. We *could* have had phone sex, damn it. Hot, heated phone sex."

An older woman who had just sat down next to me cleared her throat.

"Yeah, you could have. He did use a condom, right?"

I remained silent.

"Anna, you did not!"

"What? I'm on the pill, and I wanted to—" I lowered my voice— "feel him."

She groaned. "This doesn't sound like my baby sister. The responsible one. Who are you right now?"

"What do you mean?" I asked.

"I mean, you slept with a stranger, and now you're wishing you got his number so you could have phone sex. This move is already changing you. Come back home."

Laughing, I shook my head even though she couldn't see me. "It was fun and daring to let my guard down."

"Yeah, until nine months from now and you've got a baby, and the daddy is nowhere to be found."

"Oh, stop it. I'm on birth control, Meg. There isn't going to be a baby."

She scoffed.

"Listen, they're getting ready to board. Once I get settled in, I'll call everyone. I love you."

"Love you, too, Anna."

When my boarding group was called, I stood, grabbed my stuff, and walked to the gate. I took one more look behind me, just in case.

No one.

With a sigh, I handed my ticket over and then walked down the ramp toward my new life in Texas.

Chapter 11

Roger

THE VISE THAT had been around my chest seemed to grow tighter and tighter the farther Annalise walked away from me. I followed her into the airport. Watched as she walked up to the counter. I kept a good distance away as she walked toward security. I smiled when I saw her look back one last time once she made it through. I was off to the side, so I knew she couldn't see me. Something about the fact that she'd looked for me just one last time did something to me, though. The smile that spread over my face couldn't be helped.

She looked back for me.

It wasn't until I got to my gate later and sat down that I felt like I could breathe again. I had wandered around the airport for the last hour or so, feeling utterly lost. I scrubbed my hand down my face and cursed. "What in the hell did she do to me?"

My phone rang, and for a crazy moment, I thought it might be her. But she was up in the air flying, and we hadn't even exchanged phone numbers.

Shit. Why didn't I at least get her number?

I pulled my cell out of my bag and saw Truitt's name.

"Hey," I said, not even caring that it sounded like my whole world had just ended.

"What's wrong with you? I figured you'd be happy to be heading home."

Glancing around the airport, a small part of me hoped I'd see Annalise standing there.

Snap out of it, Carter. It isn't like you to be hung up on a woman.

"I *am* happy. How are things back home? Saryn? The kids?"

"They're good. Listen, once you get back, Dad wants us both over for dinner. He wants to talk to you."

I brought my hand to the back of my neck and sighed. "Today? I'm not going to feel like dinner at Mom and Dad's house after this flight. What's so important that he can't wait until tomorrow to talk to me?"

"Do you remember the Martin ranch that was about twenty miles outside of town?"

"Yeah. I remember it."

"They're putting it on the market. You know what'll happen if an investor gets it."

"Houses," we both said in unison.

"Is Dad interested in it?" I asked.

"No, but we both thought of you. I know you said you wanted something bigger, maybe even get some cattle from Dad."

I leaned back in my chair. Ranching had never really been on my list of top priorities, but it had piqued my interest lately, and I *did* want to move farther out.

"How much do they want for it?" I asked, dreading the answer. The price of land in Texas had skyrocketed in the last few years, with more and more investors moving in and buying up all the land.

"From what Dad told me, they want to sell local. They don't want to see their family's land get broken up into lots and sold off. Dad mentioned you were looking for some land, so they want to meet and talk about a price."

"Tonight? Dinner?" I quickly asked.

"Yes. Luke Martin and his wife will be there around seven."

Glancing up at the board that listed my flight, I saw that it was leaving in thirty minutes and nodded to no one. "As long as I don't have any delays, that should be fine. I've got a straight flight, so I'll have plenty of time to get there."

"Did you change your rental car?" Truitt asked. "You know I can pick you up, Roger. It isn't any trouble."

"No, I don't want to make you drive in. And please, this isn't my first rodeo. I rebooked it as soon as I got my new flight info."

He laughed. "Right. So, um, how did things go with your hotel buddy?"

"Good. Better than good."

"Christ. You slept with her?"

"More than once. We made an agreement: no-strings-attached sex."

"And how did that work out for you?"

The last thing I wanted to do was talk about sex with my brother while surrounded by a bunch of strangers. "They're calling for boarding. I've got to run."

"In other words, you don't want to talk about it."

"Give the kids a kiss and hug for me. Talk soon."

Before Truitt could ask anything else, I disconnected and then shut my phone down. All I wanted to do was get on the plane, order a drink, and fall asleep. Maybe once I woke up in Texas, everything would be back to normal and this strange longing would finally be gone.

The flight from Illinois to Texas was miserable. Every time I managed to fall asleep, I dreamed of Annalise. When I was awake, the guy next to me in first class tried to sell me life insurance. I couldn't wait to get off the fucking plane and get back to Boerne.

I pulled out my computer and caught up on emails, so that occupied some of my time, at least. A part of me was tempted to email the hotel Annalise worked at in New York City to see if they'd tell me where she'd moved to, even though I knew there was no way that would happen.

The moment the plane landed, I headed to the car rental desk. I drove a Ford F-250 so there was no way I was leaving it in the airport parking lot, not even in valet parking. Truitt had dropped me off, and I had booked a rental for when I came home. Truitt was just as busy as I was, and the drive into San Antonio was a bitch with all the traffic.

As I came down the escalator, the hair on the back of my neck stood up, and a strange sensation rushed through me. I glanced around, confused, but then shook it off.

I walked around the corner—and my entire world seemed to slow down and come to a halt.

I'd felt her before I even saw her. Then I heard her, and I couldn't help but smile as I walked up and stood behind her in line.

"But I had a reservation," she pleaded in her sweet voice.

"Yes, you did, Ms. Michaels, for three days ago."

"I was stuck in Chicago in a snowstorm."

The girl at the counter gave Annalise a sympathetic smile. "I'm so sorry, ma'am. If you had just called and rescheduled, we might have been able to hold a car for you. I've only got one car left now."

"I'll take that one then!"

I smiled and looked down at the ground, trying my hardest not to laugh.

"It's reserved for someone. I can't give it to you."

Annalise stood on her tiptoes and said, "I'll pay double."

The girl hesitated, then looked at me. She grinned before focusing her attention back on Annalise.

"I'm sorry, I can't. You could always check another car rental place."

At that moment, a younger man rushed past me, and Annalise and frantically asked the girl, "Do you have any available cars? No one in this damn airport has any left!"

The girl shook her head and turned to Annalise. "Maybe an Uber?"

I cleared my throat and said, "Maybe I can help."

Annalise spun around and stared at me, an openly shocked expression on her face.

I winked at her, then looked at the clerk. "I have a reservation under the name Roger Carter."

The girl typed away on her computer and then said, "Yes, Mr. Carter, let me get those keys for you."

Annalise slowly shook her head before she started to laugh. "You've got to be kidding me. *You're* the guy with the last reservation?"

I held out my hands and shrugged. "I can't help it if I remembered to call the rental car place and you didn't, princess."

Her mouth opened to say something, but all she did was smile and shake her head.

I couldn't fucking believe it. Annalise was standing in front of me. Here, in Texas—and she was fucking moving here. God, I hoped it was to San Antonio since she wouldn't be that far from me. I wasn't sure if I wanted to jump for joy or run like hell. "What are the odds we're both heading to San Antonio?" I asked.

Her eyes lit up like Christmas morning. "A million to one. I knew your accent was from the south."

The girl behind the counter cleared her throat. "I just need you to go through this paperwork, Mr. Carter."

After I initialed and signed, I looked at Annalise. "Where are you going? I'll give you a ride."

"Do you live here? In San Antonio?"

I shook my head. "No, not in San Antonio, about forty minutes outside of it."

She let out another disbelieving laugh.

"You're moving to San Antonio?" I asked. "I got the impression you were going to a smaller hotel."

The way she stared at me made my heartbeat kick up some. "Oh, I am. The town is outside of San Antonio. Thank you for offering to give me a ride, but it would probably be out of your way."

"I'm not doing anything else before dinner, and what better way to spend my afternoon than to sneak in some more time with you?"

"Do you two know each other?" the girl behind the counter asked as she handed me the keys to the rental. She could clearly feel the energy between me and Annalise.

"Yes," Annalise answered with a wide grin. "We know each other well."

I lifted a brow and fought to hide my own smile.

"It's all set for someone to come pick this up tomorrow?" I asked the girl when I finally broke my stare with Annalise.

The girl nodded. "Yes, sir. It's all arranged."

Turning back to face Annalise, I smiled. "So, are you going to tell me where I'm taking you, or do I have to start guessing all the surrounding towns?"

Annalise looked at the girl, then at me. "You have to promise me that if it's out of the way, you'll just let me take an Uber or a taxi."

I held up my hand and crossed my heart with my finger. "I promise. Where to?"

"I'm staying at the hotel I'll be working at until I can find a place of my own. The owner has graciously allowed me to have one of the suites."

"That's nice of her."

Annalise pulled out a piece of paper. "I have it memorized, but just in case... Yes, here it is. One twenty-eight Blanco Road. In Boerne..." She trailed off, looking for the name.

My breath caught in my throat. Had I heard her right?

"Do you know where that is?"

All I could do was nod. There was absolutely no fucking way Annalise was moving to Boerne.

There was no way she would be working only steps from my office.

Was I still asleep on the plane?

I looked at the counter girl, then back at Annalise. I rubbed the back of my neck and pinched myself. Yep, I was indeed awake. What in the fuck was going on?

Tilting her head, Annalise gave me a concerned look. "Roger, are you okay? You look white as a ghost."

"What's the name of the hotel you'll be working at?"

"The Montclair."

"The historic hotel," I replied.

Her eyes lit up, and she gave me a brilliant smile that stole my breath. "Yes! Do you know about it?"

I reached down and grabbed her case and placed it on top of mine. "Yes, I've heard of it."

She followed me as I started toward the rental car parking lot. "Is it out of your way? Because if it is, Roger, I can totally take an—"

"It's fine. I'm going that way."

I hadn't meant for the words to come out so cold and harsh, but I needed a fucking minute to process all of this. The only reason I'd slept with Annalise, that I'd allowed myself to open up even slightly, was because I knew I would be walking away. I knew I wouldn't have to think about the way she made my entire body feel warm when she was around. Or how she made my heart feel like it might beat right out of my chest. Or how all I wanted to do was pull her into a private room and bury myself inside of her.

"Okay, if you're sure," she said softly.

Her voice sounded so uncertain, and I hated that I had made her feel that way.

We both remained silent as we walked out of the airport to the rental lot. Once there, I unlocked the car and put Annalise's stuff in first and then mine. When I shut the trunk, I stilled. Annalise was staring at me.

"Are you angry because you ran into me again? I get why you'd feel that way if you thought what we shared in Chicago was...was... well...what it was. I swear to you, I didn't know. I mean, how could I have known you lived in Texas?!"

I nodded. "I know you didn't know, and no, I'm not angry at all. Just surprised."

How in the hell could I tell her that I wasn't prepared for her to be living in the same goddamn town as me? Working only a block away? It wasn't like Boerne was still a super-small town, but there was no way we wouldn't run into each other on occasion. There was absolutely no way I could pretend she wasn't in the same town.

"It's just, I had mentally prepared myself that this morning was the last time I was ever going to see you again, and now..."

"We run into each other at the airport," she said with a nervous chuckle as we both got into the car.

I pulled out of the parking lot and around the twists and turns of the airport until I got out to the highway.

"Roger, if you're worried I'm going to expect anything, I don't. I'm not going to pretend that what happened between us in Chicago was just a fling. I mean...for me, it was more. But I don't expect anything from you."

Glancing at her, all I could do was laugh.

Her brows pulled in tightly and she glared at me. "Is something funny?"

I laughed harder, and that made her cross her arms over her chest, let out a disgusted sigh, and turn to look out the window. "Texas is pretty big," she said. "I highly doubt we'll see each other again, so you don't have to worry about me asking for anything."

I could hear the anger in her voice, and fuck if it wasn't hot as hell. I needed to put myself in check, though. Annalise Michaels was unlike any other woman I had ever been with, and when I told her earlier that I wasn't looking for a relationship, I hadn't been lying.

What I didn't admit was that when it came to her, I could see myself breaking that rule.

We drove in silence for nearly the entire thirty-five-minute trip. Annalise had started to text someone—her new boss, I assumed. Then her phone rang, and I noticed how her hands shook as she answered it.

Why in the hell was she so nervous? Was it me who made her nervous, or the new job? She had run one of the most prestigious hotels in New York City. She had this in the bag. The Montclair was a nice hotel, one of the nicest in Boerne, but it was on the small side. Very small side compared to what she was coming from.

"Hello? Yes, Mrs. Montclair, I'm excited as well. It looks like I'm about ten minutes from the hotel. Okay, yes. Of course. I'll see you in a few minutes."

She hit End and then looked out the window.

"Did you fly in for an interview?" I asked.

"No. We did it all on Zoom. This is the first time I'm seeing the town. It's adorable. All these little stores."

"It's called the Hill Country Mile."

She faced me. "Yes, I read that. Are you familiar with this area?"

I stopped at the light and put my signal on to turn left onto West Blanco Road. "Yes, I'm very familiar with Boerne."

"Really?" she asked as I turned. The hotel was at the end of the road and sat just above the Cibolo Creek. I pulled into the circular drive of The Montclair, put the car in park, and turned to face her.

"Really. I grew up here."

Her eyes widened in shock. Yeah, I was a bit freaked out by all of this, as well, so I knew how she felt.

"You did? Oh, my gosh. Well…that's a weird coincidence." Her eyes dropped down to her hands, which were now twisted in her lap.

I nodded.

"And…where do you live n-now?" she asked as those ice-blue eyes looked up at me.

My gaze drifted down to her soft pink lips, and more than anything I wanted to forget the stupid promise I'd made to myself to never let another woman into my heart. I wanted to pull her to me and tell her how fucking happy I was that she was here. That I hadn't lost her, because I had been so damn miserable at the idea of never seeing her again. But I didn't say any of that.

"I live *here*, Anna. In Boerne. My office is one block away. My father's ranch is just outside of town. My brother lives fifteen minutes from here. My house isn't that far either. Maybe ten minutes away."

Annalise went still, her eyes growing as wide as saucers. "You're joking, right?"

I shook my head. "No, I'm dead serious. I've lived in Boerne my entire life."

She looked out the window at the front door of the hotel and then back to me. Her mouth opened and closed a few times before she closed her eyes, shook her head, and then fixed me with a sharp gaze.

"You live in Boerne, Texas. *Boerne*. The same place I'm going to be working and living?"

"Yes."

She burst out laughing before she dropped her head back against the seat of the rental car. "What in the hell? What are the odds of this happening?"

"Fate, I guess," I said with a chuckle.

She snapped her head up and stared at me. "Fate?" she whispered, then seemed to drift away before shaking her head. "I, um…I can't process this right now. I need to get in there. Mrs. Montclair is waiting for me."

"Of course."

I got out of the car and opened the trunk to take out her luggage. After shutting it, I reached for her hand and held it. "We'll talk soon, okay?"

Annalise swallowed hard and then took a step away from me. Almost as if she needed the distance. She blinked rapidly. "Yes, of course. I guess you know where to find me."

"Or you could give me your number."

She shook her head. "No, because if I give you my number and you don't call, I don't think I could… I just think… I need to go."

Reaching for her stuff, she turned and headed into The Montclair Hotel. It struck me as odd that this was the second time today she had turned and walked away from me, both of us uncertain about where our future was going.

Except now I knew where to find her…and this conversation was far from over.

Chapter 12

Annalise

MY NERVES WERE shot. I wasn't sure if it was because I was walking into a new job, new career, new life—or because Roger had just laid a giant bomb on me only moments ago.

He lives here.

Boerne.

Roger lives in Boerne, Texas.

As I opened the door to the lobby of The Montclair, I couldn't help but laugh at the cruel irony fate had dealt me. The entire flight down to San Antonio, I had resolved to forget about Roger Carter. I mean, I knew I would truly never forget him, but I could bury him away in a special place...because the last few days with him truly *had* been special. My own little fairy tale that I'd been able to live in for just a little while.

And now? Now the man of my dreams, who clearly wasn't interested in anything but a fling, was living only minutes away from me.

"Oh, God, this isn't happening," I whispered, stepping into the small lobby of the new hotel I was now general manager of. It was adorable, and the pictures I had seen of it did not do it justice. The hardwood floors were original, and instantly gave that romantic, charming feeling the hotel was going for. To my right was a sitting area with a large rock fireplace. Dark wood board and batten covered half the walls and gave it that historical look. On the opposite-end sitting area sat a French door that I knew led into the library. Behind the sofa sat a large antique table with all the brochures for the area laid out in a neat arrangement.

I glanced to my left and smiled. Another fireplace that mirrored the one on the right, but this one boasted a large vase filled with fresh flowers. A large desk and two chairs sat on this side of the lobby, along with another set of French doors that led to the restaurant.

Directly in front of me was a hallway that led to the front desk that sat on the left side, and two antique chairs sat on the right up against the staircase that led to the second floor.

I'm dreaming. I have to be dreaming.

I pinched my arm.

Nope, not dreaming.

"You really are here. No need to pinch yourself!"

I looked up and saw the owner of the hotel, Mrs. Montclair, standing in front of me with a wide smile on her face. Her grayish-blonde hair was pulled up in a bun, and she wore a black pantsuit that showcased a rather impressive figure. She had mentioned once that she ran five miles every day with her husband. *Here's hoping there's something in the Texas water because this woman looks amazing.* The closer she got, the more I found it hard to believe she was in her mid-sixties as she'd previously stated.

"Mrs. Montclair, it's so nice to meet you in person!"

I extended my hand to shake hers, but she brushed it away before pulling me into her arms and hugging me. Not just a friendly hug. A hug that said she was glad to see me.

"I was so worried about you being stuck in Chicago all alone," she said, pulling back and giving me a quick once-over. "You appear to be well. No harm done."

No harm at all.

My nerves were still rattled by the encounter with Roger, so I willed myself to give her the brightest smile I could. "I've never been better. I'm so excited to start this new adventure, Mrs. Montclair. I've already got a few ideas about how we can expand the marketing on—"

She held up her hand. "First off, you're a part of The Montclair family now, Annalise. We all go by our first names here. You can call me Patty."

With a nod, I said, "Patty it is, then."

"Second, no business right now. I want to get you settled into one of the cabins. Then we'll do a tour of everything and introduce you to the rest of the crew. Everyone came in this afternoon so they could meet you."

"That's so sweet."

Patty smiled before she motioned for me to follow her.

"As you know, we have forty different accommodations on site. Much smaller than what you're used to, but each unique in their own way."

"I'm all about the intimacy of this hotel. I'm extremely excited about the change."

Another brilliant smile spread over her face. "It is a rather charming hotel, isn't it? From the time the hotel was built in 1860 as a home for Mr. and Mrs. Philip Stein, it's stood out in the community of Boerne. Of course, being located on the Cibolo Trail has always made the property more popular."

The hotel sat on a beautiful piece of property, a stone's throw from the Cibolo Creek. It was surrounded by massive cypress, oak, and elm trees that made the hotel feel as if it was in the middle of nowhere when, in reality, it was only a block from Main Street and a plethora of retail stores and restaurants. If you looked up charming in the dictionary, this hotel would be pictured.

"I cannot wait to see it in the fall," I said, glancing around. "I imagine, with all these trees, it looks beautiful."

"Oh, it is. And spring. Just wait until spring, darling. The wildflowers that surround the gazebo in the back are stunning. You'll see why we book so many weddings back there."

We walked out the back door and stepped onto the hotel's back porch. The lobby was located in the oldest structure on the property:

the original house. Years later, two sides had been built onto the main in order to expand the hotel. A wide courtyard sat in front of me with tables, benches, rocking chairs, and a large oak tree that sat in the middle of it all. Strands of Edison lights were draped from the branches to the buildings. To the back left of the courtyard were two large grills. Next to them sat an old buggy.

"I meant to ask you when you were giving me the tour on FaceTime, Mrs....er...Patty—what's the story behind the old buggy?"

Patty had sent me video after video showing me the entire hotel and the property it sat on. Not to mention hundreds of photos.

Her eyes lit up as we walked to the roped-off item in question. "This buggy belonged to the original owners of the property. Mr. Stein bought it for his wife so that she could travel to visit friends. It was his way of showing their wealth at the time. Mr. Stein wanted to make his presence well known in town."

I glanced back at the old buggy, which was still in pretty good condition, but it didn't look anything like something you would be showing your wealth off with. I hadn't meant to, but I frowned.

Patty laughed. "Trust me, back in the 1860s, this was beautiful."

"I'm sure it was," I replied with a slight chuckle.

"Over the years, my husband and I have traveled all over the country collecting old cabins and buildings to add to the property."

We walked through the courtyard to the back half of the property, and I found myself growing giddy. It was a far cry from the Lotte Hotel in New York City, but I loved how unique this place was. Historic log cabins were arranged to the left of me, with a second small courtyard sitting in the middle. To the right was an old church house that the Montclairs had picked up from a small town in West Texas. Behind that was a red schoolhouse. Down the walkway were more cabins, all small historical homes that the Montclairs had saved from being torn down.

"I thought we would put you in the St. James chapel," Patty said.

I looked at her. "What? That's our nicest suite, Mrs....um...Patty. I couldn't even think of staying there. Honestly, I'm perfectly happy staying in one of the rooms in the main hotel."

She waved me off. "Nonsense. I want you to be comfortable, and I already had Elizabeth block that suite out for the next two months. I don't think it will take you that long to find a place, but just in case. You did mention you wanted to rent first before you purchased anything. I think that's smart. Get to know the area before you jump into anything like that."

I nodded as we made our way toward the St. James suite.

"How long has Elizabeth worked for you?" I asked. I had made a list of the employees before leaving New York, and had written down the little information Patty had given me about them next to their names. Elizabeth, for example, was the front desk supervisor. She was young, most likely in her mid-twenties. I'd met her when I had my second Zoom interview with the Montclairs. She had a warm and friendly smile that made me feel instantly at ease. I could see why Patty had made her supervisor of the front desk.

"Oh, goodness, let me see. Lizzy has been working for me since she was sixteen," Patty said. "She's twenty-five now. She started off in housekeeping and worked her way up. She's one of the hardest-working employees we have. If you need her to pitch in anywhere, she's there, no questions asked. I cannot tell you how many times that girl has cleaned up the rooms or helped out over at the River City Grill. She's even done some landscaping a time or two."

"That's wonderful. Employees like that are hard to come by, and when you do find one, it's best to hang on to them."

Patty nodded. "Trust me, if Lizzy gave her two-week notice, I'd probably double her salary just in the hope that she'd stay."

I raised my brows.

"Yes, she's that good. You'll soon see."

As we climbed the steps of the St. James, I asked, "And does she want to be promoted higher up?"

Patty unlocked the door and pushed it open, motioning for me to walk in first. I had seen this suite before, of course. During my second interview, Mr. Montclair had walked the property with his phone to show me a few rooms and three of the freestanding buildings. The St. James happened to be one of them. It was still as breathtaking now as it was when I first saw it.

One large room—that I'm sure at one time held church pews—now housed a small living and dining area. A wood wall had been built to separate the sitting and sleeping areas. And at the far end of the church sat a stunning bathroom, which featured a large walk-in shower and a claw-foot bathtub. I was already dreaming of soaking in it.

"Lizzy has a wonderful work ethic, but as far as managing The Montclair, she has a lot to learn, and lacks the knowledge that someone like yourself has to offer."

"I can understand that. I'm happy to help her learn more about the business side of running a hotel if that's something you'd like me to do."

Patty placed her hand on my arm and gave a little squeeze. "You truly are a gift. Right now, Lizzy seems to be very happy in her role here. She started dating a young man who works for the city of Boerne, and I'm not sure even *she* knows what her future holds."

Suddenly Patty grinned. "What about you, Annalise? Is there a someone special in your life?"

An image of Roger popped into my mind. "No, I'm single."

With a wink, she replied, "Well, we have a lot of handsome cowboys in our little town of Boerne."

I laughed and decided to change the subject. "I went over the budget you have set for the rest of this year and next. I have some ideas I'd like to go over with you and Mr. Montclair."

"Jim. Call him Jim."

I really wasn't in New York City anymore. "I have some ideas I'd like to go over with you both, whenever you're free."

"That sounds amazing. Let's plan on meeting at the restaurant for lunch tomorrow, and we can talk more then. As far as today goes, get settled, we'll do an official tour, and I'll introduce you to everyone. Then you're free to roam around for the rest of the day and get some food. I had Manny bring in a small refrigerator for you to use."

"Thank you so much, Patty. And thank you for being so understanding with the delay in starting."

She waved her hand again. "Pish, posh. I'm not the least bit worried. I'm just so excited to have you on our team as part of the

Montclair family. Now, text me whenever you're ready to head back to the front desk, and I'll make sure everyone is there to meet you."

"Sounds good," I said as I followed her back to the door.

Before she stepped out, she turned and faced me. "I have to ask, how do you know Roger Carter?"

I was positive my jaw hung open for a good twenty seconds. "Roger?"

She nodded. "He dropped you off, and it seemed like the two of you knew each other. I wasn't aware you knew anyone in town."

"I don't. I mean, I didn't until the other day." I laughed nervously. "Funny story! Roger was actually stuck in Chicago as well. We met there. Neither one of us even knew we had a connection to Boerne until we both ended up at the same car rental company today. And that's when we found out we were going to the same place. It's a crazy...um...coincidence."

Patty slowly nodded and gave me a look I couldn't read *at all*. "I don't believe in coincidences. I believe in fate. There is a reason for everything. And sometimes, fate meets destiny."

I drew in a deep breath and then let it out slowly. Was she talking about me and Roger? "Well, we're only friends. I don't think Roger is the least bit interested in anything other than that."

With a half-shrug, Patty turned toward the path that led back to the hotel lobby. "Hmmm. I don't think he truly knows *what* he wants. See you soon, Annalise!"

I stared at her back as she retreated. "What in the hell does that mean?" I asked to no one but myself.

After shutting the door, I leaned against it and let out a groan. Today was supposed to be the beginning of a new life. I should have been excited to start this new journey. Instead, I was confused and, honestly, a bit shell-shocked.

I rushed over to my purse, pulled out my phone, and hit my sister's number.

"So? How is it? Is the town cute? Have you been able to look around? Tell me there are cowboys, and I'll fly down tomorrow! I want to know everything!"

"Oh, my God, Meg, I'm in so much trouble. So. Much. Trouble!"

She gasped. "They fired you already?"

I jerked my head back. "What? No, I didn't get fired. My gosh, Meg, that's the first thing you think of?"

"Well, what else am I supposed to think when you call me on your first day and tell me you're in so much trouble?"

Rolling my eyes, I replied, "I don't know, but not that I was fired from a job I haven't actually started yet."

"Fine. Why don't you just tell me what's wrong then."

I took in a deep breath. "Roger lives here."

"Wait, Roger, the guy from the hotel? He lives where? In Texas?"

"Yes! Not only does he live in Texas—he lives in Boerne."

Silence filled the line, and I waited for it to sink in.

"Are you sure he lives there? He didn't follow you there like some maniac, did he? I mean, you had sex with him, but you knew nothing about him."

I growled at her. "No, he didn't follow me here. He couldn't have since he didn't even know I was coming. And the owner of The Montclair noticed Roger dropping me off and started to talk about him. She knows him, Meg. She knows him! She said it was fate we met in Chicago."

"You told your new boss you slept with Roger?"

"No, of course not! I simply told her we met in Chicago and then ran back into each other in the airport when I was trying to get a rental, and none were left so Roger gave me a ride."

"That was nice of him. Where did you run into him? I can't imagine it's a small airport."

I let out a disbelieving laugh. "Are you sitting down? Because this story keeps getting stranger by the minute."

"I'm sitting."

"I never changed my reservation for my rental car, so when I got there, they didn't have any cars left. Next thing I know, Roger is standing there with a reservation. He got the last car!"

Meg laughed. "Wait, why was he renting a car if he lives there?"

"I don't know. I think he told me, but I was so stunned he was there, I don't remember. This morning, I figured I'd never see him again. I'd prepared myself for it. And now, he's not only in the same state, but also the same damn town!"

"Oh, no, Anna. Have you fallen for this guy?"

I swallowed hard. "No."

"You are such a terrible liar. And can we get back to the fact that he had to share not only his hotel room with you but his rental car as well? Oh, and he lives in the *same town* that you're now living in? If destiny isn't playing her hand in this, I don't even know what's happening. What are the odds?"

"Um, one in a billion?"

"It's like your hearts are fated."

I sighed. "What do I do?"

"What do you mean, what do you do? It's easy—pick up where you left off. Except now you know you're having hot sex with a cowboy. Please tell me if he wears a cowboy hat." My sister made some sort of growling sound before she started laughing again. "This could only happen to you!"

I dropped down onto the sofa and closed my eyes. "He doesn't want a relationship. He told me so the last night we were together. If Mrs. Montclair knows him, other people will know him too. What if I find out he's an absolute asshole? Oh, my God, what if he's married! Or has a girlfriend?"

"He doesn't have a girlfriend, and I doubt he's married."

"But how do you know?" I asked as I stood and paced. "I can't deal with this right now. I need to get to the hotel lobby so that I can meet the rest of the staff. I need to change."

"Wait, what about Roger?"

Sighing, I replied, "I just...I just can't with that right now. I'm here to start a new job, and that's what I need to focus on."

"But—"

"But nothing, Meg. I had a wonderful few days with Roger, and I'll never forget how he made me feel, but it ended this morning. We agreed no strings attached, so this changes nothing. It changes *nothing*."

It was Meg's turn to sigh. "Like I said, you're a terrible liar."

Chapter 13

Roger

"YOU SEEM DISTRACTED."

I glanced over at my brother as he handed me a bottle of beer. "Nah, I'm good."

Truitt sat down and gave me that look that said he knew I was lying. "Want to talk about it?"

"Just tired, I think. The rental car company was late picking the car up."

"Told you I could have picked you up from the airport—you're the one who insisted on a rental."

My mind drifted back to earlier this afternoon when I saw Annalise standing at the rental car counter. I took a long drink from my beer and looked back at my brother. "Do you believe in fate, or do you think everything that happens is all a crazy coincidence?"

He smiled and leaned back. "I'm a firm believer in fate. Why?"

"Well, you're not going to believe what happened to me today," I said, rubbing at the ache in my neck.

"Try me. Dad's still on a call so he won't be joining us for a few more minutes anyway."

I set my beer on the side table, then leaned forward and rested my forearms on my knees. "Annalise, the woman I was forced to bunk with in Chicago..."

He laughed. "You regret not getting her number now, don't you?"

"I don't need her number."

"You sure about that?"

"I don't need her number because she's here."

Truitt's eyes went wide. "She came home with you? I thought you said she was starting a new job."

"She is, but her new job is here. In Boerne. At The Montclair Hotel. She's the new general manager. And to make it even more bizarre, she was at the rental car place trying to get a rental. I got the last one. I gave her a ride to the hotel."

Truitt's mouth fell open. "You're shitting me. What are the odds of that?"

"I don't know what to do, Truitt."

He frowned. "What do you mean? About what?"

"Annalise. What do I do about Annalise living in Boerne?"

"You said it was no-strings. It's not like you haven't slept with a woman before and nothing has come of it. Look at Lucy. Y'all have hooked up more than once, and there isn't any problem there."

"I haven't been with Lucy in at least a year and a half. Maybe even two."

"Really? I didn't know that. Okay, well, what's your heart telling you to do?"

I let out a gruff laugh. "My heart? When in the hell have I ever followed my heart?"

Truitt leaned forward and pierced me with a look. "You know it's okay to want something more than sex."

Narrowing my eyes, I gave Truitt a hard stare. "I don't want anything more. I have no desire whatsoever to settle down with anyone."

He scoffed. "Then why in the hell do you look so fucking miserable right now?"

"I'm not miserable. It's just...Annalise was different. The moment I laid eyes on her, I wanted her in a way I've never wanted another woman. I also knew that if I slept with her, there would be an endpoint. We were forced to walk away from each other, so it was…"

He frowned. "It was what?"

I gave a half-shrug. "It was safe. I knew this morning when she left that was going to be it. I'd never see her again, so I wouldn't have to deal with the weird-ass thoughts and feelings going on inside of me. And now she's here, and I…"

My voice trailed off again.

Truitt slowly nodded. "Can see yourself wanting more with her."

I stood and went over to the window. My silence was clearly answer enough for my brother.

"Roger, it's okay to let someone in. It's been a long time since Kerri."

With a shake of my head, I said, "I can't, Truitt. I can't."

I heard him give a long sigh. "Then you need to tell Annalise. If she likes you as much as you clearly like her, then you need to tell her you're not interested in more."

"I already did. Earlier this morning. I knew her thoughts were mirroring mine, and I had a feeling she was going to want to keep in touch, so before she asked and I broke her heart, I told her I wasn't into relationships. That I had no desire to settle down. I'd hoped it would keep her from asking, and it worked."

I faced Truitt. He was about to respond when our father walked into the room.

"Roger, how was the extended trip?"

I smiled as I reached for his hand. He pulled me into him and gave me a hard slap on the back. "It was cold."

My father let out a bark of laughter and then walked over and poured himself a scotch. "Well, you're back home now, and that's all that matters. Have you seen your mother yet?"

"No," I replied with a shake of my head. "She was gone when I got here."

Dad nodded. "She'll be back in time for dinner. Let's head to my office. I want to talk about the Martin place before Luke and Jean get here."

Three hours later, I was getting up from the table with Luke and Jean Martin after agreeing to purchase their family ranch outside of town. I had been so busy negotiating a fair sale price that I hadn't thought about Annalise for a short while. It wasn't until I was alone with my thoughts on the way back home that images of her flooded my mind. And when I found myself parked down the street from The Montclair, I wasn't the least bit surprised.

I walked into the lobby and quickly glanced around. It wasn't a huge hotel by any means. It had that small-town feel to it, and I smiled at the idea of Annalise running this place. In some folks' eyes, it would be a step down, but I was sure Annalise didn't feel that way. She would do some amazing things here.

"Roger, what a pleasant surprise seeing you here!"

Patty Montclair made her way around the counter and pulled me into a hug before I could even say a word.

"How are things going over here at The Montclair?" I asked as she pulled away. "How's Jim?"

Her eyes lit up like someone had just presented her with a diamond necklace. "Things are amazing now that we have our new general manager. Annalise is a godsend! I heard you two know each other."

How in the hell was I supposed to respond to that? How much had Annalise told Patty?

"Annalise said you two met in Chicago when you were both stuck there, then ran into each other again in the rental car line! Is something wrong with your truck?"

"No," I said with a laugh. "And yes, we did meet in Chicago, but neither of us had any idea we were going to the same place. It's a small world."

The corner of Patty's mouth twitched with a hidden smile. "That's one way to describe it."

I had no idea what she meant by that comment, and I knew better than to ask. "Speaking of which, is Annalise around?"

"She's at the River City Grill. Michael invited her to dinner."

I felt an instant rush of anger sweep through me. Michael was Patty and Jim's youngest son. He was also one of the biggest players in Boerne, and the fact that he was anywhere near Annalise boiled my blood.

"She's having dinner with Michael?" I repeated.

"Yes, he happened to stop by to check on things over at the restaurant and invited Annalise to try the food with him. I told her I thought it was a good idea since folks will be asking her how the food is, and it would be best if she's actually eaten some of it."

I nodded and forced myself to give Patty a smile. Michael Montclair had lived in New York City for a number of years while he went to culinary school, and then worked in a few of the nice restaurants in Boerne. He'd always dreamed of opening his own restaurant and had finally launched the grill near the inn just six months ago.

"I'm sure they have a lot in common since they both lived in New York," Patty said as she smiled and took my arm. "I'll walk with you next door."

A part of me wanted to turn and leave. Maybe it wasn't such a good idea to see Annalise right now. But at the same time, I didn't want her to think I was avoiding her. Then again, if she liked Michael in the least bit, maybe I was doing us both a favor.

I growled internally. Michael wasn't nearly good enough for her.

Patty cleared her throat while she waited for me to start walking.

"Sounds like a plan."

We headed out to the front porch and turned right toward River City Grill, which was located on the far west end of the hotel. The moment we stepped inside, I saw Annalise, and my breath was yanked right out of my chest. Could it be possible she was even more beautiful than the last time I'd seen her only hours before? She sat at the bar with Michael standing beside her—a little too close if you asked me.

Annalise laughed and Michael winked at her. I wasn't positive, but I thought I heard a growl come from the back of my own throat.

"Seems Michael and Annalise are getting along." Patty looked at me and then back to them.

"So it does," I stated dryly, making my way over to them. As I got closer, I could hear Michael talking.

"You've got to let me take you. I have a feeling you'll love it there."

Annalise gave him a polite smile. "That's sweet of you, but I don't think I'll have any free time to start. I'll be pretty busy with the hotel and all."

Michael leaned in closer and went to say something but stopped when I stepped up.

"I see you're already making friends, princess."

Annalise jumped while Michael took a step back.

Her face went from confused that I was there, to pissed I had called her princess, to relief that she had an escape from Michael. "Roger, I...I...wasn't expecting to see you."

"Tonight or ever?" I asked with a wicked smile.

Before Annalise could respond, Michael faced me and extended his hand. "Roger, I haven't seen you in some time."

I shook his hand. "It's been a while, Michael. How's the restaurant business treating you?"

He looked around at the crowded establishment and smiled. "As you can see, pretty damn good. I'm excited to have a place right inside my folks' hotel."

I nodded as I gave the bar and restaurant a quick once-over. "You've done a lot. I like it. Looks good."

Michael rocked on his expensive dress shoes and shoved his hands in his pockets. "Thanks, I'm pretty happy with how it turned out."

Annalise cleared her throat, drawing our attention back to her. Motioning between us, she said, "You know each other, I see."

Michael grinned. "Ever since what, middle school?"

I gave a half-shrug. "Something like that."

"Wait, how do *you* two know each other?" Michael asked.

Oh, this was going to be fun. I gave a saucy grin and started my tale. "We met in Chicago. Both of our flights were delayed because of the snowstorm up there, and funnily enough, we were both—"

Annalise slid off the barstool. "It's been a long day. I think I'll turn in. Thank you for the recommendations, Michael." Turning to face me, she said, "Good seeing you again, Roger."

I touched her arm. "If you've got a few minutes, I was hoping we could talk."

I wasn't sure what expression just crossed her face—it was gone as soon as it appeared.

"Um, sure." Annalise looked at Michael. "Have a good evening, Michael."

He gave her a resigned smile as he glanced between us. "Thank you, you as well."

I stepped to the side to allow Annalise by, then followed her out of the restaurant, across the front porch, into the lobby, and out into the back courtyard. It had been years since I'd stepped foot inside The Montclair. Never really had a reason to be here unless there was a meeting I was attending, or someone I knew from out of town was staying here and we planned on meeting at the bar in the restaurant.

Annalise walked through the garden and up the small porch of the church that sat on the back of the property.

"Are we going to confession or something?" I asked as I followed her.

Glancing back over her shoulder, she smirked. "Ha-ha, this is my room."

The structure was one of the many stand-alone buildings that the hotel had, and it sat at the back of the courtyard. Other outbuildings—mostly old log cabins and a schoolhouse—surrounded the church, making it feel like the centerpiece on the back half of the hotel property. The courtyard separated the historical main structure from the free-standing ones.

When I stepped into the building, I came to a stop. "Wow, this is amazing."

"I know," Annalise said, taking off her sweater and laying it on the back of a chair. "It's one of their grand suites, but Patty said I could stay here until I found a place."

"Are you going to rent first?" I asked.

"Yes, at least until I get to know the area and decide on where to buy."

I nodded and walked deeper into the space. There was a dining table on one side of the room with a small refrigerator against the wall. On the opposite side sat a sofa and chair. A large piece of furniture held the TV, as well as some photos of areas around Boerne.

Annalise cleared her throat, and I looked over at her. She had an expression on her face that indicated she felt just as lost as I did.

"I'm not going to lie and say I'm not glad to see you, Anna. The moment you walked away from me at the airport, I wanted to go after you if only to get your number."

A soft smile spread over her beautiful face. "I still can't believe this. I mean, Boerne, Texas! What are the chances I would get stuck in a hotel room with someone from the same town I was moving to?"

I shrugged and let out a soft laugh. "It's a crazy coincidence, no doubt about it."

Annalise motioned for both of us to sit down. "I'm not really sure where we go from here, Roger. You made things pretty clear back at the hotel."

I sat and stared at her. "Well, things have changed a bit. If you were to ask me now, I'd say the next thing we should do is exchange numbers because I honestly don't want this to end, Anna."

Her brows pulled together as she studied me. "You yourself said you don't do relationships, so what would this be? I can't... I won't be with you knowing that you're going out with other women."

It was my turn to clear my throat. "I'm not sure where this is going, and by *this*, I mean you and me. But what I *am* sure of is the fact that when I saw you standing at that rental counter, something inside of me burst with happiness, Annalise. All I know is that I desperately want to take you in my arms and kiss you, and *only* you."

Her cheeks turned the most beautiful shade of pink. She dug her teeth into her lower lip, clearly thinking about what I'd just said. When she finally spoke, I realized I had been holding my breath.

"I want you to kiss me too," she whispered softly.

We both advanced at the same time until we were face to face, our bodies so close I could feel the heat from hers.

"Fuck, what are you doing to me?" I asked before I captured her mouth with mine.

Annalise wrapped her arms around my neck and moaned as she opened to me. My fingers sliced through her blonde hair, and I tugged her head back, giving me better access to that luscious mouth of hers.

She pulled back, and her blue eyes meet mine. "Tell me this isn't a dream. Tell me you're really here."

With a lazy smile, I went in for another kiss. I tore my mouth from hers and swept her up into my arms. "How about if I show you instead?"

Her smile practically lit up the entire room. "I like that plan."

The moment I set her down on the bed, she crawled to her knees and began to undo the button on my jeans. Before I could even get a word out, my dick was in her warm hand.

"Christ, you drive me mad, Anna."

She lifted her eyes to meet mine. She slowly licked her lips, bent over, and took me into her mouth. My hips jerked, and I let out a moan as I laced my fingers in her hair.

"God, that feels...so good."

Annalise moaned, and I had to force myself not to push farther into her mouth. If I let her keep that up, I'd come. And I really wanted to be inside of her when it happened.

"Stop. Baby, I need you to stop, or this is gonna be over before we even start."

Slowly, she moved her mouth up, gave me one last suck, and then let my cock fall from her mouth.

I reached behind me and pulled my shirt up and over my head while trying to kick off my boots at the same time. Annalise also quickly undressed, and by the time I finished, she was lying on the bed naked, her hair spread across the pillows. Her eyes were hooded with desire, and the way her chest rose and fell told me she was just as eager for this as I was.

Crawling onto the bed, I placed kisses on her body and worked my way up to her parted lips.

She whimpered my name as I lowered my mouth and teased one of her nipples with my tongue, slipping my hand between her legs.

"Shit, you're so wet."

"I haven't been able to stop thinking about you all day. Please, I need to feel you inside of me, Roger. Now."

Without a second thought, I positioned myself and pushed inside of her. Her warmth nearly had me coming on the spot. After a moment of getting myself under control, I rocked in and out of her. The rhythm of our bodies moving together left me breathless. It was like she was made just for me, and I for her. Everything. Was. Perfect.

"Roger...oh, God. Yes. Yes, don't stop!"

"I need you to come, baby. I don't know how long I can hold off."

When her hand slipped between our bodies, I bit the inside of my cheek.

Annalise's entire body trembled, and I could feel her squeezing my cock as she cried out, "There, yes, I'm going to come!"

My name spilled from her lips, and I lost the battle and fell right along with her. I moved until my arms shook from the fatigue of holding myself up.

Rolling off Annalise, I pulled in long breaths.

I wasn't sure how long we lay there, both of us trying to get our breathing back to normal. But it was me who finally broke the silence.

"I wasn't expecting that," I said. "I hope you know that. I really did want to talk."

Annalise took in a deep breath and then slowly exhaled. "So, let's talk."

Turning, I propped my head up on my hand. "I don't want to walk away from you, Annalise. Not when life has brought us together again like this."

She searched my face. "I don't think I can do this. I *want* to do this, but knowing what you said back in Chicago..."

I closed my eyes for a moment and wished I could go back in time and never say what I had said to her. "Annalise, I'm not going to pretend that I'm perfect and that I won't mess up. There's a reason I've never gotten serious with anyone, and to be honest, no one has ever made me *want* to. But then you came along, and I'm feeling..."

My voice trailed off as I closed my eyes and tried to think of the words I wanted to say.

"You're feeling what?" she asked in a low voice.

"Things I haven't really ever felt before. At least, I haven't felt them in a very long time. When I was waiting in the airport, I decided that if I was meant to see you again, I would. I spent three hours on that plane making myself believe everything was okay. I could simply go back to my life the way it was before you showed up in my hotel room three days ago."

"Did it work?"

I laughed, glancing between us. "Considering I'm naked in bed with you, I'd say no, it didn't work."

We both laughed.

"When I saw you at the rental counter, my breath was nearly pulled from my chest," I said. "I won't lie and tell you that doesn't scare me because it does."

Annalise took my hand in hers. "There's a reason this all happened."

I nodded. "I suppose there is, but I want to be honest with you about all of this. I'm not sure what I can give you past this right here, us dating. I want to get to know you better, spend time with you, show you around Boerne and all my favorite places. I also want you to know that I'm not going to date anyone else. It would be you, exclusively."

A warm smile spread over Annalise's face, and she squeezed my hand. "I want to get to know you better too. And I won't ever pressure you, Roger. I mean, we really don't know each other all that well."

We both laughed again. "Then how about we start with lunch tomorrow? Text me when you're free, and I'll take you to one of my favorite places to eat here in Boerne."

She pulled her lower lip between her teeth, and I saw the excitement in her eyes. "I would like that very much. I, um…I need your phone number."

I gripped her hand harder and pulled her on top of me as she let out a squeal of delight.

"How about we exchange numbers *after* we take a shower?"

Chapter 14

Annalise

"I HAVE TO say, Annalise, you seem to be glowing this morning."

My face instantly heated as I looked up at my new boss. "Glowing?" I asked innocently.

I knew the reason why I appeared to be glowing. Roger had informed me that Texans were a friendly folk and that he didn't think it was a good idea for me to spend my first night in Texas alone.

We'd stayed up for hours last night, talking, making love, and talking some more. I finally collapsed in exhaustion after Roger buried his face between my legs, nearly making me pass out from the intense orgasm he gave me with his mouth.

I should have woken up looking like a mess; instead, even I noticed the extra pink in my cheeks this morning.

"It's all this fresh air. I went for a run this morning on the trail, and I couldn't believe how peaceful it was," I said, closing the book I was looking at. It was a list of events the hotel had already booked for the upcoming spring and summer wedding season. We had a large, separate building off the courtyard that was big enough for receptions, meetings, reunions...you name it, and we could host it.

"I imagine it's very different from New York City," Patty stated.

Laughing, I nodded. "Yes, in a lot of ways."

"Bryce told me you were looking at the event calendar."

Glancing back down at the book, I grabbed it and stood up from where I had been sitting on the sofa in the lobby. It was a nice change from my office with its one small window. I couldn't help but laugh to myself. My office in New York City had been five times the size of the one I had here at The Montclair, but I hadn't minded one bit. I loved being able to sit peacefully in the lobby and work. "Yes, I was trying to get a feel for the type of events we typically hold here. It looks like a number of weddings, and I can certainly see why with that beautiful creek-side area we have."

Patty grinned like she knew something I didn't. "Did you know that the gazebo was built by Truitt Carter, Roger's brother?"

The mention of Roger's name made my entire body tingle. "I did *not* know that."

"He did it as a favor to Jim and me. He normally only builds playhouses."

"Yes, and I hear he's very talented at it. He's even had a few famous clients, apparently."

Patty's eyes lit up with delight, but I wasn't exactly sure why.

"Anyway," I went on, "I was in the library earlier, and I wanted to mention an idea I had."

"Oh, I love new ideas, especially for the library. It's one of my favorite spots, and original to the house, you know."

With a soft chuckle, I said, "What would you think of using it to host a monthly employee game night?"

Patty stared at me, then blinked rapidly a few times before looking away.

Oh crap. Crap. Crap. Crap. She hates the idea.

"If you don't want to, that's totally fine."

She held up her hand and gestured for me to wait a moment. I held my breath, and when she finally turned around, she wiped a tear from her cheek and smiled. "That is the best idea I think I've heard in a very long time, Annalise."

I exhaled and reached for the back of the lobby's antique sofa to steady my wobbling knees. Now I just had to figure out why she was shedding tears at the idea. "Great. I thought it would be a wonderful way for the staff to let loose once a month and do something fun. I used to host a few staff-appreciation events throughout the year at my previous job, and I know how much they mean to the employees."

Patty nodded. "It *is* a wonderful idea."

"I thought maybe we could pick a different local restaurant each month to cater dinner. I know it's an additional expense to your overhead, but after looking at the budget set for this year by the previous GM, we have plenty in the miscellaneous fund."

"Yes, yes, we do. Beatrice, who was our GM before Rick, used to do things for the staff on their birthdays. I'm not sure why Rick didn't."

"That would explain why there's a large balance left."

The door to the lobby open and shut. Patty and I both turned to greet whoever it was. My heart skipped a beat when I saw that it was Roger.

Oh. My. Goodness. My ovaries exploded at the sight in front of me—Roger had a little girl on his shoulders.

"Roger, Liliana, what a wonderful surprise!"

I looked from Roger's sky-blue eyes to the little girl's matching ones. She couldn't have been more than five or six years old. I took a step back as my heart dropped to my stomach, and I reached for the sofa again.

Was this why Roger wasn't interested in a relationship with anyone? Because he had a little girl?

I quickly raced through our conversations last night. Roger had briefly mentioned one long-term relationship but hadn't offered up any information other than the fact that they'd met in high school.

"Is this her, Uncle Roger? Is this Annalise?" the little girl asked as she stared at me and smiled. "She looks like Cinderella!"

Patty and Roger both looked at me, and I suddenly felt like I was under a microscope.

With a tilt of her head, Patty said, "You know what? You do kind of look like Cinderella!"

Roger winked at me and then put the young girl down.

"Wait, did she just say 'Uncle Roger'?" I asked, not fully aware that I was speaking aloud.

Roger raised a brow. "Did you think she was mine?"

I gave a half-shrug. "I mean, for a moment I did. You have the same eyes."

He let out a boom of laughter. "Yeah, no, thank you. I'm perfectly fine being the uncle and not the dad."

A strange, unnerving sense spread through my chest. Did Roger not want kids? I desperately wanted them. It was one of those conversations you had eventually, but not this early on, especially with a guy as skittish as Roger.

"Liliana heard I was meeting you for lunch today, and she asked if she could join us," Roger said. "I didn't have the heart to say no."

I smiled and looked down at the little girl. She was staring up at Roger with a huge smile on her face. Even I could see the love she had for him twinkling in her eyes.

"Uncle Roger said I gave him *the look*."

"Oh?" I asked with a curious expression. "What look would that be?"

Liliana cleared her throat, stood up straight, drew in a deep breath, and then proceeded to give me "the look." Her lower lip jutted out, and she somehow managed to make her baby-blue eyes turn misty, all the while trembling her bottom lip. My heart melted on the spot, even though I knew it was a fake pout. I couldn't even imagine what one of her real ones might look like.

"Wow. I don't know anyone who could say no to that," I said with a bubble of laughter.

"I could," Patty announced. "But you don't have to pout today, Liliana. I've got some chocolate cookies right out of the oven next door at the restaurant. How about we get one, and you can take it to go and have it after lunch?"

"Oh, yes! May I, Uncle Roger?" Liliana asked, already halfway out the door with Patty.

"Why do you even ask, Lil?" Roger called out right before the front door shut. He laughed and then turned back to me. "She's something else."

Smiling, I replied, "She seems like a sweet little girl. Your brother Truitt's daughter?"

"Yes. She has a little brother, Nolan. He's a little heartbreaker in the making."

I chuckled.

"Do you still have time for lunch today?" he asked.

Taking a quick peek at the time, I replied, "Yes, as long as it's a quick one. I have a meeting at one with the company that launders our linens."

"You're in luck, then. We aren't going far to eat. We're going to eat right on the corner at The Dienger Trading Company. Best breakfast in town, by the way."

"That's perfect. Let me go grab my purse."

He held out his hand. "Lunch is on me."

"Are you sure?"

"Of course, I'm sure." Roger motioned for me to walk ahead of him out the door. "We'll have to grab Liliana first. If she knows there are cookies and desserts over there, you better believe she'll sweet-talk someone into giving her a box-full."

Laughing, I said, "Sounds like a clever girl."

"She is—takes after her mother in that sense."

"What traits Did she get from Truitt?"

Roger paused for a moment before stopping altogether and turning to face me. "Truitt isn't her father. Saryn was married before. She divorced the jackass, and he wanted nothing to do with Liliana. The crazy thing is, he turned out to be my and Truitt's half-brother. Our father had an affair early on in his marriage, and that dickhead—I'm sorry, Tim—was the result of that affair. Truitt and I never knew Tim was our brother. We only found out a few years ago."

"Oh, wow."

Roger let out a humorless laugh. "Yeah, imagine our surprise. Liliana has my father's blue eyes."

"I suspect you do as well. I don't think I've ever seen such a light shade of blue before. Sometimes your eyes look like ice."

He winked. "When I'm horny?"

With a shake of my head, I gave him a playful push.

"Boerne has grown a lot over the years," he said, changing the subject. "We've tried to keep that small-town feel to it, though. Lots of folks aren't from around here originally, but a lot are. And I have to warn you, when the locals see me with you, tongues are going to wag."

I folded my arms over my chest. "In a good or bad way?"

He lifted one shoulder. "Both, I imagine."

The door to the River City Grill opened and Liliana came rushing out, Patty on her heels.

As she handed the box of cookies to Roger, she said, "Uncle Roger, I got the three of us one chocolate cookie each! Can we eat them in the bazeba?"

I looked over at Patty, who simply smiled. Roger softly tugged on Liliana's pigtail. "Of course, we can."

"Bazeba?" I asked.

"Gazebo," Patty and Roger said in unison.

"Ah." I nodded, then looked at Liliana and grinned. "I think eating dessert in the gazebo is a fabulous idea."

Liliana jumped for joy and reached for both my and Roger's hands. She tugged us toward the door. "Come on, I'm so hungry I could eat a cow!"

Lunch with Roger and Liliana had turned out to be one of the best ones I'd ever had. He was so sweet and attentive to her, and it was clear she simply adored him. He somehow managed to balance his attention between the both of us, and I felt my heart nearly bursting. Not to mention my ovaries. By the time we had made it to the gazebo, I was positive there was no other man on this earth like Roger Carter, and little Liliana seemed to agree with me.

It had been exactly two weeks since I'd arrived in Boerne—and Roger wasn't kidding when he'd said tongues would wag after people saw us together.

Since we'd been spotted together on more than one occasion, I'd become the talk among the locals. Or at least that was the case according to Elizabeth, who seemed to know everything and everyone.

"It's my duty as the front desk lead to keep informed on things, and that includes gossip," Elizabeth told me over our breakfast of bagels and coffee.

I smiled as I took her in. She was younger than me but seemed to have an old soul. We truly clicked almost immediately. Her light brown hair was pulled back in a ponytail, and it swooshed back and forth every time she got excited and spoke.

"Do you know a woman came up to me in HEB yesterday and invited me to play Bunco?" I asked. "When I told her I had no idea what it was, I thought she was going to pass out."

Elizabeth laughed. "Well, considering you've been spotted out several times with Roger Carter in the last couple of weeks, they're curious about you."

"Why, though?"

Elizabeth took a quick look around the courtyard and then gave me a warm smile. "Roger hasn't really been known to date women more than once. As a matter of fact, I don't think I've ever seen him out on a date before. You know, Patty is really good friends with his mother, Janet Carter."

I shook my head. "I didn't know that."

"Yep. She's known Roger probably since he took his first step. But back to why people are curious about you—I think they're simply curious about the woman who's finally caught his eye."

I nodded as I let her words settle in. "When we first met, he told me he wasn't interested in any kind of long-term relationship."

Elizabeth raised a brow. "He seems to have changed his mind. How do you feel about that?"

It didn't take long for Elizabeth and me to become friends. She was easy to talk to, and I was beginning to get used to her no-nonsense, get-to-the-point attitude.

I gave her a half-shrug. "I'm not a hundred-percent sure. I really like him a lot, and I think there's a reason we were brought together. I'm just…"

"Worried you'll fall more than he does?"

I lifted my gaze to meet hers. There was no judgment whatsoever in her eyes, only understanding.

I rubbed my hands together nervously and forced myself to stop fidgeting. "He's been very upfront and honest with me about his feelings. I just can't help but wonder if maybe I'm just a challenge in some way. But maybe it's stupid to think that. He seems to be just as enamored with me as I am with him."

"Is the sex good?"

I was positive my eyes nearly popped out of my head. "Did you really just ask me that?" I asked with a nervous laugh.

Elizabeth waved off my shock. "Please, I'm not blind. I see the way the man looks at you and you look at him. The moment I saw you get out of his car on your first day, I knew there was something between y'all. When did you find out he lived in Boerne? I mean, what a small world for y'all to have a fling in Chicago only to both end up in the same town."

"A fling?" I asked with a mixture of confusion and amusement. How did Elizabeth know Roger and I had slept together in Chicago?

After another quick glance around, she went on. "If I were in your shoes, stuck in Chicago for a few days with a man as good-looking as Roger, I'd have a fling as well. Okay, maybe not since I'm engaged, but we're role-playing here, so I'm pretending to be you."

I giggled. "It's that obvious, huh?

A triumphant smile appeared on her face. "Girl, yes."

I rolled my eyes.

Elizabeth took a sip of her coffee. "Now, spill the beans. I want to know everything!"

"Oh, no. You've already admitted you're a gossip."

With a dramatic gasp, she looked at me in mock horror. "I said I was in the know, and I am. I listen, darlin'. I don't talk. That's my number-one rule. I don't mind hearing the juicy stuff, but I'm not a gossip spreader. Whatever you tell me stays with me."

I bit my lower lip, trying to decide if I should tell her the whole story of how Roger and I first met. It would be nice to talk to someone about it other than my sister, Meg.

"Fine," I said with a sigh. "But if you tell anyone, I'll never share anything with you ever again."

She lifted her finger and crossed her heart. "I swear to keep what you say to myself. I mean, I may tell my boyfriend, but men don't gossip."

I gave her another roll of my eyes before clearing my throat. I decided I needed someone else to analyze this whole thing. "The hotel accidentally booked Roger and me in the same room."

"What do you mean, the same room?" she asked. "How is that even possible?"

With a shake of my head, I told her the whole story, then laughed as I said, "The first time I ever laid eyes on Roger Carter, he was…"

My cheeks flamed with embarrassment.

"He was what?!" Elizabeth asked as she bounced in her chair. "Tell me!"

"You swear you won't tell anyone else this?"

"I already did the whole cross-my-heart thing. Sheesh, is that not good enough anymore?"

I opened my mouth to say something, then closed it and shook my head slightly. With a breath in, I word-vomited everything. "He was naked. I scared him, and he jumped out of bed, which scared me, then the light came on, and he was…completely nude."

"Whaaat? Naked!" Elizabeth shrieked, and I quickly looked around. "I bet that was a sight to see! Is he big?"

"Shhh!" I whisper-shouted. "Gah, I knew I shouldn't have told you."

"Did you jump on him? I mean, I love my boyfriend and all, but Roger Carter naked in a hotel room. I don't know *any* woman who wouldn't jump on him right then and there."

I jerked my head back and stared at her. "No! Of course not. We actually started to argue."

She blinked rapidly before she found her voice. "Let me get this straight: Roger was naked, and you started to *argue* with him?"

"He was in my room!"

"It sounds like you were in *his* room."

I glared at her. "It was my room."

She gave me a look that said she was right, and I was wrong. "Okay, whatever. Who cares whose room it was. What did y'all argue about?"

I sighed. "I wanted to know why he was in *my* room, and he wanted to know why I was in *his*."

She nodded and pulled her brows in as if deep in thought. "When did the sex come into play?"

"You are direct, aren't you?"

With a no-nonsense smile, she motioned for me to keep talking.

"I'm not exactly sure how it happened. We agreed we wouldn't ask each other anything personal, it would be a no-strings-attached kind of thing." I swallowed hard as I looked down at my teacup and whispered, "A fling."

"Wait, you didn't know he was from Boerne that whole time?"

I shook my head. "I had no idea where he was from. We didn't share any information with each other. Then, when the day came for us to leave, we said goodbye, and I got on the plane for Texas."

A burst of laughter came from her. "Then how was it he dropped you off here?"

I sighed. "It's a long story, but to get straight to it, I didn't have a rental car, he did, and he offered to drop me off where I needed to go."

"If this story is written in a book, sign me up to read it!"

I rolled my eyes. "It would be a crazy story, that's for sure."

"So, Roger ended up giving you a ride. When did y'all figure out you were going to the same place?"

"At the rental car counter. He asked where I was going, and I told him. His reaction now, of course, makes sense. Back then, he just seemed shocked or distracted."

She sat up and clapped her hands in excitement. "He didn't say anything when you told him Boerne?"

I slowly shook my head. "Nope. Nothing. He didn't tell me until he pulled up in front of the hotel, and then he dropped the bomb on me."

Elizabeth dropped back in her seat again and slowly shook her head. "Wow. What are the odds of that?"

Laughing, I replied, "I have no idea. Now, we both live in the same town and...well...I honestly don't know where things will go from here, but I think I can say I'm hopeful."

She smiled. "Should be interesting to see."

Something in her tone of voice made me feel unsettled. "Why do you say that?"

Her eyes met mine. "Listen, I really like you, Annalise. All I know about Roger is what I hear from friends of mine and the gossip mill."

"And what do you hear?"

She looked unsure, all of a sudden.

"Elizabeth—what have you heard?"

With a sigh, she gave me a sympathetic look. "He likes being single. He's always been a one-night-stand kind of guy. I know he's hooked up with my older sister's friend Lucy a few times, but it's more sex than anything."

I knew Roger wasn't an innocent and had most likely been with his fair share of women, and he'd even told me he didn't date often. No relationships. But hearing it from someone else made my stomach feel queasy.

"Did they date?" I asked, not even sure why I wanted to know. Whatever Roger did in his past was in his past. But was Lucy the one serious relationship?

"No, like I said, it's always just been a casual thing. They're friends but nothing more. I think *she* wanted more, but Roger made it pretty clear they weren't headed down that road, according to my sister."

I chewed on my lower lip.

Elizabeth leaned forward and gave me a small smile. "Listen, I don't think that's the case with you. I see the way Roger looks at you. He really likes you, Annalise. I didn't mean to put doubts in your mind."

"I know you didn't, and whatever Roger did in the past is his business. Just like mine is."

"Exactly! And it sure seems like he's changed his mind and wants something more with you. At least, it sounds like it."

I nodded and glanced down at my watch. "I've got to go do the schedule for the next few weeks. Talk to you later?"

"Yep, talk to you later."

As Elizabeth walked back toward the hotel, I found myself wondering who this Lucy girl was…and why I suddenly felt so threatened by her.

Chapter 15

Roger

"ARE YOU SURE you want to come with me?" Annalise asked as we walked out of the front entrance of The Montclair.

"Yes. I want to help you find a place and make sure the area is safe."

She smiled that brilliant smile of hers, the one that made my stomach feel like I was on a rollercoaster staring down a straight drop.

"Okay, well, I've got two houses to look at for renting. One isn't far from the hotel, and the other is a few miles out of town."

We headed over to my truck that I'd parked right down the street. I opened the passenger door and held my hand out for her to climb up.

"Patty is taking me to look for a car tomorrow," she said. "I'm sure you're sick of driving me everywhere."

I pulled her toward me before she could get up into the truck. "I like driving you around."

Her eyes sparked with heat as she stretched up onto her toes and kissed me. "Do you?"

I nodded, leaned in, and brushed my lips across hers again. "It means I get to spend more time with you." Then I took her mouth in a searing kiss that left her swaying a bit in my arms. I loved how she reacted to my kisses.

We broke apart, and I helped her up into the truck. I started to walk around the front of it when I heard someone call my name.

"Roger?"

Turning, I saw Lucy and a few of her friends walking up from Main Street.

I quickly looked at Annalise in the truck. She had a warm smile on her face. I turned back to look at Lucy.

"Hey, Lucy. Where are y'all heading?"

Lucy swung her gaze to Annalise and smiled before focusing back on me. "River City Grill to celebrate Mary's new promotion at the hospital."

"Nice." I headed back around the truck and called over my shoulder, "It was good seeing you."

"Good seeing you too."

I was about to open the door when Lucy spoke again. "So, the rumors are true. You're dating."

Christ, why are people so interested in my fucking life?

"Yeah. We're in a bit of a rush. I'll introduce you some other time."

Something moved over Lucy's face, but I couldn't read the expression. "Sure, see you around."

After I got into the truck, I expected Annalise to ask me who Lucy was. For a moment, I swore she was about to. She glanced at Lucy, a slight wrinkle appeared between her eyes before she cleared it away and faced me. She smiled as she gave me the address of the first house she was set to look at.

Annalise didn't seem like the type of woman who would be jealous, and truth be told, she had nothing at all to be jealous *about*. I'd met Lucy in the ER when my brother Truitt had gotten hit by a branch and thought he'd broken his dick. Yes, he actually thought he might have injured his junk. It was the best and worst hospital visit I'd ever had thus far. But there was nothing there feelings-wise for Lucy. She had been a fun time, and that was it. I always knew, though, that if I had offered up more, Lucy would have most likely been up for exploring that possibility. I hadn't been the least bit interested, though.

Annalise wasn't kidding when she said the first house was close to the hotel. She could walk to work if she wanted.

"This is super-cute," she said after I opened the passenger door for her, and she jumped out. A newer-built home, the one-story limestone house looked simple enough. "It's so big!"

I frowned. "You think?"

Turning to look at me over her shoulder, she said, "You should have seen where I lived in Manhattan. You probably couldn't fit this garage in there."

I laughed. "I always forget you moved here from New York."

An older woman walked out of the house, heading our way. "Annalise, it's good to see you again." The woman turned to me and extended her hand. "Nancy Whitmore, I'm the real estate agent Annalise is working with."

I shook her hand. "Roger Carter, it's a pleasure to meet you."

"Ah, you're the friend Annalise mentioned. I'm glad you were able to make it."

Before I could respond, she spun on her heels and walked up to the door. "I think you'll really like this open floorplan. I'll let the two of you walk around the house first before I come in and join you. I'll be right outside."

"Thank you, Nancy," Annalise said, stepping into the large living room.

I whistled as I followed her. "Wow, this is a huge living room."

Annalise smiled. "I like the fireplace. I've always wanted one."

I looked over at the fireplace, and that made me realize I hadn't brought Annalise back to my house yet. In the nearly three weeks she'd been in Boerne, I'd always gone to her suite. Something didn't feel right about bringing her to my house. I knew things would end in sex, and the thought of making love to her in a bed I'd slept in with other women just felt...wrong. Anna was special to me, and the women I had brought home were simply there for one reason. Sex. Suddenly, a strange feeling came over me. It almost felt like guilt.

"Look at this archway, Roger. Isn't it beautiful? I love how the space just flows into the next room."

I followed her into the large dining room that connected to the kitchen.

"Kitchen's kind of small, don't you think?" I asked as she walked up to the island.

"Yeah, I do think it's pretty small. There's hardly any counter space."

We walked through the three bedrooms and the two-and-a-half baths. When we stepped into the backyard, I heard Annalise gasp.

"A gazebo! I love gazebos!"

I laughed. "You've got one at work."

She looked back at me. "I know, but having one in my own backyard would be so amazing!"

I glanced around the large, grassy area. I lived in a similar neighborhood, with neighbors so close you could practically reach out and touch them. Now that was I buying the Martin ranch, I wouldn't have that problem for much longer.

As we made our way back into the house, Nancy appeared in the living room. "Well, what do you think?"

I kept my mouth closed and didn't share the fact that I thought the kitchen was too small and that the neighbors could see into almost every single window, not to mention the backyard.

"It's cute, but I don't think this one's for me," Annalise said.

Nancy nodded. "Not a problem. Let's head on out of town and stop at the other listing I pulled for you."

When we got back to the truck, I asked Annalise what she hadn't liked about the house.

"The kitchen was too small. After living in cramped spaces in New York, I want a large kitchen. I don't need a bonus room or anything like that."

"Fair enough." I started my truck, and we headed to the next house. This one was about fifteen minutes outside of Boerne.

The moment we pulled up and Annalise saw that it was in the middle of nowhere, she turned to face me. "There is no way I'm living in this house all alone."

I looked past her at the two-story home. It was older, a for-sure fixer-upper. "It's...charming."

"Charming? It looks like it's straight out of a horror movie, Roger!"

Nancy got out of the car and waited for us. Instead of getting out, Annalise rolled down her window. "Nancy! This looks like someone with an ax is going to jump out at any moment!"

Nancy's smile faded, and she turned and stared at the house for a few moments before looking back to Annalise. "Well, you did say you'd be interested in a historical home."

"Oh, my God, I'm going to be living at the hotel forever."

"I've got one more I can show you," Nancy offered. "I pulled an extra one, just in case."

I pointed to her. "That is the sign of a good real estate agent right there."

"Is it out this way or closer in town?" Annalise asked.

"It's right down from the hotel. They are thinking of selling it, but right now, they're only renting."

Annalise smiled. "As long as they can rent it out for the year. That gives me more time to get to know the area and maybe buy a house of my own."

Nancy's smile was back. "Yes, they're not planning to sell for at least a year, they told me. Follow me, then!"

Fifteen minutes later, we were pulling up to a house about two blocks from The Montclair.

Annalise gasped, and I knew we had a winner. The house was an older home and boasted that historical charm she loved. It was a one-story, white, Victorian-style house with a large front porch.

When we walked into the house, we faced a hallway that led to a big living room. The kitchen and eating area were right off that, offering the big, open space Annalise wanted.

"The kitchen is huge!" Annalise breathed with a wide grin.

"Do you like to cook?" Nancy asked.

"I love to cook, but I worked so much back in New York that I never really had a chance—plus, my kitchen was a quarter of this size."

The primary suite was huge, and the attached bathroom was nearly as big. A large, walk-in shower stood next to an even more impressive claw-foot tub.

Annalise ran her fingers over the edge of it. "I want the house just for this tub."

"Looks like it fits two," I whispered as I walked past her.

A large wooden patio sat right off the back door. The yard wasn't nearly as big as that of the first house's, but the privacy more than made up for the lack of size.

"What do you think?" Annalise asked me.

"It's close to work."

She nodded. "Is your place very far from here?"

I suddenly felt like a complete asshole for never bringing her over to my house. "Yeah. We can swing by when we're done here."

Her eyes lit up. "I would love that."

After Annalise and Nancy worked out her application, Annalise walked back over to me. "All done. I've got the rest of the afternoon off from work, so I don't have to rush back."

My entire body heated at the idea of being alone with Annalise. "Do you want to grab some lunch before we go to my place?" I asked.

"Sure. I've been dying to try that barbecue restaurant right off Main."

"Which one?" I asked.

She looked up in thought, then snapped her fingers and said, "Klein Smokehaus, I think it's called."

"That place is freaking amazing. Yes, I'm all for getting some to go and bringing it back to my house."

She did a little clap with her hands before we turned and headed to my truck.

After ordering brisket sandwiches with potato salad on the side, we were on our way.

I turned into the driveway of my house and drove around to the back where the separate garage was. "I used to live in a townhouse, but I bought this place a few years ago when I got tired of hearing my neighbors fight all the time."

"Oh, wow. How old is this house?"

"It was built in 1879."

Annalise got out of the truck and grabbed the bags from the restaurant. "This lot is stunning. Look at these trees."

I looked around at the large elm and pecan tree that stood on each side of my house. "Yeah, the lot was one of the features that sold me on the place. That, and there's a home office here. I hate being stuck at my office over on Main. Neighbors are still a bit too close, though."

Annalise nodded as she looked over her shoulder at the house next door. The lot was a good size, but I could still see the houses on either side of me. "I bet this is a much more enjoyable place to work."

We walked through the back door that led into the mudroom. From there, we went straight into the eat-in kitchen. Annalise stilled when she walked into the space.

"What's wrong?" I asked.

Her eyes were as wide as saucers as she looked around the kitchen. "This kitchen is magnificent. I mean, it's so big!"

I laughed. "Well, maybe you can put it to good use, seeing as I hardly ever use it."

She turned and looked at me, a twinkle of excitement in her eyes. It made me happy to know I was the reason it was there.

"Do you want to eat in here or the game room?" I asked. "That's where I spend most of my time."

I could tell she was intrigued by the notion of checking out my personal space.

"Let's eat in the game room. Should we get silverware and plates?"

I shook my head. "No, we're good. Unless you want a plate for your sandwich."

"No, I'll be fine," she said as she waited for me to lead the way.

We walked through the main dining room and the largest living room. I hardly ever set foot in that room either.

Motioning for her to head up the steps, I said, "It's upstairs. Second door on the left." Annalise started up the stairs and I tried like hell not to stare at her perfect ass.

The moment she walked into the game room, she nearly dropped the bags she was carrying. "You have a pool table?"

"I do. You play?"

With a slight shrug, she replied, "Not that often, but I have a time or two."

She suddenly turned and looked at me. I knew that expression—and my entire body trembled with anticipation.

"Want to make a wager?" she asked.

I raised a brow in question. "What kind of wager?"

"Best out of three pool games. Winner gets to pick where we have sex next."

I swallowed hard. Where would Annalise want to have sex in my house? My bedroom? Fuck. No way was I doing that. I couldn't make love to her in a bed where I had been with other women.

She picked up one of the cue balls and examined it. "I mean, how hard is it to hit this little ball with a stick?"

A slow smile spread over my face. I was totally going to win this one.

Chapter 16

Annalise

I WATCHED AS Roger took our food out of the bags and set it all up on the small coffee table in the game room. I'd nearly died when I saw the pool table. And when he took the bait, I fist-pumped internally. He didn't need to know that my father had started teaching us all the game from the moment we were tall enough to make a shot.

I glanced around the space, taking it all in. There was a fully stocked bar on one wall, with a large sectional and coffee table in front of it. On the other side of the room were old video game machines, such as Pac-Man and Donkey Kong, with a closed door next to them.

"What's behind that door?" I asked.

"The theater room."

I let out a whistle. "Man, oh man, you've got everything here."

Roger grinned. "It was all here when I bought the house. The games, the pool table, the bar. The guy who lived here before me had a number of things done to the house. He wanted it to be perfect for his bachelor ways, yet good enough to sell to a family when the time came."

"He just happened to sell it to another bachelor."

Roger glanced over at me. "He was a client of mine, and I helped him with a...problem he had."

I tilted my head as I studied him. "Tell me you're not one of those types of lawyers."

"And what type would that be?"

"The bad kind. The kind who work for the type of people who don't believe in the law."

Roger laughed, letting his head fall back. "God, no. I mostly work for large corporations around San Antonio and Austin. I'm also on the payroll at my father's company, which is one of the largest cattle companies in Texas. He owns pretty much everything southwest of Boerne."

"Goodness. Are you a cowboy underneath the suit?"

Roger tipped a pretend cowboy hat. "Why, yes, ma'am, I am. Does that turn you on?"

Lord, just looking at him turned me on. "No," I replied, and he gave me a fake pout. "Your intelligence turns me on. And your smile—oh, and your dimples."

"My dimples, huh?" Roger asked as he handed me my food. "Do you mind if we just sit on the floor and eat?"

"Not at all."

One bite into the brisket sandwich, and I let out a moan that made the corner of Roger's mouth twitch.

"Keep that up and I'm going to take you right here on top of all the food," he said.

I feigned innocence. "Now that would be a waste of all this yummy food."

He rolled his eyes. "I haven't really asked you how you're liking Boerne so far. And the job. You've been at The Montclair three weeks now. I'd think you'd have a good feel for things by now."

I set my sandwich down and took a drink of water. "I love it. It's so completely different from New York. I'll be honest with you, though. I think you've made the transition easier for me."

He pointed to himself. "Me?"

"Yes," I said and reached for his hand. "Just having someone here that I know. Of course, the sex helps as well."

He gave me a fake shocked expression. "Why, Ms. Michaels, are you using me for sex?"

My conversation with Elizabeth popped into my mind, and quickly I swept it away. "Of course not."

We finished dinner and then talked for a little bit while our food settled.

"I'm actually going to be selling this house soon," Roger announced.

That made me sit up and take notice. "Sell it? Why?"

"I'm going to buy a ranch close to my father's. It's about twenty miles outside of Boerne."

"Wow, are you getting into ranching, too, like your father?"

He let out a bark of laughter. "Not anytime soon. I would like to put some cattle on it, but not until things slow down for me at work. Right now, I'm too busy. I do love the country, though, and I miss it. Plus, this ranch has been owned by the same family for a few generations now. None of us wanted to see an investor come in and break it up into lots."

"I don't blame you for that. From what I've been reading and hearing from some of the locals, that's happening a lot...families selling off their large ranches to people from out of state."

Roger nodded. "And then they break them up into small lots and sell them at crazy prices. Folks are buying them up, though, so that's one of the reasons I'm buying the ranch. Plus, I really do love being in the country."

"I'm sure it's beautiful."

A look passed over his face. Was it regret of some sort...? "I'll show it to you when the sale is final. You can help me decide on paint colors."

"I'd love that." We sat in comfortable silence for a bit, and then I glanced over at the pool table. "Ready to play?"

A slow, sexy smile spread over his face. "Do you need me to show you how to hit the ball?"

I gave him a neutral expression. "If you want to."

Roger stood and held his hand out for me. After helping me up, he laced his fingers with mine and guided us over to the pool table.

My stomach always felt full of butterflies whenever Roger took my hand or touched me when I wasn't expecting it. I placed my hand over my middle to settle it down.

"Let's pick out our cues. Those are the sticks," he said with a wink.

I walked to the rack on the wall that held about ten cue sticks. I looked for the smallest length and found it. I waited, though, and let Roger get his first. He reached for the one I had my eye on and handed it to me. With an innocent smile, I took it and followed him to the end of the table and watched as he set up the balls.

"Come here," Roger whispered in a voice so seductive, I almost dropped the stick and climbed him.

He smiled, and his dimples came out in full force. He leaned over the table and prompted me to do the same. "This is called your bridge hand."

I mimicked his stance. "Okay, bridge hand."

"Hold it like this."

I did as he said. When he leaned his body over mine and covered my hand with his, I knew I wasn't going to have to fake missing this shot. The man made me turn to jelly whenever he touched me.

"Now, you're going to hit it right in the middle of the ball, like this." He pulled the cue stick back and then gently hit the middle of the ball. "Of course, you'll want to hit the ball harder."

"Okay, I think I've got it."

"You can make the ball go whichever way you want by hitting it at different spots on the ball. Just watch me a few times."

He picked up the cue ball and then lined it up.

"Can I try?" I asked, right when he leaned over the table to take the shot.

"You want to break?"

"Break what?" I asked, desperately trying to keep a straight face.

He laughed. "No, that's what it's called." He waved it off and stepped to the side.

"Here goes."

"Hit it hard. You want to spread the balls out onto the table. If you make a solid or a stripe go in, that's your ball."

I nodded, leaned down, and fumbled awkwardly with the cue stick at first—before I placed my hand solidly on the table, pulled back, lined up my stick, and hit the cue ball as hard as I could.

Balls went everywhere, and I sank two. A solid *and* a stripe.

Daddy would be so proud.

I moved around the table and took it all in before I found my next shot. "Are we calling shots ahead?"

When Roger didn't answer, I turned to look at him. His chin was practically to his chest and I had to bite my lip to keep from laughing. "Calling shots?" I asked again.

All he did was look at me, then narrow his eyes. "Yes, we'll call shots."

"Good."

Turning back to the table, I said, "I'll take solids, number four in the left corner."

Of course, I did exactly what my father had taught me and sank the four ball.

"Motherfucker," Roger whispered from behind me.

This time, I let a little giggle slip free as I moved around the table and pointed out my next shot. "Seven, side pocket."

The crack of the two balls hitting was a sweet sound, but hearing my ball drop in was even sweeter.

Roger walked toward me. "You little lying brat."

I glanced over my shoulder to him. "I didn't lie." Then I focused back on the table and said, "Three ball, back right."

Another ball in.

"You said you didn't know how to play!"

Leaning against the table, I smiled. "*No*, you asked if I wanted you to show me how to shoot, and I said you could if you wanted to. You can't blame a girl for letting a handsome man teach her how to shoot a pool cue, now can you?"

His mouth opened, then closed, then opened again. "You'd make an excellent lawyer. Do you know that?"

I tossed my head back as I let out a deep laugh.

Roger walked up to me, and I found myself holding my breath. "I want to up the bet," he said.

I raised one brow. "Really?"

"If I win, I get to fuck you right here, with you bent over this table."

My legs went weak, and I had to hold myself up against the side of the table. "And if I win?"

His eyes turned dark. "I'll do anything you want."

I pulled my lower lip between my teeth and thought about what I wanted. "What if I want the same thing as you?"

A slow smile spread over his face. "Do you?"

The pulse between my legs grew, and I had the urge to squeeze my legs together to ease it. I tried to speak, but my answer came out as a whimper. "Yes."

He leaned in closer, and I closed my eyes and opened my lips slightly, inviting him to kiss me.

And then the heat was gone—and I opened my eyes.

"Take your shot," Roger said matter-of-factly.

"Wh-what?" I asked, shaking the daze away.

He pointed to the table. "Call your next ball."

I pushed off the table and glared at him. "I see what you did there. You thought you could render me sex-stupid."

He looked befuddled for a moment before he laughed. "Sex-stupid?"

"Yes. Press your body to mine, talk to me about how you want to fuck me bent over the pool table, almost kiss me... You wanted me to lose my touch."

Roger swallowed hard and reached down to adjust himself. "God, Anna. Don't talk like that, or I'll take you right now."

Spinning around, I studied the table. "One ball, side right pocket."

Hit. Sank.

I moved to the other side of the table and made the mistake of glancing up at Roger. My breath stalled in my chest.

He studied our game, his brows pulled in slightly, a soft smile playing at the corners of his mouth. He'd put on a baseball cap and... turned it backward. When in the hell had he put that on? And, oh dear heavens above, why was it so freaking attractive?

I had to pull my eyes away from him and look at the table. Where was my shot? There!

"Six ball, off the side, into the back left pocket."

"There's no way you'll make that shot."

I positioned my hand and looked up at him. Our eyes met. "Care to wager on it?"

He smirked. "Why not? But let's make it interesting."

My heartbeat picked up. "Go on."

"If you miss, you have to let me tie you up and...explore."

"Tie me up?" I squeaked out. "As in...tie me up with something?"

All he did was nod.

I lifted a brow. "Is there something you want to tell me, Roger? Are you into kinky stuff? Because now would probably be the time to alert me."

He chuckled. "I've never tied a woman up before in my life. Never had the desire to."

"But with me, you do?"

Roger drew in a long breath before he exhaled, letting his eyes move over my entire body. "With you, I so very much want to."

I swept my tongue over my suddenly dry lips. The idea of Roger restraining me turned me on so much, I could hardly think. That wanton woman from Chicago was back. "Okay, I accept."

"And if you sink it?"

A wicked thought came to my mind. "I get to tie *you* up."

He laughed. "I do love the way you think, Ms. Michaels."

I turned away from him and took in a few deep breaths before I focused on my shot again. As I lined it up, I had a strange thought.

What do I want more? To tie up Roger, or to have him tie me up?

"You're trying to decide which you'd prefer, aren't you?" he asked with a smirk on his face.

"As a matter of fact, I am. I can't decide."

He walked over to the pool table and studied it. "I tell you what, you sink it, we'll do both."

My eyes lifted to his, and I smiled.

He shook his head and chuckled. "That confident, huh?"

With a deep breath in, I slowly exhaled, lined up the shot, and hit the cue ball. I barely missed the pocket.

"Oh, damn. Sucks for you," Roger said, then he quickly got to work sinking five of his balls in a row until he missed the eleven in the back left pocket.

I managed to sink the rest of mine and studied the eight ball. I had zero shots.

"What's the matter, princess? No shot?"

I glared at him before attempting to bank the cue. I barely missed the eight.

Roger puffed out his chest and said, "Let's get this over with now so I can have some fun with you."

Rolling my eyes, I let out a dramatic sigh.

Roger lined up the cue ball and then hit and sank the eight.

"I hate losing," I grumbled. "I believe we said best out of three."

He tossed his cue stick onto the pool table and stalked over to me. He picked me up, tossed me over his shoulder, and smacked my ass.

Laughing, I tried to get down, but he quickly moved through the house and into a bedroom that didn't appear to be his own.

"Strip down. I'll be right back."

Before I had a chance to utter a single word, he was out the door. I glanced around the room as I sat up in the bed. Was this a guest room? Had he just been that eager? I turned to see the wrought-iron bedframe and smiled. Maybe that was it.

Slipping off the bed, I walked over to the dresser and opened it.

Empty.

I checked the closet next.

Empty.

Before I had a chance to think about it more, the door opened, and Roger walked in, stark-ass naked with something around his neck. As he moved closer, I laughed.

"Are those your work neckties?" I asked.

He flashed me a wicked smile and motioned for me to get on the bed.

"Lie down, Anna."

I completely forgot what I was going to ask him as I let my eyes travel down his perfect body. His large, muscular chest led to a narrow waist. Washboard abs gave way to that famous "V" women went mad over. And his dick...oh, my goodness. It stood erect, bobbing against his body and perfect in every way.

Dropping onto the bed, I moved to the middle and bit down on my lip. I had never done anything like this before, and I was both nervous and excited.

"Roger..." I started to say as I sat up, and he went completely still.

"We don't have to do this, Anna."

I smiled when I saw the tenderness in his eyes. "I want to. It's just, I've never done this before, so..."

His hand cupped the side of my face. "Neither have I."

"Why me? What made you want to do this with me?"

He frowned and broke eye contact with me for the briefest of moments. Something moved across his face, and I wanted more than anything for him to share his thoughts with me.

When his eyes met mine again, he spoke so softly I could barely hear him. "I want to explore every inch of your body and memorize everything. Every moan, whispered plea, how your body reacts to my touch. I want to know it all. And I want you to feel me touching you, to memorize what it feels like to have my hands and mouth on your body."

Swallowing hard, I let out a nervous laugh. Was it my imagination, or did that almost sound as if this would be our last time together?

I knew Roger had said he wanted to see where this went. I couldn't help but keep thinking about his words back in Chicago. It was stupid; he was trying and being so vulnerable, so why did something feel off?

He leaned in and kissed me softly on the lips while he ran his hand down my arm. Pushing me back onto the bed, he lifted my arm over my head, then reached for one of his neckties. He tied my left wrist to the headboard, ensuring I could slip out if I wanted to. Then he kissed along my neck, down my chest, and took one of my nipples into his mouth. I arched my back and moaned.

He went to work tying up my other hand. When he held up a third necktie, I raised my brows in question. "Blindfold?" A rush of wetness spread between my legs, and I had to rub them together to ease the throb.

"Lift your head."

I did as he asked and blew out a shaky breath when he placed the necktie over my eyes.

"Is that okay?" he asked.

"Y-yes," I breathed out.

Then his heat was gone.

"Roger?" I asked in a panicked voice.

"I'm right here, princess."

The tension eased out of my body when I felt him. His hands moved slowly up each leg, gently spreading me open to him. The fact that I couldn't see what he was going to do next made my body thrum with an awareness I never knew I possessed.

I jumped when he placed a kiss on my inner thigh. His hand landed on my lower stomach, and I felt my breath pick up.

Kiss me there, I silently urged.

"You're trembling, Anna."

"I want...I want..."

My voice trailed off as he blew hot air between my legs. A low moan escaped my lips, and I could not believe how much I needed to feel his mouth on me.

"What do you want?" he asked in a raspy voice.

"You...or, um...I want...oh, Roger, please. *Please.*"

"Do you want my mouth on your pussy?"

I sucked in a breath. "Yes," I hissed.

And then he was there, sucking, licking. His hands cupped my ass, lifting so he could taste me better. It. Was. Heaven.

"Roger!" I cried out, tugging on the restraints. "I...I want to..."

He teased my clit with the tip of his tongue while he slipped his fingers inside of me.

What did I want? Him. My hands in his hair. Touching him.

Fuck, I wanted to touch him so badly, it was driving me insane.

"Un...tie me...please!" I gasped.

"Are you sure?" he asked. Then he put his mouth back over me, and I fell hard.

His name felt as if it was ripped from my very chest. My body trembled, the orgasm starting from the tips of my toes and rushing up my body. Stars exploded behind my eyes, and even with the blindfold on, it felt like the room lit up.

Ripple after ripple of pleasure rolled through my body as Roger kept up his endless teasing with both his mouth and fingers.

"Stop. Can't. Breathe. Stop!"

He pulled away, and I was suddenly left with nothing but cold air swirling around me. The heat of his mouth, his body, was instantly gone.

Suddenly, the blindfold was gone as well. I blinked my eyes open, and before I could adjust to the light, his mouth was on mine.

God, the way this man kissed.

I would forever be ruined because if I was sure of anything, it was that no man would ever be able to make me feel the way Roger did. Not with their kisses, their touch, or their lovemaking.

"I'm going to fuck you now," he rasped against my mouth.

The only thing I could do was nod and whisper, "Yes."

Chapter 17

Roger

MY ENTIRE BODY shook as I stared down at the goddess tied up on the bed.

When I removed the blindfold and those blue eyes blinked open, a pain so beautiful—yet so fucking frightening—hit me in the chest and left me nearly unable to breathe. The way Anna looked up at me made me feel something I hadn't felt in a very long time.

Truth be told, I wasn't sure I had ever felt this way before.

The love in her eyes screamed out her feelings for me. They begged for me to make love to her, and as much as I wanted to, I couldn't. Not now. The moment those eyes met mine, I knew...I was falling in love with her. Emotion pounded in my chest. I couldn't make love to her, not with my heart feeling this way. I would not let myself get hurt again. I couldn't. No, there was absolutely no way I could make love to her right now, no matter how much I wanted to. So, I did what I did best.

Leaning down, I took her mouth with mine and kissed her until we both needed air. Those eyes still pierced through me as if she was looking right into my goddamn soul. She didn't need to utter a word; it was clear to me.

She had fallen in love with me.

With my mouth inches from hers, I softly said, "I'm going to fuck you now."

Her head barely moved as she whispered a response to my crude words. "Yes."

I'd never moved so fast in my life. I quickly untied one of her hands, turned her over, grabbed her free hand, and pushed it back over her head as I slammed into her hard and fast.

"Roger!" Annalise cried out.

"Did I hurt you?" I asked, my stomach dropping. I was losing control. *Fucking asshole.*

"No. No, I just...you're so deep like this, and I wasn't...expecting that."

I closed my eyes and tried to gain my composure. I was such an asshole for entering her that way. I slowly pulled out before pushing back in hard. We both moaned as I went in as deep as I could.

"Roger...I need..."

I pushed back in again. Harder.

"God, please," she whispered. "I need my other hand free."

Without even thinking, I reached over and pulled the tie loose. "Grab the bed and don't look at me."

She glanced over her shoulder with a confused look on her face. "What?"

My cock twitched inside of her as I closed my eyes and tried not to lose myself anymore. I looked at her and said, "I need you to not look at me, Annalise. I can't go slow right now. I can't."

Her eyes softened—and there it was again. That look of love. I squeezed my eyes shut. What she said next nearly broke me.

"Don't. Don't hold back. I want you, Roger."

That was all I had to hear. My eyes snapped open and I saw her hands on the bed frame and that ass tilted up, waiting for me. I pulled almost all the way out and pushed back in. Then I grabbed her hips and lost control.

I fucked her liked a man in need, or an asshole attempting to chase away his own feelings. It wouldn't take me long to come, and even though I was acting like a total prick, I needed *her* to come. It was the only thing I needed...for her to experience pleasure.

I slipped my hand around her front until I found her clit. A few circles, and I could feel her body winding up.

"Oh...yes...I'm going to come!" she cried out.

"That's it. Come, Anna. I need you to fucking come. Now!"

The sound of my name ripped from her lips threw me over the edge. I sped up. Our bodies slammed together, mixing with our moans of pleasure. She called out my name once more, and I came so hard, I thought I was going to pass out.

I pumped hard and fast until every ounce of my cum had spilled into her body. Then I stilled as I stared down at her.

Her head had dropped to the bed and she pulled in breath after breath. She was perfect. Her wavy blonde hair fell around her. The skin on her back was so soft and smooth. I ran my hand down the middle of her back and then cupped her beautiful ass.

I could hear her breathing hard. When I started to pull out of her, she gasped.

I had acted like a goddamn savage because I was afraid of my own feelings. Pushing my hand through my hair, I closed my eyes and counted to ten before I pulled out of her more slowly. Annalise collapsed onto the bed.

"Are you okay? Did I hurt you?"

She let out a few mumbled words, but I could only make out, "I'm okay. Just burns a little."

I moved and sat on the edge of the bed for a moment before I got up and walked toward the door. A feeling of numbness came over me as I realized what I had done. Instead of making love to her like I'd wanted to, I had fucked her. Even if she'd enjoyed it, I had done it for all the wrong reasons. To avoid my own fucking feelings.

"Goddamn it," I whispered.

"Roger? What's wrong?"

Without answering, I walked out of the spare bedroom and down to my room. One look at myself in the mirror, and I froze. I had just left Annalise in the spare bedroom. Walked away like she was nothing.

"What the fuck did I just do?" I whispered, staring at myself. I turned around to go back but then stopped.

A light knock on the door made me jump.

"Roger?" Annalise cracked open the door and saw me.

Our eyes met in the mirror. What would she think of me now? With the way I had just acted? Treated her?

She let her eyes wander around the room. When they landed on my bed, they widened, then filled with...sadness.

Guilt slammed into me for a plethora of reasons. The way I had just left her alone. The stupid idea that I couldn't make love to her in a bed I'd shared with other women. For the way I was feeling. Confused...so fucking confused. My head swam, and I couldn't talk to her right now. I needed a few minutes to get my head on straight.

"There's a bathroom next door to the guest bedroom," I said. "You can shower in there if you want."

The look of pain on her face nearly brought me to my knees. She didn't say a word, only backed out and closed the door.

Click.

I stood perfectly still, trying to hear if she was still there. After five minutes of standing in the middle of my bedroom naked, I moved to the door and opened it.

She wasn't there.

I let out a breath, shut the door, and then made my way to my bathroom where I took a hot shower as fast as I could.

After dressing, I went in search of Anna. I needed to be honest with her about how I felt. The only problem was, I wasn't sure I could be honest with myself.

I couldn't find her anywhere. Not in the game room, not in the kitchen. My heart started to pound in my chest as I called out her name. I took the steps back upstairs two at a time and pushed open the door to the guest bedroom.

Annalise sat on the edge of the bed. She was dressed and had pulled her hair up into a ponytail. She'd never looked so beautiful. Her head slowly rose, and our eyes met.

"Why did you bring me into this room?" she asked.

"What?"

"This room. Why did you bring me into this room, Roger? Why not down to your bedroom? You could have easily tied me up to your bed frame. Why in here?"

My thoughts raced for an answer. "It was closer."

Her head tilted ever so slightly. "What happened?"

"What do you mean?"

She stood quickly and sent me a withering glare. "Don't play fucking stupid with me, Roger. What in the hell happened with you? You just left me in here like I was nothing but a woman you paid to fuck."

I jerked my head back as if she'd slapped me across the face.

"You bring me to a spare bedroom, you tell me not to look at you, then you simply walk out and tell me to take a shower without you?"

I rubbed at the back of my neck. "I...I needed a couple of minutes."

Her brows pulled in tightly. "For what? You needed a couple of minutes for what? Is this some sick little game you like to play? How many other women have you tied up and done this with?"

My eyes widened in horror. "None. I told you, I've never tied up a woman before. I wouldn't lie to you."

Tears started to build in her eyes. "Who were you thinking about?"

I stared at her, unable to even form words.

"You tell me not to look at you, then you treat me like a mistake."

I shook my head. "No, Anna."

"Someone not even worthy enough to be in your own bed. Is that why you never brought me here to your house? Because I'm not good enough for your bed?"

"No, that's not..." I took a step toward her and stopped.

"Who is she?"

I ran my hand down my face. "There isn't anyone."

"Who is she?" Annalise asked again softly.

I stood there like a fucking fool. Maybe it was better if she thought there was someone else. Things were getting too complicated. My feelings for her were growing into something I could not allow. I was fucking falling for her, and knowing how she felt about me... I couldn't process it right then.

When I didn't give her an answer, she wiped a tear away and started for the door.

My heart screamed out, *Stop her.*

I lifted my hand, then closed it into a fist and let her walk past me.

Closing my eyes, I attempted to make sense of the emotions that swirled around in my heart like a tornado.

The sound of the front door slamming snapped me out of my daze. I ran down the steps, through the house, and out the door.

"Where are you going?" I called out as she started down the long sidewalk toward the street.

"Home."

I started toward her. "Annalise, you can't walk home."

She spun and shot me a look of pure anger. I stopped in my tracks. "I don't need your help getting home."

"How—?"

At that moment, a white Toyota Camry pulled up. Annalise turned and practically ran for it. I leaned down to see who it was, but all I could tell was that a woman was driving.

"There isn't anyone, Annalise!" I shouted right before she shut the door and the car drove off.

I watched the road until I could no longer see the car.

"Fuck!" I shouted, pushing my hands into my hair. "Fuck! Fuck! Fuck!"

It took every ounce of strength I had to walk back into my house. The urge to go after her was so strong, I nearly drove my fist through the wall. But how in the hell could I explain it all to her? The reason I didn't want her in my bed. Why I couldn't let her look at me with such love in her eyes when all I'd wanted to do was hide from my own feelings. And to do that, I ended up fucking her instead of making love to her like I had wanted to.

"Christ, you're fucked up, Carter," I whispered as I walked into the kitchen and grabbed a beer. I headed out to the back porch, where I spent the next few hours trying to drink my feelings away.

I stood in front of the large window in my office and stared at the people walking down Main Street. Almost all of them were tourists. Another reason I wanted to move farther out of town. My eyes caught on a woman with blonde hair walking down the street, and I immediately knew it was her.

Just like I knew she usually walked to the Bear Moon Café nearly every day for lunch.

Just like I knew every morning at seven she went to Black Rifle Coffee and ordered the same drink: a chai tea latte.

The ache in my chest grew with every step she took. When she'd passed the parking lot and moved out of view, I turned and walked back over to my desk.

It had been two weeks since she'd gotten into that car, which I now knew belonged to Elizabeth, her coworker at The Montclair.

Two weeks since I'd watched that tear slip from her eye and trail down her face before she wiped it away.

Two weeks since I'd realized I had fallen in love with her and acted like a coward because of it.

A knock on my office door startled me out of my thoughts.

Could it be Annalise? I doubted it.

"Roger?"

It was my brother's voice, and I released the breath I'd been holding. "Come on in."

The door opened, and Truitt walked in. He gave me a quick once-over and then shut the door. "Dad said you were in today."

I nodded and pretended to be looking over a contract.

"Saryn wants to know if you're free to join us for dinner tonight."

With a forced smile, I shook my head. "I can't tonight. I've got a bunch of contracts I need to look over for the city. They're trying to purchase some land and turn it into a park."

Truitt sat down in a leather chair on the other side of the desk. He looked around my office, which made *me* look.

There wasn't anything special about this space. It housed my desk and two large leather chairs that sat opposite mine. To the left was a small conference table and a sofa. My degrees were in frames and hanging on the wall, along with a few personal photos that were placed around the office. That was my mother's doing, not mine.

On the right side was a small bar cart, where I kept scotch, whiskey, and my father's favorite gin. There was also a door that led to a private bathroom. Since the building housed my office, Truitt's, and our father's, we'd had a small gym put in. It was nice having it handy, and allowed me not to have to go to a public gym and work out. Truitt used to do so all the time before he married Saryn. My father hardly ever used it, so it was mainly my own personal gym now.

I had been hitting it up at least twice a day lately. If I wasn't on the Peloton, I was lifting weights until I could hardly move. Anything to keep my mind off Annalise.

"Do you want to talk about it?" Truitt finally asked.

"Talk about what?"

He sighed. "Come on, man. Everyone can see how miserable you are, Roger."

"I'm not miserable."

He raised a single brow in question. "Really? How many times this week have you gotten shit-faced?"

I laughed. "What kind of question is that?"

"One that I think you're afraid to answer."

"Fuck you, Truitt. Not everyone wants the fairy tale life you have."

He stared at me for a few moments before he leaned forward. "You know Kerri would have wanted you to be happy."

Truitt might as well have reached across the desk and punched me in the chest.

"This...this has nothing to do with her." I fought to keep the memory of Kerri's last moments out of my head.

"Really?" he asked with a disbelieving laugh. "You say it, but do you believe it, Roger?"

Our eyes met, and I realized I was holding my breath.

"What happened between you and Annalise? For the near month you let her into your life, you were the happiest I had ever seen you. And it's not just me who thinks that way. Saryn, Mom, Dad, we all saw it. Hell, even Lil saw it."

I slammed my fist down on the desk. "You didn't see shit because there was nothing to see! I had fun with her, things got too serious, and that was it. I'm not looking for that."

"For what? Happiness? A woman to wake up to every morning and to kiss every night? Having someone in your life to share the ups and downs with? You act like you don't care, but I see it on your face, in your eyes. Roger, you care about her. Why are you so afraid?"

I swallowed hard and looked away.

It only took Truitt a few moments before he said, "You love her, don't you? That's why you pushed her away."

With a shake of my head, I said in a hoarse voice, "No, I don't love her."

He scoffed. "You always were a fucking terrible liar. For fuck's sake, are you *that* afraid of opening up your heart that you'll sit here and deny it and push her away in the process?"

I snapped my head back up to look at him. "I'm not denying anything. I don't…I don't…love her. I don't want a relationship. I don't want to be tied to one woman. If I want to go out tonight and pick up some random woman, I can. I like my life, Truitt."

He leaned back and crossed his arms. "So, how many women have you been with since Annalise came into your life?"

I couldn't look him directly in the eyes and lie again. The last lie nearly took everything out of me.

"I thought so."

With a sigh, I asked, "What do you want from me? You want me to pour my heart and soul out to you? What good would that do either of us?"

"It might make you open your damn eyes and see what you're throwing away. Christ, Roger. It was fate that brought you two together. How do you not see that? What are the odds that the woman you got stuck in Chicago with ends up moving to the very town you live in? A million to one! And you're really okay with just walking away from her?"

I steeled myself for another lie. "Yes. I'm okay with that."

His silence finally made me look at him. He fixed me with a hard stare. "Then you'd be okay if she moved on. Met someone, dated them, got married, all while you watch from the sidelines."

I felt anger rush through my veins as I clenched my fist and then slowly opened it. "If she meets someone she's happy with, then that's great."

Even I could hear the lack of sincerity in my words.

Truitt dropped his head and slowly shook it. He stood and looked out the window for what felt like an eternity before he focused back on me. "Will you be at the fundraiser dinner tomorrow night?"

Standing, I nodded. "Mom will kill me if I'm not."

Truitt laughed softly.

"Tell me it's not black tie," I said.

"Okay, it's not black tie. But you better get your tux pressed if it needs it."

I let out a groan. "Christ, I hate these things."

Truitt started for the door, then stopped. "Mom's going to ask me if you're bringing anyone."

For the briefest of moments, I thought about asking Annalise. But I highly doubted she would even take a phone call from me right now, let alone go to a charity dinner. "No, just me."

"Are you sure?" Truitt asked.

I shot him a dirty look. "Just me."

Without another word, Truitt opened the door, said his goodbyes, and then left me alone once again.

Seconds later, my phone went off in my pocket and I pulled it out to see it was a text from none other than my mother. She'd known about me dating Annalise, of course. I'd had every intention of introducing them eventually, despite putting my mother off every time she asked.

Mom: Truitt just told me you're coming solo to the dinner tomorrow night. Is this true?

Exhaling, I typed out my reply. *It's true. It'll just be me.*

Mom: Press your tux and be sure to shave this time!

I couldn't help but laugh as I dropped my phone on the desk and walked back over to the window. What I needed to do was go for a run in the fresh air. Clear my head.

I quickly changed into shorts and a T-shirt, put on my running shoes, and walked down to the Cibolo Trail, where three miles of paved trails ran along the Cibolo Creek. I thought back to Chicago and the bet with Annalise. She'd probably kick my ass on this trail. The two times we'd run it together, I knew she was holding back for my benefit.

I sighed. The hard surface pounding under my feet was exactly what I needed to get my shit back together.

Chapter 18

Annalise

"ANNALISE, I'M NOT sure this is such a great idea," Bryce said from below. He was looking up at where I stood on the very top of a ladder, attempting to hang the last of the Edison lights on the gazebo.

"Nonsense, these are going to look beautiful on the gazebo at night. Especially with how they sweep out to the cypress trees."

He sighed for the millionth time. "Not the lights—you on this ladder. Patty is going to kill me if you fall and get hurt."

"If you keep nagging me, I *will* lose my train of thought and fall." Another sigh.

"For the love of all things, Bryce, stop sighing." I reached up onto my toes and stretched as I said, "Just one more inch and I've got it."

"Oh, God. You're going to die."

I hooked the wire and smiled. "See? I didn't die," I mused as I glanced down at Bryce. When I looked back up again, my heart stopped, and I had to reach out and grab the roof of the gazebo for support.

Roger.

He was running on the Cibolo path, a determined look on his face. I started to step down when I saw a woman move into his path. Roger stopped, pulled out his AirPods, and smiled at her.

"What are you doing?" Bryce asked.

I waved him off. "Shh!"

He quickly stopped talking.

The girl looked like she laughed, and then Roger did as well.

"Well, he certainly seems okay," I grumbled.

"Who seems okay?" Bryce called up to me.

"Hush, Bryce!" I scolded.

Then I nearly fell off the ladder when she reached up and kissed him.

She. Kissed. Him.

He did turn his face at the last minute, and she kissed his cheek before he stepped away. But she had definitely gone for his mouth.

Why had she looked so familiar? Then I remembered she was the same woman who had spoken to Roger when I was in his truck. I felt my heart drop. Was she the one he had been thinking of the last time we were together? Judging from his body language, he didn't seem too happy to see her. Who was she, then?

Suddenly, Bryce appeared in front of me, and I nearly screamed. He had climbed up the other ladder and was eye-level with me.

"Who are we spying on?" he asked. "I love a good peek."

"No one."

"Mmm, hmm, so it's just a coincidink that Roger is standing there talking to Lucy."

I nearly fell again when I turned my head to look at Bryce. "First off, what are we, in first grade? A grown man in his early thirties does not say coincidink."

"This one does. And who are you to talk? You're spying on your ex."

I rolled my eyes and looked back at Roger. "So that's Lucy, huh?"

"You know who she is?"

I shook my head. "No, I just heard she's Roger's..." I couldn't finish my words.

"Fuck buddy."

My entire body felt as if it had deflated. "Thanks, Bryce."

"Let me rephrase that. She *used* to be his fuck buddy. I'm pretty sure they haven't hooked up in a long time."

Turning to him, I asked, "And how do you know?"

He gave me a half-shrug. "She's friends with my sister, Kate. They're both nurses. That's how Lucy met Roger. His brother Truitt ended up in the ER."

I thought about all the stories Roger had told me about his brother being accident-prone. "Which time?" I laughed.

"I think the time Truitt thought he broke his dick."

Roger had told me that story but had failed to mention Lucy. Ugh, why did I even care? It was way before I was in the picture.

Hello, jealousy. Please go away now.

Suddenly, as if he could feel my eyes on him, Roger turned and looked up the hill toward the gazebo. It sat at the back of the hotel and was a popular spot for weddings—and you could easily see it from the trail.

I quickly pretended I was doing something. Bryce did the same, and we both pointed and mouthed words at each other.

"Wait, why are we not actually talking?" Bryce asked.

I wanted to die but was so glad he was willing to play along with me. I was going to kiss him when we got off these ladders. If we made it down without falling and breaking something.

"I don't know why. Let's just get down."

"Thank you!" Bryce stated as he started to make his way down.

I slowly stepped off the top of the ladder, but I only made it down one step before a voice called up, "You know you can hire people to do that kind of stuff."

I glanced down and saw a well-dressed, handsome gentleman about my age staring up at us.

Smiling, I replied, "What fun would that be?"

The stranger chuckled. "Ah, a woman who likes to live on the wild side."

"Can you get down now, please?" Bryce asked as he held his hand up and motioned for me to keep going.

I chanced one more look at the trail. Lucy and Roger were still there, but he was looking at me while she spoke.

Jerk.

Asshole.

Stupid, good-looking jerk of a man.

When I reached the last few steps of the ladder, I felt a set of large hands grip my hips.

I stepped off the last rung and turned to get a better look at the stranger. "Thank you, but I had it."

I couldn't help but wonder if Roger had seen that. A part of me—the stupid, childish, jealous part—wanted him to see it.

"Well, if you had fallen and broken a leg, that would have stressed out Patty. And no one likes to have Patty stressed out."

"Here, here," Bryce said under his breath as he folded up each ladder.

"I'm sorry, you are?" I asked, holding out my hand.

He took it and gave me a brilliant smile, then lifted it to his mouth and kissed the back of it. Any normal woman would probably giggle or swoon at such a handsome man acting so chivalrously.

I was clearly not normal because it had zero impact on me.

Then he winked and smiled even wider. He had dimples.

I was such a sucker for dimples, but apparently my love for them now only pertained to one asshole of a man who just so happened to be yards away talking to his…fuck buddy.

"Is it just me, or are you angry about something?" the man asked.

"Me?" I asked in mock surprise. "Angry?"

He nodded. "You keep muttering under your breath, and I'm catching words like 'jerk' and 'asshole.' And one I probably shouldn't repeat."

My cheeks got hot, and I pressed my hands to them in an attempt to hide my embarrassment. "I'm so sorry. That was all supposed to be said in my head, not out loud."

He laughed. "No worries. Whoever he is, it's his loss."

Okay, that was sweet, and I could admit it made me swoon the tiniest bit.

"I'm Annalise Michaels, the general manager at The Montclair."

His brows shot up. "Just the person I was looking for."

"Really?" I asked as I started toward the hotel, the stranger walking alongside me. The urge to turn and glance back at Roger and Lucy was strong, but I ignored it. I would pat myself on the back later. For now, I needed to figure out what this man wanted with me.

"Yes," he said. He placed his hand on my lower back, gently leading me toward the back steps—the second time this man had placed his hand on my body without permission. "The name is Rick Klien."

I stopped and faced him. "Patty's nephew. She told me you were coming to town."

He laughed. "Yes, my mother is her sister. I'm a little bit more than just her nephew, though. I'm also her lawyer."

I instantly frowned.

Rick drew his head back. "Yikes. By that look on your face, I see you don't like lawyers."

"What?" I asked with an amused laugh. "Don't be silly. I just don't trust them."

He raised his hands. "Fair enough."

We started walking again, and I asked, "What brings you to Boerne?"

"My aunt and uncle are thinking of purchasing the land across the creek. They asked me to look over some paperwork. Instead of doing it back and forth, I thought I'd just come to town."

Turning, I glanced back toward the creek. I could no longer see the part of the trail Roger had been on, but I could see the land across the creek. Well, at least a little of it through the trees. The large cypresses blocked most of the view. "Why would they want that land?"

"They're thinking of building a house there, above a potential wine bar. That way, they can be close to the hotel and indulge in one of their favorite pastimes: wine."

I chuckled because Patty mentioned her love of wine often. She had already signed me up for a wine-of-the-month club. I didn't have the heart to tell her I hated wine. "That would be lovely, to have a little wine bar for the hotel guests to walk over to."

He nodded. "Yes, it would."

"You mentioned you live out of town. Where do you live?"

"Not far, just a couple hours away in Austin."

"I haven't been to Austin yet. I just bought a car the other day, finally, and made my first trip into San Antonio."

"Where did you go?" Rick asked as he opened the door to the lobby and motioned for me to go in first.

Sighing because my life was so completely pathetic, I replied, "The Riverwalk and the Alamo."

"Did you enjoy yourself?"

With a half-shrug, I looked up at him. He had eyes like the color of honey. They were pretty. I forced myself to stop staring and cleared my throat.

"Um, yes, I did."

"Why the long, dramatic sigh then?"

"Oh," I said with an embarrassed laugh. "No reason. It's just…it would have been more fun to go with someone and not by myself."

His eyes seemed to sparkle as he nodded and then said, "Well, when you decide to come to Austin, call me. I'll show you all the best places to eat and all the hot spots to hit."

I gave him a polite smile. "Thanks, but I'm actually planning on going next month with my parents. They're flying down and staying a week."

"Bring them along."

I walked around the front desk and stood next to Elizabeth, suddenly feeling like I needed to distance myself from Rick. "Thank you, that's nice of you. Let me go grab Patty from the back office for you."

He waved me off. "Don't bother. I'll just head on back."

I stepped to the side while he made his way around the desk and through the doorway. Once he was gone, I glanced at Elizabeth. She gave me a knowing smile.

"Why are you looking at me like that?"

She lifted one shoulder. "No reason."

"Liar."

Giggling, she glanced over my shoulder at the office doorway and then back at me. "He likes you."

I gave a humorless laugh. "Don't be silly. He's simply being nice."

She rolled her eyes. "Maybe he'll still be in town tomorrow night to attend the charity dinner."

Groaning, I walked back around the counter and headed over to the sitting area of the lobby. I picked up a pillow from an antique sofa and punched it. "Ugh, I don't want to go to that thing."

"Why not? It's the perfect place to meet people. And we bought you an amazing gown. The single guys in Boerne aren't going to know what hit them when they lay eyes on you."

I worried at my lower lip, and Elizabeth walked up to me and squeezed my arm. "Are you afraid Roger will be there?"

Nodding, I said, "I am, but I have to face him sooner or later."

She gave me a sympathetic smile. "I'm sorry. I know how much you really liked him."

My heart felt as if someone had reached into my chest and squeezed it as hard as they could. It always felt like that when I thought of Roger.

Before I had a chance to respond, Rick walked back out into the lobby with Patty.

"You'll go then?" Patty asked.

Rick seemed displeased about something, but he nodded anyway. "For you, yes."

Patty beamed with happiness. "Wonderful. We can all go together."

Running his hand through his hair and sighing, Rick glanced my way and gave me a halfhearted smile. "I better head on over to the real estate office."

Patty clapped him on the back. "You do that. See you tomorrow!"

Once Rick was out the door, Patty spun around and pointed at me. "I just arranged a date for you tomorrow night."

My mouth dropped open, and Elizabeth mumbled, "Oh. No."

"What!?" I choked out, following Patty back to her office.

"You need a date for the charity dinner."

I vehemently shook my head. "I do not need a date, Patty. As a matter of fact, I am very much *against* having a date."

Patty laughed. "Oh, honey, don't worry. I made it perfectly clear to Rick that he was only allowed to *act* as your date to make a certain man jealous."

I was positive I had a look of horror on my face. From the way Elizabeth was slinking away, she must have known about Patty's plan.

"I don't want to make anyone jealous! Patty, what have you done?"

Acting as if she couldn't hear me, Patty grabbed her purse and rushed toward the front door. "I need to go visit Janet and make sure everything is in place for tomorrow!"

"Wait, Patty," I said, taking her arm and pulling her to a stop. "I'm not into playing games like that. I won't pretend to be with him. If you ask either of us to play that part, I won't go."

Patty sighed and then rolled her eyes. "Fine, but he's already planning on going."

I closed my eyes and took in a deep breath. By the time I opened them, Patty was out the door.

I whirled around and looked at Elizabeth.

She held up her hands. "I didn't know anything about this, I swear. But if I'm being honest, it's pretty clear how miserable you are, and…well…Roger hasn't been around in a few weeks. Of course, she noticed."

"I moved out of the hotel a week ago! I'm not even living here anymore. How does she know I'm not seeing someone else? I could be sleeping with a different guy every night."

Elizabeth stared at me, then fell into a fit of laughter.

I brought my hands to my hips. "What? I could!"

That made her laugh even harder, and she leaned over and grabbed her stomach.

"Okay...like that's believable," she said between bouts of laughter.

I let out a growl and stomped away like a five-year-old. Maybe I would suddenly come down with the flu, or something, and not even have to go....

As I made my way into my office, I settled on a plan. "Yes, that's what will happen. I'll get the flu."

Chapter 19

Annalise

THE FLU IDEA didn't work. It had been worth a try, though.

"You look beautiful! Did you get that Brazilian wax like I suggested?" Patty asked.

I glared at her in the full-length mirror in front of me. She had shown up at my house at eight in the morning after I'd called to tell her I wasn't feeling good. She'd brought every known remedy she could find and made me try them until I finally broke and told her I was fine. Then she'd talked me into going *and* getting waxed.

"I don't even want to talk about that with you," I huffed as I crossed my arms.

Her eyes met mine in the mirror. "Oh, honey. I know I'm your boss, but I'd like to think I'm a mother figure to you as well."

I let out a humorless laugh. "I can promise you, I would not be talking to Mom about a Brazilian wax."

"I have the perfect earrings for this outfit. Now, where is that bag?" Patty asked as she spun around in a circle, not even paying attention to what I'd just said. "I bet it's in the car. Be right back!"

I glanced over at Elizabeth, who was putting her hair up in a French twist.

She smiled back at me. "You got the wax job, didn't you?"

I nodded. "It was awful. At one point, I swore my belly button was attached to my clitoris. When she tore that paper off, I felt it rip from the inside all the way up to my belly button. I actually demanded a mirror so I could make sure it was still there."

Elizabeth lost it laughing.

"It's not funny. Did you know all the places they wax? I wasn't even aware my ass *had* hair that needed to be waxed."

She let out a snort-laugh. When she finally got herself under control, she said, "Now imagine Patty getting that done."

The image flashed through my mind, and I screamed as I covered my face with both hands.

"What in the world?" Patty asked, walking back in. "What are the two of you talking about?"

Elizabeth pushed the last bobby pin into her hair before she turned and said, "Annalise thought her clitoris was pulled off during her wax this morning."

Patty flashed me a satisfied smile. "Good, you got it done. You'll thank me later."

I snarled my lip at her. "I'm pretty sure I'll be cursing you until the day I die."

Patty gave a rumbling laugh and then forced me to turn around, holding up a pair of diamond earrings.

"There, these are the perfect finishing touch for your dress."

I gasped. "Are those real diamonds?"

She nodded.

"And you had them in your *car*?" I asked.

Elizabeth walked up and handed me a glass of wine. I still hadn't grown a taste for it and usually sipped at the same glass for hours. But today was different. Today it was a sweet, bubbly dessert wine, and I'd already had more than four glasses. At least, I had stopped counting at four. Patty had brought four *bottles*, thinking we would drink all of them while getting ready for dinner. So far, we'd nearly polished off three.

I was starting to feel the effect, so I shook my head. "No more for me. I'm starting to feel it."

Shrugging, Elizabeth downed the glass. "This isn't New York City, Annalise. We can leave diamonds in our cars."

"It's not Mayberry either," I countered.

Elizabeth poured another glass as she said, "That's true."

Clearly, I was a lightweight when it came to wine.

Patty stepped back and covered her mouth, studying me. "Oh, you look beautiful."

I turned and looked at myself in the mirror. It was a version of myself I don't think I had ever seen before. Oh, sure, I'd dressed up for plenty of fancy parties in New York, but beyond the gown, there was something very different about the woman staring back at me.

She looked happy, yet her eyes screamed of sadness.

As for my outfit, the top of the light blue gown was satin with appliqued beadwork that dipped down to the skirt. I stared at the deep V-neck and wondered, again, if I was showing too much cleavage.

"You're not showing too much, so wipe that frown off your face," Elizabeth said.

"How did you know I was thinking that?"

"You're staring at your chest."

Patty huffed. "If I had perky boobs like that, I'd be staring at them as well."

The three of us laughed as I lifted the blue tulle skirt.

"You look like Cinderella going to a ball," Elizabeth gushed.

I forced a smile. "If only I believed in fairy tales still."

"What?" Patty asked. "How can you not believe in them?"

I sighed and turned to look at the back of the dress. The straps crossed up at the top near my shoulders, and the back was open damn-near to the top of my ass, where more beadwork started—and all I could think was *How in the hell am I going to sit down?*

"Because Prince Charming doesn't exist," I said, meeting Elizabeth's gaze in the mirror. She looked equally beautiful in her gown of emerald green. And Patty was rocking a black, off-the-shoulder dress with a slit so high, I actually thought I saw *her* Brazilian wax job.

Elizabeth walked up and rested her chin on my shoulder. "That's not true. I've met mine."

"You're an exception to the rule," I said, letting my fingers run over the empty space at my neck. "Do I need a necklace?"

"No," Patty said in a low, seductive voice. "A woman keeps her neck bare so men can dream about kissing it in a dark corner somewhere."

Elizabeth snorted again. Okay, maybe the wine was getting to her.

"Are you sure you don't write naughty romance novels, Patty?" Elizabeth asked.

Patty winked at her, then turned and put on a pair of earrings that hung nearly to her shoulders.

My doorbell rang, and Elizabeth gasped as she ran for the door. "That's them!"

Patty's husband, Jim, along with Rick, and Larry, Elizabeth's boyfriend, had agreed to pick us up at my house. I wasn't even sure how my house had become the go-to spot for everyone to get ready, but Patty and Elizabeth had shown up hours ago and proclaimed a girls' day of getting fancied up. I knew it was Patty's way of making sure I actually went tonight, even though she had proved her point earlier this morning.

I watched while Patty followed Elizabeth, calling out, "Lizzy! Do not run in those heels. You'll break a leg."

My heart swelled, and I fought to keep my tears at bay. The last month and a half had been hard, being away from my sister and mother, but Patty and Elizabeth had truly become my second family. After everything that had happened with Roger, my world felt like it was both falling apart and beginning. If that were even possible.

The drive in the limo was eventful. Elizabeth was well on her way to being full-on drunk. Patty was starting to plan a ball at The Montclair simply for an excuse to dress up again, and Rick put his hand on my leg one too many times. And it was only a ten-minute drive to the Cana Ballroom, where the charity dinner was being held.

I sucked in a breath as we walked into the ballroom. It looked like a dinner Cinderella would attend. Round tables with six chairs apiece were set up throughout the room. White linens were draped over tables laden with blue and cream china. Crystal wine glasses caught the light from the small tea lights on every table, as well as from the dozens of chandeliers that hung throughout the room.

"This place is beautiful," I whispered, wrapping my arm around Elizabeth's.

"I know. It's like a magical land in here, isn't it?"

I nodded, taking everything in.

"Look at those flower arrangements," I added. "The simple white flowers look so elegant. We need to remember that for the next function we have at The Montclair."

"No talking business!" Patty said over her shoulder at me.

I couldn't help but laugh.

"Why are you sticking to me like glue, Annalise?" Elizabeth asked.

"Because Rick keeps getting a little too handsy. I don't think he got the memo that we're not really on a date."

She giggled and glanced over her shoulder at him. "He seems to be focused on someone else right now."

"Oh, good! Is she pretty?"

"Umm…not that kind of focused. He's talking to Mitchel Lawrence who also happens to be a lawyer."

I sighed. "Damn."

As we made our way through the ballroom, Jim and Patty stopped numerous times to introduce me to different people. Every now and then, I glanced at the tables to see if I could find ours.

My eyes caught on the name Roger Carter—and then I ran right into Jim's back, throwing him off slightly. The man standing next to him reached out to help steady him.

"Jim, I'm so very sorry!" I said, trying to right myself as well. When I looked up at the gentleman who had helped him, I froze.

I'd seen blue eyes like that before.

"It's okay, sweetheart," Jim said. "Truitt, Saryn, I'd like to introduce you to our new general manager at The Montclair, Annalise Michaels."

Both Truitt's and Saryn's mouths dropped open for the slightest moment before they recovered and smiled at me.

"Annalise, it's so nice to finally meet you," Saryn said, reaching her hand out to shake mine.

"The pleasure is all mine." I turned and looked at Roger's brother, swallowed hard, and extended my hand. "Truitt, it's a pleasure meeting you."

The corners of his mouth twitched, and then he smiled and shook my head. "The same for me, Ms. Michaels."

"Please, call me Annalise."

Truitt and Saryn exchanged a glance before they both focused their attention back on me.

"I can certainly see why my brother hasn't been himself the last few weeks," Truitt stated. He took a sip from the drink in his hand.

I frowned at him while Saryn laughed softly. "Ignore him. I want to hear all about what you think of Boerne. It has to be so completely different from New York City."

"Um, it is," I said, trying with all my might not to look around the ballroom. At the same time, I worked to calm my racing heart.

"There you are." Rick walked up and handed me a glass of wine. "Our table is over there, in the back corner closest to the stage."

I forced a smile. "Thank you, Rick."

When I looked back at Saryn and Truitt, they both seemed slightly disappointed. It was Saryn who broke the awkward silence. "You're here with a date?"

"No," I said quickly, glancing over at Rick. "He's not my date. He's the nephew. Um, Patty's nephew."

Rick lifted his drink and smiled. "We're not on a date. My aunt strong-armed me into coming."

Truitt chuckled. "Sounds like Patty."

Rick rolled his eyes and took a drink.

Saryn stretched her hand out to Rick. "It's a pleasure to meet you. I adore your aunt and uncle."

Rick shook her hand. "They're two of a kind."

It was Truitt's turn to shake Rick's hand, and I couldn't help but notice the look of relief on his face.

Rick and Truitt started talking about Truitt's custom playhouse business while Saryn pointed out Roger and Truitt's parents to me.

"Would you like to meet them?"

I went to answer when someone behind Saryn caught my eye.

It was Lucy. She was dressed in a light purple ball gown, and her hair was down in long, soft-looking curls.

I quickly found myself scanning the room for Roger again. When I couldn't find him, I let out a breath I hadn't even realized I was holding.

Would he really show up with a date? He probably didn't think I would be here, so it was possible.

Just as I was beginning to relax, I saw Roger walk up to his parents. He was alone, or at least, for a split second, I *thought* he was alone. Then a woman suddenly appeared at his side as if out of thin air.

She was beautiful, with dark auburn hair. She almost seemed to have a glow surrounding her whole body. It was as if she was there but wasn't there.

I blinked a few times to make sure I wasn't imagining it.

She gently put her hand on Roger's shoulder, but he seemed unmoved by her touch as his mother spoke to him. When her eyes turned and found mine, I stood motionless, her gaze holding me captive.

She was too far away for me to hear her speak, but I caught her words anyway.

"Don't give up on him…he loves you."

A breeze blew in from the open balcony doors—and she floated off with it.

I squeezed my eyes shut and quickly opened them, but she was gone.

Was I losing my damn mind now? Had she even really been there?

Suddenly I felt dizzy, and I swayed slightly.

Truitt reached out for me, and so did Rick.

Saryn was by my side in an instant. "Are you okay, Annalise?"

I tried to speak around the lump in my throat. When nothing came out, I simply shook my head.

"I'm going to take her outside for some fresh air," Saryn said, guiding me away from the two men toward the open terrace.

The moment I stepped outside, I dragged in a deep breath and quickly walked all the way to the end of the terrace. It overlooked the Texas Hill countryside, and the views were breathtaking, but that wasn't what still stole my breath away.

"Who was she?" I whispered, looking out at the oak and cedar trees swaying in the wind. The deep blue sky seemed so dark and expansive with the remaining clouds of pink and orange stretching across the horizon.

"I didn't think he'd told you about her."

Saryn's words caused me to spin and look at her. "So, there *is* someone else?"

A look of confusion crossed her face. "Wait, who are you talking about?"

"Who are *you* talking about?"

Her brows drew in tight as she walked up next to me and placed her hands on the railing. "Kerri."

My heart pounded so hard in my chest, I had to place my hand over it. I drew in a long, deep breath and steeled myself for her answer to my next question. "Who is Kerri? Is that who was standing with Roger just now?"

"What do you mean?"

I glanced back to the open doors that led into the ballroom. Echoes of laughter drifted through, along with mumbled conversations. I stared into the room, willing the woman to appear again. "The woman who was standing next to Roger in there only moments before we walked out. I swore she spoke to me."

Saryn followed my gaze, then looked back at me like I was crazy. "Are you taking any pain medications or muscle relaxers, by any chance?"

I scrunched up my face. "What? No! Why would you ask me that?"

She rubbed at her temples. "Sorry, the nurse in me comes out sometimes." She reached down and took my hands in hers. "Kerri was Roger's fiancée."

My mouth dropped open as I stared at her, dumbfounded.

"By your reaction, I'm going to guess that he *hasn't* told you about her."

"Was?" I managed to ask.

Saryn looked down and pressed her lips into a tight line before staring back up at me. "He'll probably never forgive me for telling you this. He doesn't talk about her—ever."

I suddenly no longer wanted to know about this Kerri. If Roger was still in love with her, his commitment issues would make total sense.

"Kerri died in a car accident when Roger was twenty-three."

I gasped and jerked one hand free from Saryn's grip to cover my mouth. "Wh-what?"

"Let's sit down," Saryn said, taking me by my elbow and gently leading us over to a bench. "Roger wasn't with her, but he saw the accident happen. He ran to her and got her out of the car, but she... she..."

I felt a tear slip free and trail down my face. "No," I whispered softly as Saryn nodded.

"She died in his arms. Truitt said Roger changed that day. Locked up his heart and tossed away the key. Vowed he would never allow himself to fall in love again. He started to drink a lot, spent a lot of time with women. At one point, they were afraid he'd drop out of law school. I guess Truitt sat down with him one day and told him Kerri wouldn't want to see him throw his life away. So, he got his act together, finished law school with honors, and joined a firm in Boerne before he went off on his own."

"Where does Lucy play into all of this?" I asked.

Saryn drew her head back in surprise. "Lucy?"

I nodded. "Yes, do you know her well?"

She opened her mouth, closed it, then opened it again and cleared her throat. "Well, you see, Roger hasn't been a choir boy,

Annalise. He's been with a number of women. Lucy and Roger met a few years ago. They've had a few..."

"Hook-ups?" I added for her.

Her eyes met mine. "Yes. But trust me, there isn't anything there. At least not on Roger's side. He's been open and honest with Lucy that he was only in it for...well...um..."

"Sex."

"Yes," she said in relief. "I'm sorry, I don't mean to hurt you by saying that. I don't think they've been together in well over a year."

"I know about his past. Roger is a very handsome man, and he never claimed to be an innocent. But I thought...he made it seem like..."

She took my hand in hers. "He made it seem like what?"

The back of my eyes stung with unshed tears. I had to focus on my breathing because I knew the moment I opened my mouth, sobs would come out instead of tears.

Saryn pulled me into her arms and hugged me. "Oh, sweetheart, he really broke your heart, didn't he?"

I lost the battle, and a sob slipped free, along with those stupid tears.

Wiping them away, I drew back and sniffed, staring down at my empty hands. "I'd kill for a tissue right now."

"Use the back of your hand. No judging here."

I let out a half-sob, half-laugh as I did just that, then tried to carefully wipe away the tears from my face. I'd look like a clown by the time I went back into the ballroom if I didn't get myself under control.

With a deep, shaky breath, I went on. "He made it seem like he wanted something more with me. And I really thought things were going that way. Then one day he brought me to his house. And he acted so strangely. We played pool and made this stupid bet and things got a little...you know. Instead of taking me to his bedroom, he brought me to the spare room. The sex that time was different. I thought in a good way...but it was the way he acted afterward that changed everything."

"What do you mean?" she asked with a hard look on her face. "Did he hurt you?"

I quickly replied, "No! No, he would never hurt me. He grew distant. Very distant. He walked out of the room and pretty much locked himself up in his own room, leaving me alone. I had never felt so used in my life. That's the only word I can think of to describe it. We argued, and I asked him who he was thinking of, and...." My voice trailed off. "Oh, God. Was he thinking of Kerri?"

Saryn quickly shook her head. "No. No, Annalise, I don't think that was it."

"What else could it be? How in the hell am I supposed to compete with a woman who's gone? Who is clearly always going to own his heart?"

"I don't think that's it. I think it's something deeper for Roger. It doesn't have anything to do with Kerri. At least, not all of it."

I met her gaze. "I think he meant to push me away that day."

Saryn and I both turned and stared out at the darkening night sky. My mind was a whirlwind of thoughts and different emotions. Maybe the best thing I could do was forget about Roger, or at least resign myself to only having a friendship with him. I still cared about him and wanted him in my life. Could it be only as friends? I wasn't sure.

"I wish I knew what to tell you, Annalise. But I'm not in Roger's head. What if you talk to him?"

I sniffled and wiped my nose with the back of my hand again. Ugh. I was heading straight to the ladies' room to wash my hands and freshen up my face.

"If he's gone this long holding her memory in his heart like this, then I seriously don't think me talking to him will change anything."

"I'm telling you, Annalise, I don't think it's because he's still in love with Kerri. He cares about you, more than I think even he knows. I know he does. Truitt said Roger has been miserable the last two weeks. He stopped by to see the kids the other day, and when they weren't occupying his time, he simply sat there and stared out at the countryside. Please, please just talk to him. There's a reason you were brought into his life."

I quickly stood, drawing in a breath as I straightened. "You weren't there, Saryn. He wouldn't let me look..." I let my voice trail off before I cleared my throat and kept talking. "I'm not going to try to compete with a woman who isn't even alive." I looked away, attempting to regain my composure. "I deserve more than that. I deserve a man who wants me and who can give me all of him, not only a small part."

She also stood. "I understand that, but—"

I shook my head as fast as I could. Maybe I hoped if I did it fast and hard enough, the last half hour would simply slip free, and I could forget all about Roger and Kerri's past. I wasn't sure if knowing about her helped ease my pain or caused more of it. The mysterious woman who had been next to Roger entered my mind again. Had I conjured her up somehow? A chill ran through me, and I looked at the trees swaying in the wind.

He loves you...go to him.

After closing my eyes for a brief moment, I focused back on Saryn and cleared my throat. "I better get back in before Patty sends out a search party. Thank you so much for telling me about Kerri. It definitely clears up a few of the missing pieces."

She gave me a soft smile. "I really wish you would talk to him."

"I appreciate the advice, but if Roger truly wanted to work things out, he'd have come after me. He knows where I've been the last few weeks. I can't fight for both of us, not when there could possibly be someone else standing between us forever."

Turning away from Saryn, I quickly headed back inside the ballroom. With my head down, I somehow managed to find the ladies' bathroom. One look at myself in the mirror, and I groaned.

Elizabeth walked into the bathroom and stood next to me. She opened her clutch and said, "Look at me."

I did, and she grimaced. "Damn men," she whispered. She pulled out a few things, plastered on a smile, and said, "It's nothing that a little bit of lipstick and mascara can't fix."

I exhaled and looked at myself in the mirror. I looked tired, and no amount of makeup could fix my broken heart.

Letting out a ragged breath, I whispered, "I wish it were that easy."

Chapter 20

Roger

I LIFTED THE whiskey to my mouth and downed it all in one drink, then placed the empty glass back on the bar.

"Another one?" the bartender asked.

"I think he's had enough," Truitt's voice said from behind me.

Looking at him over my shoulder, I smiled. "Last time I checked, I don't need someone watching over me."

Truitt glared. "Yeah, well, I'm certainly not going to let you get drunk at a charity dinner our mother worked hard at putting together. Get your shit together and go talk to her."

I looked back at the bartender. "I'll take another."

"Damn it, Roger."

Turning in my seat, I shot my brother a look that I hoped conveyed how close he was to getting punched in the face. "I don't need or want your advice."

Truitt sighed, grabbed me by the arm, and pulled me through a door. I tried to pull him to a stop, but he just looked at me said, "Don't make a scene."

He then proceeded to drag me down a hallway and into a small room. He shut the door, folded his arms across his chest, and glared at me.

I balled my hands into fists. "Move, or I'll knock the shit out of you."

"Do it. Then I can knock some fucking sense into *you*."

I started to say something but turned away before I really *did* hit him.

"She's here, you know."

With a gruff laugh, I replied, "I know she's here. She was the first fucking person I saw when I walked in. She's also with a date."

"He's..."

Truitt's voice trailed off, and I looked back over my shoulder at him. "He's what?"

He shook his head. "Are you going to sit back and let some other guy sweep in and take her?"

My entire body trembled with anger. "Who. Is. He?"

"If you're so fucking worried about it, go find out."

I turned my back on him again. "I don't care who he is."

"Then why do you look like you want to murder the guy every time you catch a glimpse of him?"

I huffed.

Truitt sighed, and I could feel his eyes burning into my back. "Roger, Kerri is gone."

I closed my eyes, and my body sagged. "It's not just about Kerri. The last time Annalise and I were together, I...I fucked up."

"Do you want to talk about it?"

I walked over and dropped into a chair, dragging my hands down my face. "I can't take the guilt, for one thing."

Truitt pulled up another chair and sat down in front of me. "About Kerri?"

Leaning back, I let out a long breath. "That's part of it. I avoided bringing Annalise to my house because the thought of making love to her in my own bed made me feel...not good about myself. I couldn't bring myself to be with her in my room."

Truitt frowned. "Why not?"

I shrugged. "All the women I've slept with in that bed. It didn't feel right. I don't know how to explain it. I didn't want to tarnish what I had with Annalise. Anyway, we were at my house, and things got…heated. I took her to one of the spare bedrooms. I wasn't myself, and I lost control." I held up my hand. "Before you ask, I didn't hurt her. But I wanted her in a way I haven't ever wanted anyone before. It was this desperate need. Then she looked at me—and I saw it. I saw the way she felt about me in her eyes, and I suddenly felt it too. It scared me, the realization that she was falling for me, and I was for her. Something happened, and I tried to push it away by acting like a fucking asshole."

"What did you do?"

"I fucked her, but it was how I did it. I wanted to pretend my feelings for her weren't what they were. I told her not to look at me, Truitt. I tried to pretend like it all meant nothing."

I scrubbed my hands down my face and exhaled. Truitt waited for me to keep going.

"Afterward, I felt like such an asshole. I was rough, and I knew she was sore but wouldn't tell me. I walked out of the room and left her there." I closed my eyes tightly as I said, "God, Truitt, I was a dick, and she accused me of things…things that nearly brought me to my knees."

"What things?" he asked.

I opened my eyes and looked at my brother. "She said I treated her like a paid hooker."

"Ouch," Truitt said.

"She assumed I told her not to look at me because I'd been thinking about another woman."

"Why did you lose control like that?"

I clenched my jaw together so tightly it ached. "I don't know. We made this stupid bet playing pool. I tied her up. It was different, and it turned me on, and when she looked at me with such love and trust in her eyes… I think I knew I had fallen in love with her…and that fucking scared me. I needed to take back control. To do what I did best. So, I took her from behind, and I lost myself in her. But I didn't want her to see me like that. I didn't want to see the trust fade away. I don't fucking know… Maybe subconsciously, I wanted to push her away."

"Because you're afraid of loving her, or because you're afraid you still have feelings for Kerri?"

I wiped away a tear that had suddenly appeared. "I don't have feelings for Kerri. Not anymore."

"Then what in the hell is your problem? Why do you push everyone away? Why did you push Annalise away?"

"When I lost Kerri, it felt like I lost a piece of myself. I vowed I would *never* let another woman have that kind of power over my heart again. With Annalise, though...everything feels so different. If I gave Annalise my heart, she'd have the power to destroy me."

"What do you mean?"

I leaned forward and rested my elbows on my legs, dropping my head into my hands. "God, I don't know, Truitt! The first time I saw her, something happened. I don't even know how to explain it. It wasn't like when you see a beautiful woman and you want to explore her body, spend a few hours in bed with her, and then move on. With Annalise...she brings out this whole other side of me. She makes me feel so goddamn *happy*. My heart beats differently when she's near me. I don't know how to put it into words. I feel something more powerful with her—and that scares the living shit out of me. I won't lie and say it doesn't make me feel a bit guilty because I never felt that with Kerri. And I truly thought Kerri was my soulmate."

"Roger, have you ever stopped and thought about how Annalise came into your life? That maybe *she's* your destiny? Your soulmate? There's a reason you two met."

I jerked my head up and met my brother's gaze. "She said the exact same thing."

Truitt shrugged. "I'm just saying, if life gives you a chance at happiness, at love, at being with someone who makes you feel like your heart is stronger simply by having them at your side, then why in the hell would you not hold onto it with all you've got?"

I could feel my eyes building with tears once more. "What if she gets taken away from me? I survived Kerri leaving me. I won't survive if I let Annalise in and lose her."

"Then you have to ask yourself something. Is it better to have loved her and had her in your life, for however long you get? Whether it's fifty years or five? Or would you rather let her go and *never* know what loving her would be like?"

Truitt stood and placed his hand on my shoulder. With one strong squeeze, he said a million things at once. Then he let go and opened the door to walk out. Before he stepped out, he stopped and looked back at me.

"And just so you know, Rick isn't her date. He's Patty's nephew, and he's here to help them with a purchase they're making. He's a lawyer."

I groaned and rolled my eyes. "Christ, lawyers are the worst."

Truitt let out a soft laugh. Then the door clicked shut, and I was plunged into a solitary silence.

I wasn't even sure how long I sat in the small room before I finally made my way back to the ballroom. By the time I got there, the tables had been cleared and people were either dancing or out on the terrace.

With a quick look around, I soon found Annalise. She looked beautiful in the soft blue gown she was wearing. She was talking to Jim and Patty, and they said something that made her laugh. The sound carried across the room and sent a jolt of heat through my entire body.

"She looks like a princess, doesn't she?" a familiar female voice said from behind me. I turned to see my mother standing there.

"Yes, she does."

"Saryn introduced her to your father and me earlier. Interesting, the way the two of you met. What are the odds, I wonder, that two people traveling would meet, get stuck in a hotel together, then end up living in the same city?"

All I could do was nod and repeat her words. "What are the odds?"

I could feel her staring at me, and I heard the slow intake of her breath before she spoke. "You know, all I've ever wanted was for the two of you to find happiness. Love. Real love. The kind of love that pulls the air from your very lungs when that special someone simply walks into a room."

I turned and looked at my mother, who was still watching Annalise.

"Roger, life doesn't give us a whole lot of opportunities to find that kind of love." She met my gaze. "Some of us have it and don't even realize it until we've almost let it slip through our fingertips."

"Love does nothing but cause pain," I mumbled.

She let out a sarcastic laugh. "I guess you and I would know that more than anyone, wouldn't we?"

I pulled my gaze away from her and found Annalise again. "I don't think I even know how to love, Mom."

She rested her hand on my arm and gave it a slight squeeze. "If you could only see what I see every time you look at her, you'd eat your own words."

I closed my eyes for a moment. "She'd be better off if I just left her alone."

"Maybe. But take a long look, Roger. Because if you let her go, *this* is your life. Standing back and watching. Observing how she moves, who she talks to, the man she leaves with when the party is over. If you can live with that, then I guess you should leave her alone."

She lifted her hand from my arm, turned, and walked away without saying another word.

A waiter walked by carrying a tray of champagne. I took two glasses and started toward Annalise.

A few more people had joined her by the time I approached. Annalise had her back to me, so I patiently waited for a pause in the conversation to speak.

Finally, Patty saw me. "Roger! What a pleasant surprise."

Annalise spun around, nearly knocking the two glasses out of my hands.

God, looking at her up close only confirmed how beautiful she was. Her blue eyes seemed to catch every twinkle of light in the room. Her blonde hair had been pulled up into ringlets of curls on her head. I smiled as I thought back to that first night and the pigtails she'd had in her hair.

I held up a glass. "Champagne?"

She looked confused for a moment before she hesitantly reached out and took it. "Thank you."

A male voice cleared his throat, then said, "Annalise, I believe you promised me a dance so you could tell me some places to eat in New York City."

Annalise and I both looked at him.

"Yes, I'm sorry." She looked back at me. Was she waiting for me to tell her to dance with the guy? That sure as hell wasn't going to happen.

When I didn't say anything, she turned back to him. He spoke before she could.

"Shall we?" he asked.

With a smile that didn't quite reach her eyes, Annalise nodded.

The fucker took the glass I'd handed her and gave it back to me, then offered her his arm.

As they walked toward the dance floor, Annalise looked back at me and said something I couldn't hear over the music.

I watched while he took her into his arms and they began dancing. I finished my drink, then hers, and set the two glasses down on a table as I made my way out of the ballroom.

Chapter 21

Roger

SOMEONE POUNDED ON my front door, and I bolted off the couch, hitting my knee on the coffee table.

"Fuck!" I yelled out as I hopped on one foot, holding onto my knee. It hurt so badly, I wouldn't be surprised if I'd broken my kneecap.

The doorbell started to ring, followed by more pounding. I glanced at the clock to see it was two in the morning. I was going to kick whoever's ass was at my door.

"This better be fucking good," I said as I opened the front door—and found Annalise standing there.

She looked pissed. Very. Pissed.

She stepped through the threshold, lifted her hand, and then slapped the living shit out of me.

I brought my hand up to my burning cheek. "What the fuck was that for?"

"You left! You asshole, *you left!*"

I stared at her, confused. "What are you talking about?"

"You left the charity dinner!"

I rolled my eyes, turned, and walked toward my kitchen. The front door slammed, and I heard her heels on my hardwood floors as she followed me.

"You seemed perfectly fine when I left," I said. "How long did it even take you to notice I was gone?"

"Why did you leave?" she asked. I wasn't sure if it was my imagination, but her voice sounded like it might have cracked.

I opened the fridge, took out a beer, and then looked at her. "You left to go dance with some jackass. I wasn't going to just stand there and wait."

Her mouth fell open. "I told you I'd be right back!"

"I didn't hear that."

Her hands balled into fists. "You arrogant asshole. You ignored me all night, then came up with a glass of champagne and I was supposed to...what? Fall at your feet? Beg you for a dance, a conversation, a simple hello?"

"It works both ways, Annalise. You could have come to me too."

Her eyes turned dark with anger. "You might as well have opened your door and kicked me out of your house the last time I saw. You never even bothered to give me an explanation for your behavior. Why should I have to be the one to seek you out when you acted like a dick? Treated me like..."

Her voice trailed off.

I let out a gruff laugh. "Are we in fucking middle school right now and arguing about who didn't talk to who first?"

Her head snapped back like I had struck her, and her eyes lost some of their fire. "I thought...."

"You thought what?"

Annalise pressed her lips together tightly, and it wasn't hard to notice her chin wobble. Oh, shit. Was she about to cry? God, why was I such an asshole?

She turned away, a dazed expression on her face. She looked down at the floor, then around the kitchen until her eyes finally met mine. "I...I guess I was wrong."

"About?"

I hated the coldness in my voice. I drew in a breath and let it out before I softened my tone. "You were wrong about what?"

Without a word, she turned on her heels and started to leave.

"Wait, where are you going now?" I asked.

She reached for the door, but I put my hand on it, slamming it shut. "Annalise, wait. Stop walking the fuck away."

When she looked up at me and I saw the tears on her face, I stumbled back a few steps.

"Why are you crying?" I asked.

Her eyes locked with mine, and we just stood there for a few moments, neither saying a word. I wasn't even sure we were breathing. Then she laughed a strange, distant laugh.

"I don't even know why I came here. Patty and Jim dropped me off at home, and the first thing I did was grab my keys and start driving here because clearly, I am the biggest fool who ever walked this earth."

I frowned. "What are you talking about?"

"Everyone kept saying how amazing it was, the way we met. God, everyone, including myself, kept filling my head with words like fate and destiny. We were meant to be. And just as I was about to give up, you walked up to me. I had the smallest bit of hope that maybe, somewhere in your heart, you had let me in."

Her voice cracked as a sob slipped free.

"I remember thinking a few weeks ago about how we met and how I was falling for you so fast and so hard. I knew in Chicago I would never be the same again. That my heart would never be the same. My sister said we had fated hearts."

My own heart hammered in my chest. "Fated hearts?"

Annalise wiped at her tears. "But I can't compete with her."

"Who?"

"Kerri."

I thought my knees might buckle out from under me. "Who told you about her?"

She shook her head. "It doesn't matter anymore. This stupid dream of mine, my Prince Charming sweeping in and carrying me off into the sunset...what a joke. I let myself believe it for those few days in Chicago. Then, when you were at the airport, I was so stunned that we had been brought back together. But...but you can't even let me into your own bed. Why? Because of *her*? Because you've already given your heart to someone else? If that's the case, Roger, tell me now. Tell me so I can put myself out of this constant...m-misery I'm in. Tell me so I can let go of this stupid fairy tale I've made up in my head."

I took her hands in mine. "That wasn't it. Now that I look back on it all, it's so fucking stupid, but I didn't want you in my bed because I'd slept with *other* women in that bed. It didn't feel right to be with you there. You're so different, so special. I...I don't know how to explain it without making me sound like a crazy man who's had woman after woman in and out of my bed. I mean, I've slept with other women, of course, but—"

She held up a hand. "Please, just stop. You don't think I know you've been with other women, Roger? I'm not naïve, for fuck's sake. I know I'm not your first. That makes no sense to me at all."

"Maybe it is stupid, but in my head, it made sense. What I have with you feels pure, and I thought it would ruin it." I scrubbed my hands down my face and sighed. "That next day, I bought a brand-new bed."

Annalise frowned. "I don't know if that's the stupidest thing I've ever heard, or the most romantic." She shook her head and waved a hand in front of her. "No, it's not romantic. I don't know *what* it is."

She turned away from me. "I don't care about your past, Roger. Who you slept with, how many times... Whatever... It was the *past*. It was all before me, and I don't care. What I do care about is whether you'll ever be able to open your heart to me. Because if you're going to pine for a woman who isn't even here, I don't think I can play seconds."

Every part of me wanted to scream out and tell her she was wrong. She was *so* wrong. But I stood there, not uttering a single word because I couldn't seem to make my mind come up with the *right* words. I knew, deep down, why I held back. I was fucking terrified to give her that much power over me. How in the hell did I explain *that* to her?

Her eyes met mine.

With a sniffle and a shake of her head, she opened the door and walked away from me, and I let her go.

Again. All because I was too much of a coward to admit to her how scared I was to give her my heart.

After I'd managed to down nearly an entire bottle of whiskey, I stumbled to my bed and fell into it face-first with a bottle of gin clutched in my hand. It didn't take long for me to fall asleep. Visions of Annalise came and went in my dreams. Her smile, her laughter… her tears.

I rolled over and sat up in bed when I heard a noise.

Blinking rapidly, I stared at the woman sitting at the foot of the bed.

"Kerri?" I whispered, quickly realizing I was dreaming since there was no way she was actually sitting on my bed.

She smiled. "Are you really going to let her go?"

"Annalise?"

Laughing, she said, "Yes, Annalise. Are you an idiot?"

I opened my mouth, then snapped it shut. I pressed the heels of my hands into my eyes and rubbed them.

When I opened them again, Kerri was still there.

"Why are you afraid to let her in? I know you love her, and it's okay if you love her more than you loved me."

I shook my head. "No, I don't love her more. It's…it's a different love. God, I'm so sorry, Kerri. It feels…so much stronger than what we shared. I'm so sorry."

"It's supposed to be different, Roger. It's okay that it's different, that it's stronger. Everything happens for a reason."

I swallowed hard. "What did you say?"

She moved and knelt at the bottom of the bed, just like she used to when she wanted to talk to me about something important. "Everything that has happened in your life up until now has been for a reason. I died in that car accident for a reason. You got stuck in Chicago for a reason. Annalise ended up in that hotel room with you...*for a reason.*

"Fate, Roger. Fate brought you back together here in Boerne." She laughed. "My goodness, Roger. Do you need to be knocked upside your head for you to see it? No woman has ever made you feel the way she does because your journey was to find *her*. To find Annalise. Her path and your path led you to each other. Our love didn't work out because it wasn't meant to be. Your heart has always belonged to her, and you *have* to be brave enough to hand it over to her now."

"When I lost you, Kerri, I was devastated. What if...?"

A soft smile moved over her face. "Love isn't easy, darling. But to never give it a chance would be even more devastating. Your hearts are fated for one another. Open up and let her in."

"Wait—Annalise said the same thing."

I squeezed my eyes shut and opened them again, only to find Kerri drifting away.

She blew me a kiss and then said, "It's time to wake up now, Roger. You have to go get her. She's leaving...wake up now... She's leaving! Roger! Wake up!"

I sat straight up in bed and looked around the room.

"Fuck, you scared the shit out of me, Roger."

I turned to find Truitt next to my bed, a panicked look on his face.

"What happened?"

He held up the empty bottles. "Well, for starters, it looks like you drank an entire bottle of whiskey *and* gin. No wonder I couldn't wake you up."

I scrubbed my hand down my face and felt the stubble along my chin. "Shit, I had the strangest dream...it felt so real."

"As much as I would love to analyze your drunken dreams, you need to get up and get dressed."

Dropping back onto the bed, I groaned. "Go away, Mom. I have a hangover."

Truitt pulled the blanket and sheets down. "Roger, Annalise is leaving."

That made me sit up again. The room spun, and I had to cover my mouth to keep from throwing up. Once everything settled, I looked at him. "What do you mean, she's leaving?"

"Patty called Mom, who called Saryn, who told me I needed to find you. Annalise called Patty this morning and told her things weren't working out. That she was going back to New York City."

I flew out of bed.

"God Almighty, dude! Give a guy a warning before you flash your dick at him!"

"Call it payback for the time you made me go to the ER because you thought yours was broken."

Truitt called out to me as I rushed into the bathroom, "If I remember right, I believe you not only won money because of that ER trip, but you got laid as well."

I turned on the water, splashed my face, brushed my teeth, and then made my way to the closet. "Is she driving? Flying? Do we know where she is?" I asked, not even recognizing my own voice. I sounded panicked.

"Patty just left her rental house. She's there right now packing up some things, then she plans on catching a flight out this evening."

I jerked my jeans on one leg at a time, reached for a T-shirt, and slipped it on. "Wait, is she just leaving her new car here? What about the house? She just signed the lease on it. Is she breaking that?"

Truitt shrugged. "I don't know. All I know is what Patty told Saryn. She's leaving on a flight out."

With a quick glance at my clock, I saw it was nearly noon. I grabbed my wallet and truck keys and started down the hall.

"Shoes?" Truitt asked.

"Fuck," I said as I turned and ran back into my bedroom to pull on a pair of cowboy boots before making my way back through the house.

I was opening the door to the garage when I heard Truitt call out something about my shirt. I ignored him, got in my truck, and broke every traffic violation to get to Annalise's place. I hadn't even been there since she'd moved in.

When I pulled up and saw a car parked in the driveway, I let out a sigh of relief. I raced up the sidewalk and knocked on the door while ringing the doorbell simultaneously.

Annalise opened the door, staring at me with a stunned expression.

"Don't leave!" I said.

"What?" she asked, letting her eyes move over my body. "Why is your shirt inside out?"

I glanced down and saw that it was indeed inside out and on backward. I jerked my head up and took a step closer. "Please don't leave. Don't leave me, Anna! I beg you to give me another chance!"

Her brows pulled down in confusion. "Roger, what are you—?"

Before she could say another word, I cupped her face in my hands and pressed my mouth to hers. I ran my tongue along her lower lip, and when she opened to me, I deepened the kiss.

Annalise moaned into my mouth as I walked us back into her house, kicked the door shut, and pressed her against the wall.

She dragged her mouth from mine and gasped for air, looking up at me. "What's wrong?" she gasped between breaths.

"Don't leave. I don't think I can live without you."

Her eyes widened, and she looked as if she was going to say something, but I spoke again.

"I love you." My voice cracked, and I cleared it before I said it again. "I love you, Annalise. Maybe it's too soon to say that, but I don't want you to leave without knowing. I only want you. It's only *ever* been you. I know that with every fiber of my being. My heart only beats because *your* heart beats."

"What?" she whispered, her eyes filling with tears.

"I've been a complete asshole. I tried to deny how I felt about you because it scared me. The idea of letting you have my heart, knowing you had the absolute power to destroy me...I wasn't ready to admit it, but I am now. I want to give you everything. Every part of me. My heart, my soul, my love. Everything. Please, don't leave! Give me another chance. You were right. We were meant to meet in that hotel. Our lives played out like they did so that you and I could meet in that damn hotel room. I'm sorry I hurt you. I'm so sorry. If you'll just give me another chance, I swear to God I will guard your heart and never, ever hurt you again. Just...just don't go. Please."

Tears streamed down her face, and I brushed them away with the pads of my thumbs.

"I love you, princess."

She laughed and shook her head. "I love you, too, Roger."

I crushed my mouth to hers again. She wrapped her arms around my neck, and I picked her up and carried her into the living room.

"Where's your bedroom?" I asked.

"Down the hall, last door on the left."

I had never moved so fast in my entire life. Once we got into the bedroom, I slowly let her slide down my body until her feet hit the floor.

"I want to make love to you, Anna."

She nodded and whispered, "Um, okay."

Laughing, I kissed her on the forehead, then the tip of her nose, on each corner of her mouth, along her chin, and down her neck.

Her hands worked to undo my jeans while I reached for her shirt and pulled it over her head. She did the same with my shirt and giggled as she tossed it onto the floor. "Did you get dressed in the dark?"

I kissed down her neck and across her exposed breasts. "Something like that. I was in a hurry to get here."

She laughed when I swept her off her feet and brought her over to the bed. After I set her down, she lay back and worked on her leggings while I kicked off my boots and pulled my jeans off.

"Commando again. I like this."

"Again, was in a rush to get here."

I covered her body with mine and kissed her once again. She wrapped her legs around me and tilted her hips.

I started to rise. "Let me make you come first."

She pulled me back down. "No, I want you inside me, now."

"But—"

Annalise put her finger against my lips and gave me a look that would have brought me to my knees had I been standing. "Please, Roger. Don't make me beg."

She'd never have to ask me twice.

Moving my hand between her legs, I played with her while our kiss deepened. No way was I going to be a savage and push inside of her, not until her body was ready.

Annalise wasn't having any of it though. She reached between us and guided me to her entrance. "Roger..."

My name from her kiss-swollen lips was like a sonnet. I would never tire of hearing it.

"Okay, princess. We'll do it your way."

I slowly pushed inside of her, both of us groaning at the feel of our bodies connecting and becoming one.

"I've missed you," she whispered against my chest, then she leaned up to kiss me.

I nuzzled my face into her neck and inhaled. She smelled like roses. It was such an intoxicating scent. "I've missed you like crazy, Anna."

I moved slowly as we touched and kissed like it was our first time together.

"Don't ever leave me, Annalise. Please."

She framed my face with her hands and our eyes met. "I'm not going anywhere, Roger. I promise. I'm yours. I'll always be yours."

Something inside of me broke free. I moved my hips in a slow rotation, making Annalise gasp and lift her own hips.

"Yes," she whispered. "Oh, God, yes."

"That's it, princess. Come for me."

I lifted her leg and hooked it around my hip as I rolled again, pushing in deeper.

Her eyes snapped open and our gazes locked. One more thrust and I knew she was going to fall apart.

She arched her back and cried out my name as she squeezed and pulsed around my cock.

"Shit, Annalise...I'm going to come."

Her hands fisted in the sheets and she looked up at me again. What I saw in her eyes practically made my heart burst from my chest.

She loved me—and it didn't scare me. She was mine, and I was hers, and I had no intentions of ever letting her go.

"I love you," we both said at the same time before I captured her mouth with mine and spilled myself inside of her.

I lay on my back and stared up at the ceiling while Annalise traced patterns on my chest. Everything in the world felt so right when she was in my arms.

"Roger...what made you think I was leaving?"

I glanced down at her head on my chest and ran my fingers through her wavy hair. "Truitt told me you were getting on a plane this afternoon and heading back to New York."

She stilled. "Who told *him* that?"

"Patty called my mom, who called Saryn, who told Truitt he needed to find me. Truitt came over and woke up my drunk ass."

She turned her head and rested it on the back of her hand. "You were drunk?"

"After you left last night, I downed a bottle of whiskey, and I think a bottle of gin, like an idiot. What I really wanted to do was come after you, but I wasn't sure how to tell you I loved you."

One of her brows arched up. "'I love you, Annalise' would have been a good place to start."

I laughed. "I guess it would have been."

She crinkled her nose, and it was the most adorable thing I'd ever seen. "I hate to tell you this, but you were played."

I frowned. "What do you mean?"

Annalise moved and sat up, facing me as I straightened and leaned against the headboard. "I never told Patty I was leaving today."

"But...you were home. What were you doing home if you weren't packing up to leave?"

She laughed and covered her mouth before dropping her hand to her lap. "Today's my day off. I told Patty I'd be home all day painting the spare bedroom."

I felt my mouth drop open. "They lied?"

Annalise shrugged. "I'm going to guess it was Patty who pulled that one out of thin air. It was her idea to have Rick come to the charity dinner last night, hoping it would make you jealous."

"Whaaat?" I said as Annalise giggled. "Well, that shit worked. If it wasn't for Truitt, I probably would have punched the little bastard."

She covered her mouth again and laughed. Then she reached for my hand and laced our fingers together. "For what it's worth, I was going to call you today. I didn't like how we left things last night."

I pulled her to me, and she snuggled against my side. "You're not second. I want you to know that. I think part of the reason I was so freaked out about us was because of the way you made me feel. The feelings I have for you. Before you walked into my life, I had zero desire to be exclusive with anyone. But the thought of you being in another man's arms...it nearly drove me mad last night. I just needed to figure out how to put the past behind me and learn to trust my heart in someone else's care.

"And that night in the spare bedroom... I wasn't myself, and it had nothing to do with Kerri or anyone else. You looked at me, and I saw how you felt about me clear as day. I was lost in that moment. I couldn't bear for you to look at me like that, with such love and trust in your eyes. I *did* want to just fuck you senseless, but for all the wrong reasons."

She looked up at me and smiled. "Thank you for telling me that."

I shrugged.

Annalise ran her finger over my jaw. "I think I always knew we'd be together. Even back in Chicago, something told me that it wasn't going to be the last time I saw you."

Leaning down, I kissed her forehead. "Like you said, fated hearts."

She brought her hand to my chest again. This time, she placed it flat over my heart and sighed. "I cannot wait to see where our journey takes us next," she whispered.

Moving quickly, I flipped her over and moved on top of her. Her legs instantly opened to me, and I teased her entrance while I kissed her.

"You know where I see it going?" I asked, placing soft kisses over her face and neck.

"Where?" She giggled and squirmed under me.

"A wedding."

Her body froze. "A wedding?"

"Yep, but not just any wedding. A princess deserves a fairy tale wedding. After all, everyone does say you look like Cinderella."

She moved her fingers lazily over my back. "She wasn't a princess until she married the prince."

I shrugged. "Minor detail."

With a soft exhale, she said, "I like that thought process. Not anytime soon, though, right?"

"Oh, I don't know. How long does it take—" I pushed inside of her— "to plan a wedding?"

Annalise's breath grew faster. "I'd say…six months?"

I lifted her legs and moved faster. "Six months it is, then. That's probably good because according to my mother, my sperm is dying every day, and if we want kids, the wedding should be sooner rather than later." I pushed in deeper and rotated my hips.

"Roger," she gasped, her fingers digging into my shoulders.

"Do you like that, princess? The idea of my baby growing inside you?"

Her eyes sprang open and she screamed out my name as her orgasm hit.

When she finally came back to me, I leaned over, kissed her gently, and whispered, "I'll take that as a yes."

Chapter 22

Annalise - Six months later

PATTY AND MY mother both stood back and looked at the gazebo that I had decorated with the help of Saryn and my sister, Meg.

My mother clucked her tongue and then said, "I don't know. Something's missing."

Sighing, I looked at Meg for help, but she slowly backed away. Saryn had also taken off. It hadn't taken her long to realize that the combined force of my mother and Patty was not something anyone wanted to deal with.

"Mom, nothing is missing. This is how I want it."

"White flowers? No color?" Patty asked.

"Yes. White flowers. The chairs have blue and white hydrangeas on them, and the reception tables will have colorful floral displays. I want to keep the wedding simple."

Meg finally stepped forward. "If you think about it, Mom, it makes sense. Her dress is tinted blue, so standing in the middle of all that white will make her stand out even more."

That thought made Patty's eyes light up. "Yes! I totally forgot her dress was Cinderella-blue."

My mother rolled her eyes. She couldn't understand why I hadn't gone with a traditional white wedding gown. When I tried to explain that the blue was more for Roger than me—because he'd called me princess once, and I'd jumped all over him—she just looked at me, confused.

Never mind that the diamond Roger gave me when he asked me to marry him was also light blue.

Meg leaned in and whispered, "Now we know why Jax lives in Ireland and got married over there."

I tried to hide my laugh, but it slipped free. Patty and my mother both turned to me with raised eyebrows. Clearing my throat, I said, "The gazebo is done. I like it. It's staying that way."

"Oh, someone grew some balls in the last thirty seconds," Meg said.

My mother shot her a withering look.

"I think I'll go see if Saryn needs any help with the balloons," she said, quickly walking away.

Her words took a minute to sink in. I turned to her and called out, "Balloons? What balloons?"

"That was my idea," Mom said as she brushed by, following Meg. "Do not use up all the helium singing, Meg!"

Patty gasped and took off toward the main entrance of The Montclair. "Oh, dear, I left Jim and Truitt with the helium!"

I sighed and leaned against the gazebo. I only had a little bit of time before I needed to go get ready for the wedding. We were having it at sunset.

"Bet you wished we'd eloped now."

Spinning around, I smiled when I saw Roger standing there. I practically threw myself into his arms. "Let's do it! Let's just run away and go somewhere else and get married."

He laughed. "Your father would kill us, seeing as he insisted on paying for half of this fairy tale wedding of yours."

"We can pay him back."

Roger set me down, then took my face in his hands and kissed me softly before leaning his forehead against mine. "We're getting married in a few hours, princess."

My stomach dropped and I felt a rush of happiness.

Roger took my hand in his and walked us into the gazebo. "The flowers are beautiful."

"I'm glad you like them," I said, looking around at the hundreds of white and cream-colored flowers that adorned the gazebo. "My mother thinks it's boring."

He shook his head, then looked at me. "I'm not supposed to be talking to you right now."

I shrugged. "Are you nervous?"

He paused for a moment as if truly thinking about the question. "No, I'm not. Not at all. I thought I would be. Are you nervous?"

Smiling, I shook my head. "No. I'm glad the day is finally here. I do have something I want to talk to you about, though. I've been debating if I should tell you before or after the wedding."

He lifted his brow. "That sounds intriguing."

I twisted my fingers nervously in my lap and drew in a deep breath.

Roger reached for one of my hands and took it in his. "Hey, what's going on? Talk to me."

"Annalise! Annalise!"

We both turned to see Elizabeth heading toward us.

"You need to get in here *now* so you can start getting ready!"

I held up my hand and called back, "Give me five minutes."

She scowled. "You're not even supposed to see him yet!"

"Five minutes!" I yelled back.

Tossing her hands up in the air, she replied, "Fine! But when your mother comes looking for you, don't say I didn't warn you."

I shook my head and turned back to Roger. "I found out something this morning."

He frowned. "Damn it! I'm sorry, I didn't mean to see your dress! I walked into the room, and it was hanging up, and I saw the blue sticking out, and…I peeked. I couldn't help it. It looks beautiful, though, and I can't wait to see you in it."

"You saw my dress?"

Roger drew back some. "Shit. That wasn't what you found out?"

"No! I can't believe you peeked at my dress. I wanted it to be a surprise, Roger."

"It will be! I didn't see you *in* it!"

Jerking my hand from his, I stood and started to walk away.

"I'm sorry! Come on, princess, it was an accident! Wait—you didn't tell me what you found out."

Glancing back over my shoulder, I smiled and casually called out, "I'm pregnant."

Roger's smile instantly disappeared and then reappeared on his face. I faced forward and kept walking toward the front of the hotel. I figured everyone was either in the courtyard setting up or busy somewhere else. No one would be in the lobby. I headed up the steps and across the front porch. By the time I reached the main entrance, Roger was right behind me.

He grabbed my arm and pulled me to a stop. When he looked down at me, my breath caught in my throat. He had tears in his eyes.

"Did you just say you're pregnant?"

I swallowed hard and nodded.

"But…you just stopped taking the pill a few weeks ago. The doctor said it might take a while."

With a half-shrug, I replied, "I haven't been feeling good the last few days, and I kept thinking it was from all the wedding planning. But it's not. I took a home test this morning."

His eyes bounced around my face, maybe in an attempt to see if I was serious or kidding with him. "We're going to have a baby?"

I let out an unsure chuckle. "Yes."

Roger pulled open the door to The Montclair, took my hand, and immediately turned to the right. We went into the library, and he shut the door.

"What are you doing?" I asked as he started to undo his pants.

"I'm making love to you right now."

My eyes widened. "Right now? Here? In the library? Hours before we're supposed to get married?"

Roger wrapped his arms around me, pulled me to him, and picked me up.

"I fucking love it when you wear dresses."

He slid my panties to the side and pushed inside of me as he pressed me against a wall of books.

"Oh God," I gasped when he started to move fast and hard. I had to bite down on my lower lip to keep from moaning.

"A baby," Roger panted, going deeper, harder.

"Yes," I whispered. "Faster, Roger! I'm so close."

He buried his face in my neck, and I wrapped my legs tightly around him.

"Our baby," he said as he pulled back and met my gaze.

All I could do was nod. I moaned, feeling my orgasm build. Roger sealed his mouth over mine and moved faster, and we both came at the same time. He swung me around, pushed me against the other side of the library wall, and started to move inside of me again. My eyes went wide, but he only picked up his pace.

"What's the magical number?"

I panted between words. "I'll tell…you…when you…hit it."

Shortly after Roger made me come three times, we were a panting mess, lying on the floor of the library on our backs, both of us trying to catch our breath.

Roger turned his head toward me. "Do you know what the first thing I'm going to do is after we get married?"

My head fell to the side as I looked at him. "What?"

A brilliant smile spread across his face, displaying those dimples I loved so much. "I'm going to tell my mother my sperm is perfectly fine."

I tiptoed out of the library and made a beeline to the cabin where everything was set up for me to get ready. I peeked over my shoulder to see Roger heading upstairs. The groom and groomsman were getting ready in one of the grand suites in the main part of The Montclair.

The moment I stepped into the chapel cabin, all eyes swung to me. My mother gave me a look that said she had been two seconds from sending out a search party. Patty jumped into action and started bossing people around. Elizabeth, Saryn, and Meg all gave me goofy smiles.

"What?" I asked.

Meg slowly shook her head. "You couldn't wait."

"What are you talking about?" I asked as the hairdresser motioned for me to sit down in the chair she had pulled out for me.

"Don't even," Meg said. "It is totally written all over your face."

"Not to mention your hair is a mess," Elizabeth stated.

I looked at the three of them in the mirror. They all stood behind me now. Saryn leaned in and whispered, "You told him, didn't you?"

She was the only one I had told about the pregnancy test so far. Not that I didn't trust Elizabeth or my sister; it was just that Saryn and I had grown so close in the last few months. It was Saryn who'd shown up this morning with a bagel and strawberry cream cheese for me...along with a pregnancy test. She said I had a glow about me that gave it away.

Of course, she would know, considering she found out just yesterday that she's expecting another baby. They hadn't been trying, but it was a blessing, nonetheless.

With a wicked smile, I winked at her.

She laughed and shook her head. "Let me guess—he pulled you into the first room he could find."

It didn't take the others—including the hairdresser—long to figure out what we were talking about. I nodded.

"Where?" Meg and Elizabeth both asked.

My cheeks felt hot, and I closed my eyes before I said, "The library."

"Oh, God!" Elizabeth cried out.

"What is it, Lizzy?" Patty asked.

She held up her hand and waved Patty off. "Nothing. I just remembered something I forgot to do at the front desk."

Patty gave her a warm smile. "It's your day off. Stop thinking about work."

Elizabeth nodded, then turned and pinned me with a glare. "I love that room! I eat my lunch in there!"

Meg, Saryn, *and* the hairdresser all giggled.

Placing her finger and thumb against the bridge of her nose, Elizabeth asked, "Just tell me it wasn't on the table."

"It wasn't," I quickly said. "I think it was up against Texas history, then biographies, and once again by the romance section."

Elizabeth threw her hands in the air. "I'm going to have to find a new place to eat now."

The day turned into a beautiful fall evening in Texas, with a soft wind blowing the leaves on the trees. Occasionally, one or two leaves would float down to the ground while Roger and I exchanged our vows surrounded by a sky painted with purple, pink, and orange. It was so breathtaking, it almost looked like a painting.

Roger cried when he saw me, and I cried when I saw him. When my father placed my hand in Roger's, he promised Daddy he would love me forever and never allow anything or anyone to hurt me. My father finally lost the battle to keep his tears at bay. He grabbed Roger around the neck and pulled him in for one of those manly hugs. He whispered something in Roger's ear, which made me laugh. Then, with a slap on the back, my father took his seat next to my mother.

Meg stood as my maid of honor, and Truitt was Roger's best man. We didn't have anyone else in our wedding party. Partly because I was still so new to Boerne, and with my brother Jax not being able to make it over from Ireland, we felt it best to keep it small and simple.

The reception, on the other hand, was anything but. The Carters knew a lot of people. I swore half the town of Boerne was there.

Toward the end of the night, Roger walked up to me and placed his mouth against my ear. "Are you ready to leave, Mrs. Carter?"

I turned in his arms and smiled at him. "I've been ready to leave since we cut the cake."

He laughed and kissed the tip of my nose. I loved when he did that. Then he placed his hand over my stomach, and those dimples popped out.

"If you keep touching my stomach, people will guess why," I said.

"I can't help it. I'm in awe of the fact that you have my child growing inside you."

"*Our* child." He rolled his eyes, and I hit him playfully on the chest. "Seriously, can we leave now?"

"Yes. I've already asked Truitt to bring your car around to the front of the hotel."

"And we're staying at a hotel in San Antonio tonight?" I asked.

Roger nodded. "Yes."

"And you won't tell me what time our flight leaves tomorrow?"

He narrowed his eyes at me and slowly shook his head. "I know you, Annalise. You'll look up every flight at that time to figure out where we're going."

Sighing, I leaned into his body. "Fine. You win. I'll let you surprise me."

He kissed me softly on the mouth. "Thank you. Now let's get the hell out of here."

Chapter 23

Roger

I WASN'T SURE how I'd lucked into marrying the most beautiful woman ever, but I had. The moment I saw Annalise in that soft-blue wedding gown, with her bouquet of blue and white flowers, I fell even more in love with her. Last night in our hotel room, with her hair a mess, her makeup smeared, and a scowl on her face that should have had me running for my life, I fell even more in love with her. I made love to her for nearly half the night, and fell asleep with my hand resting on her stomach. By the time I woke, I was even more madly in love with my wife, and I knew I would keep falling. Over and Over.

"Is this blindfold really necessary, Roger? You already made me wear one—and headphones—at the ticket counter. I can't even imagine what people are thinking," Annalise said as we made our way to our gate.

"It's a surprise. When we get to the gate, I have to put the headphones back on."

Sighing, Annalise stopped walking. "Nope. I'm not doing it. I feel like an idiot. I know people are staring at me!"

I glanced around the airport and, sure enough, people were giving us strange looks.

"Okay, you're right. People *are* looking at us kind of strangely."

Annalise reached up and pulled the blindfold off, blinking a few times as she adjusted to the light.

A guy walked by and said, "Dude, save the kinky stuff for your hotel room."

I laughed as Annalise's face flamed.

Lacing my fingers in hers, I started for our gate. I could practically feel the excitement coming off Annalise's body.

"Hey, you know what?" I said. "You once told me that you make a damn good ice cream sundae. How come you've never made one for me before?"

She looked up at me and grinned. "You remember that?"

"Of course, I do."

"How about I make you one when we get back home?"

Annalise and I decided to purchase the Martin Ranch together, and construction for our house was already underway. She had moved out of her rental and in with me while the house was being built. With any luck, it would be finished in plenty of time before the baby arrived.

"When do we find out how far along you are? The due date, all of that?" I asked.

"I've got an appointment the day after we come back from our honeymoon. It's at two in the afternoon. I knew you'd taken that day off already, so I figured that would be okay."

Lifting her hand, I kissed the back of it. "That's perfect."

I stopped walking, causing her to do the same. "We're at our gate," I said.

Annalise did a little hop, then turned to look at the flight information. With a frown, she said, "Orlando? Do we change planes there?"

"Nope. That's our final destination."

I could see the wheels spinning in her head as she tried to think of why I would be taking her to Orlando. Then it dawned on her... and she slowly turned to look at me.

"I mean, where better to take Cinderella on her honeymoon than to Magic Kingdom?"

Annalise nearly knocked me over when she threw her body against mine. She held on to me tightly before letting go. She looked up at me, and I smiled and reached down to wipe her tears away.

"You remembered."

I placed my hand on the side of her face, and she leaned into it. "I love you, princess."

"I love you too."

Epilogue

Roger - A few years down the road

I STARED AT the baby in my arms in utter awe. She was perfect. Just like her brother before her had been.

"She's so beautiful," Annalise whispered as I sat down on the bed next to her.

"Me see, Daddy! Momma, me see!" Matt cried out, practically clawing to get out of my father's arms.

"Remember your inside voice, Matt." My mother held Carrie up on her hip. Carrie was Truitt and Saryn's two-year-old daughter, born on the exact same day as Matt. Nolan and Liliana stood off to the side with Truitt and Saryn.

Annalise held her hands out for Matt. My father handed him to her, and Matt crawled right in between me and Annalise.

"Do you want to hold her your baby sister, Matt?" I asked.

He nodded and held out his arms. Annalise and my mother had been working with him on how to hold the baby the right way, making sure he knew she was going to be very delicate.

I was positive we all held our breath as I lay Millie in Matt's arms after my father propped a pillow under him.

I watched our son stare down at his newborn sister. Tears filled my eyes when he started to rock softly and sing to her. No one knew what he was singing, but Millie opened her eyes and stared at him. Their connection was instant.

I heard a soft sob come from my right, and I turned to see Annalise wipe one tear and then another away.

I placed my finger under her chin and lifted her head until her eyes met mine. "Thank you for making me so happy," I said.

She shook her head. "Roger, you're the one who makes us so happy. You've made my fairy tale come true."

I glanced at our son and daughter and smiled before I looked back at Annalise.

"Just think, it all started with a snowstorm and a stranded princess."

The End

And they all lived happily ever after.

Fated Hearts is the conclusion of the Southern Bride series. I hoped you have enjoyed reading these books as much as I have enjoyed writing them.

Other Books by Kelly Elliott

What's next from Kelly?
The Seaside Chronicles series, coming August 2022
House of Love series coming late 2022, early 2023

Stand Alones
The Journey Home*
Who We Were*
The Playbook*
Made for You*
*Available on audiobook

Boggy Creek Valley Series
The Butterfly Effect*
Playing with Words*
She's the One (releases on November 30, 2021)
Surrender to Me (releases on January 25, 2022)
Hearts in Motion (releases on March 22, 2022)
Looking for You (releases on May 3, 2022)

Meet Me in Montana Series
Never Enough*
Always Enough*
Good Enough*
Strong Enough*
*Available on audiobook

Southern Bride Series
Love at First Sight*
Delicate Promises*
Divided Interests*
Lucky in Love*
Feels Like Home *
Take Me Away*

*Fool for You**
*Fated Hearts**
*Available on audiobook

Cowboys and Angels Series
Lost Love
Love Profound
Tempting Love
Love Again
Blind Love
This Love
Reckless Love
*Series available on audiobook

Boston Love Series
Searching for Harmony
Fighting for Love
*Series available on audiobook

Austin Singles Series
Seduce Me
Entice Me
Adore Me
*Series available on audiobook

Wanted Series
*Wanted**
*Saved**
*Faithful**
Believe
*Cherished**
*A Forever Love**
The Wanted Short Stories
All They Wanted
*Available on audiobook

Love Wanted in Texas Series
Spin-off series to the WANTED Series
Without You
Saving You
Holding You
Finding You
Chasing You
Loving You
Entire series available on audiobook
*Please note *Loving You* combines the last book of the Broken and Love Wanted in Texas series.

Broken Series
*Broken**
*Broken Dreams**
*Broken Promises**
Broken Love
*Available on audiobook

The Journey of Love Series
Unconditional Love
Undeniable Love
Unforgettable Love
*Entire series available on audiobook

With Me Series
Stay With Me
Only With Me
*Series available on audiobook

Speed Series
Ignite
Adrenaline

COLLABORATIONS
Predestined Hearts (co-written with Kristin Mayer)*
*Play Me (*co-written with Kristin Mayer)*
*Dangerous Temptations (*co-written with Kristin Mayer*
*Available on audiobook